"Besides telling the very real story of what everyone of Middle Eastern decent went through after 9/11, it is so well-written—lyrical, even; a joy to read. It will change the lives of children through knowledge and, hopefully, empathy."
—*Nancy Lee Cecil*, author of *Raising Peaceful Children in a Violent World*

"A thoughtful novel that invites the reader to see the world from a different perspective, and a much-needed contribution to children's literature shelves in the wake of hysteria or predispositions to assume the worst about all Muslims in the wake of 9/11."
—*Midwest Book Review*

"Holm's storytelling is honest, believable, and compelling. His characters lead the reader to feel compassion for Mohammed and his family, especially in light of the injustice and hatred they encounter. …*How Mohammed Saved Miss Liberty* shows teens and young adults the complexities of relationships, and the possibility for good will toward friends, neighbors, and humanity."
—*ForeWord Reviews*

"There is almost nothing about the Statue of Liberty that Mohammed bin Hasan Ahmed Al-Fulani—known as "Hamed," the "only kid in Pioneer Middle School with a permanent tan" and its only Muslim—doesn't know. As a member of the Young Engineers Club in his small Ohio school, he is intensely looking forward to its trip to New York. And although it is almost derailed by the Sept. 11, 2001 terror attacks, the club manages to get there, where Hamed's fantasies take over."
—*Arizona Daily Star*

Also By **M. S. Holm**

When Your School Bus Goes to Mexico
The Arborist
Driller

HOW MOHAMMED SAVED MISS LIBERTY

The Story of a Good Muslim Boy

M. S. Holm

Great West Publishing
USA

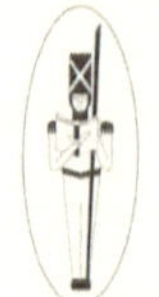

Sentry Books

Sentry Books
An imprint of Great West Publishing

How Mohammed Saved Miss Liberty
(The Story of a Good Muslim Boy)

For information about this title or to order other books and/or electronic media, contact the publisher.
www.sentrybooks.com
sales@sentrybooks.com

Library of Congress Control Number: 2007939023

Publisher's Cataloging-in-Publication
(Provided by Quality Books, Inc.)

Holm, M. S., author.
    How Mohammed saved Miss Liberty : the story of a good
Muslim boy / M.S. Holm. -- Revised edition.
    SUMMARY: A fourteen-year-old middle school boy
questions his Muslim identity after 9/11, only to make a
surprising discovery about himself and his place in
America.
    Audience: Grades 7-12.
    ISBN 978-0-9796199-9-1

    1. Muslim teenagers--United States--Juvenile fiction.
2. September 11 Terrorist Attacks, 2001--Juvenile
fiction. 3. Statue of Liberty (New York, N.Y.)--
Juvenile fiction. 4. New York (N.Y.)--Juvenile fiction.
I. Title.

PZ7.H73228How 2016   [Fic]
                         QBI15-600233

ISBN: 978-0-9796199-9-1

Map of Liberty Island by Sarah Garibaldi

Printed in the United States of America.

For Muñeca,
who dreams

THE NEW COLOSSUS.

NOT LIKE THE BRAZEN GIANT OF GREEK FAME,
WITH CONQUERING LIMBS ASTRIDE FROM LAND TO LAND;
HERE AT OUR SEA-WASHED, SUNSET GATES SHALL STAND
A MIGHTY WOMAN WITH A TORCH, WHOSE FLAME
IS THE IMPRISONED LIGHTNING, AND HER NAME
MOTHER OF EXILES. FROM HER BEACON-HAND
GLOWS WORLD-WIDE WELCOME; HER WILD EYES COMMAND
THE AIR-BRIDGED HARBOR THAT TWIN CITIES FRAME,
"KEEP ANCIENT LANDS, YOUR STORIED POMP!"
    CRIES SHE
WITH SILENT LIPS. "GIVE ME YOUR TIRED, YOUR
    POOR,
YOUR HUDDLED MASSES YEARNING TO BREATHE FREE,
THE WRETCHED REFUSE OF YOUR TEEMING SHORE,
SEND THESE, THE HOMELESS, TEMPEST-TOST TO ME,
I LIFT MY LAMP BESIDE THE GOLDEN DOOR!"

———

THIS TABLET, WITH HER SONNET TO THE BARTHOLDI STATUE
OF LIBERTY ENGRAVED UPON IT, IS PLACED UPON THESE WALLS
IN LOVING MEMORY OF
EMMA LAZARUS
BORN IN NEW YORK CITY, JULY 22, 1849
DIED NOVEMBER 19, 1887.

Original bronze plaque mounted in the base of the Statue of Liberty

THE GOLDEN DOOR

◆

It was a September morning in Ohio. Mohammed sat near the window in his eighth-grade social studies class. His book lay open on the desk as he listened to his teacher, the goofy-haired, history-loving Mr. MacDonald—known as Mac in the middle school—talk about America's first settlers. "They could not have picked a worse spot," Mac said, pointing to a map of Virginia. "Swampy. Mosquitoes. Bad drinking water. The Powhatan at their backs. This was no picnic in the park."

Out the window Mohammed observed a blue sky that was bright and clear. He saw his reflection in the glass—brown face, kinky black hair, bushy eyebrows. A white undershirt peeked unfashionably out from his button-down collar. He was the tallest kid in the eighth grade. He was also the school's only Muslim.

"Newcomers to America could not have been met with a more unfriendly welcome," continued Mr. MacDonald.

Mohammed thumbed through his book, looking at the pictures: General Grant on a horse, Winnebago Indians camped in Wisconsin. He stopped to study the picture of two well-dressed men handcuffed together. Always fascinated by crime, Mohammed read the caption: "Nicola Sacco and Bartolomeo Vanzetti stoically await their fate."

The classroom door opened, and Mr. Vander Bogart, the principal, stepped in. Known as the Vander among middle schoolers, he nodded stiffly to the students before he drew close to Mac and spoke in a low voice. Mac stared at the floor. When the Vander left, Mac turned to the class. "Mr. Vander Bogart informed me that something has happened in New York and Washington—something terrible. Several airplanes have flown into buildings."

Someone gasped. Students began to talk at once. Mohammed glanced out the window. *Had Mac said New York?*

Mr. MacDonald turned on the classroom television set. When the screen lit, the social studies class went silent. Mohammed immediately recognized the World Trade Center towers. He had a poster of them in his room. But the towers on the screen were burning. Sirens wailed in the background as a voice said, "What you are seeing is live coverage of an attack…" Then the students saw the replay. Fourteen-year-old Mohammed bin Hasan Ahmed felt a chill run up his spine as he watched an airliner crash into the South Tower and explode in an orange fireball.

"Jesus!" someone blurted. Mac didn't notice. His mouth was open. The scene on the television switched to Washington, where a smoking hole gaped in a building. "That's the Pentagon!" exclaimed Mitch Redding, whose father was in the Army Reserve.

Then the towers were back on the screen. Clouds of black smoke billowed from their wounds. Flocks of papers fell from the sky. The figures of men flew by windows, their ties uplifted as they dropped to the ground. On crowded streets fire engines raced toward the burning buildings. Men and women, their faces upturned, watched and wept.

In Ohio eighth-grade faces stared wide-eyed. No one spoke. "Oh my God!" cried the voice from the television as the first tower collapsed with a thunderous roar. When the second tower fell, the voice said, "Good Lord, this is unbelievable!" But Mohammed believed it. Live television didn't lie.

As ash and smoke filled the screen, Mac stepped back. Girls covered their faces. Boys stiffened in their chairs. Mohammed swallowed hard. In spite of the death and destruction he had just witnessed, his first thought was, *So much for the trip to New York.*

The trip by the Young Engineers of Pioneer School, the YEPS, was scheduled for October. Led by club adviser Miss Cutter, they were to see New York engineering firsthand—bridges, buildings, subways, tunnels. The towers.

For Mohammed the trip would be a dream come true. Already he knew more about New York than any other Young Engineer. His bedroom was decorated with travel posters of the city. One wall had a Rand McNally map of Manhattan with colored tacks identifying important landmarks. He could name the thirty-six bridges and arches in Central Park. He knew the city had 722 miles of subway tracks. He was also a fourteen-year-old expert on the Statue of Liberty—Miss Liberty.

Her proper title was *Liberty Enlightening the World,* and she was the largest metal statue on the planet. Erected on an island in New York's upper harbor, she faced the sea with a look of cold command, her lit torch lifted to the sky. Her skeleton was a great iron trestle. Her skin was hammered copper turned green from a hundred years of aging. She was a goddess and a storybook giant, colossal and cloud scraping.

Mohammed knew her better than he knew prepositions or polygons. He was a walking Statue of Liberty encyclopedia. He knew the number of steps in her spiral staircase (171) and how many windows were in her crown (25). He knew her gilded flame was lit by sixteen powerful lamps and that her iron skeleton could withstand winds of 125 mph. He knew Bartholdi was her sculptor, Eiffel her engineer. Mohammed even knew Miss Liberty's shoe size (879). He could name the mine near Stavanger, Norway, where her copper had been excavated (Visnes), and he knew that a Senegalese immigrant (name unknown) had made the last successful suicide jump off Miss Liberty.

He knew she was more than a statue. She was symbolic and poetic. She was hope and welcome. She was an American cathedral. She had also been on the itinerary for the club's trip that October. But so were the towers he had just seen fall.

The loudspeaker crackled. The Vander spoke. "Due to the unprecedented events of this morning, classes have been canceled. Please go home and pray for America."

No one cheered. The bell rang. Heavy feet shuffled from the room. Mac rolled up the map of Virginia.

On the bus Norman Hazelton, Mohammed's best friend, said he felt sick. "All those people…" he muttered, shaking his head.

At home Mohammed's mother sat near the television, her eyes red. When she pulled him close, he could smell her tears. "Bery bad," she croaked. Mohammed's four-year-old sister, Nura Maryam, played with dolls on the floor. "Don't tell Daddy," she said. "Mommy cry."

He sat beside his mother. On the TV they watched the confusion live, the panic replayed. News details emerged: four planes, thousands missing, thousands dead, the president on

Air Force One. Many of the same words were repeated: *hijackers, suicide mission*. The announcer kept saying *terrorist attack*.

"*Terroristas*," said his mother, shaking her head.

Mohammed wondered whether his father knew the news. There was no television or radio at the garage. "I'm going to the station," he announced, standing up.

"No go outside," replied his mother, stopping him by the arm. "No safe."

He almost smiled. "Nothing is going to happen here, Mom. This isn't New York."

His mother held his arm. "*Siéntate!*" she ordered. And Mohammed sat.

When Mohammed's father arrived, his face said he knew. Hasan Ahmed's features were often shadowed by deep thought, but tonight they looked darker than usual. His heavy eyebrows gave an ominous shade to tired eyes. His gray-black beard looked unusually scruffy. After making his sunset prayer, he sat silently at the supper table. Mohammed was full of questions.

"Did the hijackers fly the planes?" he asked.

His father said he didn't know.

"Did they have guns, Abi?"

"I couldn't say," he answered.

"Who could have done such a thing?" Mohammed asked finally.

"Eat supper," his mother said, and Mohammed knew what that meant. It meant his father didn't want to talk.

That night they watched the president address the nation. Mohammed tried to listen, the terms familiar now: *mass murder, shattered lives, acts of terror*. The president said the word *evil* many times—more than he said the word *good*—and like Mr. Vander Bogart, he asked everyone to pray.

When the speech was over, Hasan Ahmed turned off the television. "This will be trouble," he said before he rose from the couch and climbed the stairs.

Mohammed said nothing. He went to the bathroom to perform *wudu*, the ritual washing of hands, face, and feet before prayer. Next he changed into clean pajamas to make himself presentable before God. In his room he laid his prayer mat before the wall nearest to Mecca. When his family had moved into the house—his very first night in this bedroom—his father had placed the mat on the floor and stood him before the wall. "When you pray in your room," he had said, "you should always face this wall." Pointing beyond the wall, he had added, "The city of Mecca lies in that direction. It is where the Prophet Muhammad, peace be upon him, was born, and it is our holiest city. No matter where you are in the world, you must always pray toward Mecca."

Now in his darkened room, he raised his hands to his ears and began his prayer with *"Allahu Akbar."* God is greater. He kept his eyes down, reciting in Arabic the opening chapter from the Koran, the Muslim holy book.

Bismi Allahi alrrahmani alrraheemi
Alhamdu lillahi rabbil 'alamin

He had learned his verses in Saturday Koran classes, but his father had taught him the prayer positions—how to bow, when to kneel, where to put his hands. "All your prayers must be done this way," his father had said the first time he had guided him through the movements. Mohammed had been seven at the time.

The silence of the house was immense. Mohammed whispered the words quickly, finishing his first prayer, starting the second. He moved smoothly through each posture as he recited the memorized passages at the right moments. Mohammed knew the purpose of prayer was to present himself before God as a humble servant. He knew, too, that prayer was a duty to be performed without hurry five times a day. But some nights he sped up, just to finish. Like tonight.

He gave his blessings with a quick look to his right and left. Then he opened his eyes and sat back on his legs. He stared at the Rand McNally map of New York City. It, too, was on the wall nearest to Mecca. Even in the dark he could make out the colored tacks—a solitary silver one marking Miss Liberty, two white tacks on the towers.

He would leave them in place.

In spite of his prayers, he began to worry. Would the Young Engineers' trip to New York be canceled? Would there be anything *left* to visit if it wasn't? And what had his father meant by "This will be trouble"?

The next morning Norman was not at the bus stop. Mohammed recalled what his best friend had said about feeling sick.

High schoolers chatted nearby. "My money is on the Taliban," one said. "I bet Saddam is behind it," suggested another.

Mohammed knew the Taliban were the men who had blown up the Buddha statues in Afghanistan. *Taliban* was a word he had learned in Koran classes that meant "students." As for Saddam, he knew they weren't talking about his uncle, Saddam Ahmed. They meant Saddam Hussein.

In social studies Mac started a discussion on yesterday's events. "This is a terrible tragedy," he said. "How can we help?"

No one raised a hand to answer. Mac studied the eighth-graders' faces. "Merrill, what should we do?" he asked.

The class looked at Merrill. Mohammed looked at Merrill, but he was thinking, too. He might be next.

Merrill scratched his head. "Send flashlights, maybe?" Puzzled faces turned to Mac. *Flashlights?*

"Good!" boomed Mr. MacDonald. "Practical. Rescuers will need them." He wrote *flashlights* on the blackboard.

"Food," said Edgar. Edgar's appetite was legendary in the cafeteria.

Mac wrote *food* on the board. "Nonperishable, of course."

"Gloves," blurted another student. *Gloves* went on the board.

As Mac wrote, he continued the discussion. "Priscilla, how do you think we should respond?" he asked.

Everyone looked at Priscilla. Everyone but Mohammed. He secretly adored Priscilla Smith. He had already noticed the black ribbon pinned to her blouse. "I think we should write letters telling them how sorry we are," she said.

Students in the front clapped. Mac added *letters* to the board. "To whom?" he asked.

"The fire department," replied Priscilla.

"Families," said several students at once.

Mr. MacDonald said, "A school I know was affected—Public School 89. I'm sure those students could use some encouragement." His gaze fell on the back row. "Mitch, what do you think we should do?"

Mitch sat up. "My dad says we should bomb 'em."

Those next to Mitch nodded. Mac looked surprised. "Bomb who?"

"Osama and his Muslim buddies," answered Mitch.

Everyone nodded. Mohammed nodded, too, perplexed. *Osama? Muslim buddies?*

"Let's not blame anyone yet," Mac advised.

"It was on the news," added Ralph Trumbull, Mitch's buddy. "The hijackers were Muslim."

Mohammed stiffened. He recalled what the high schoolers had said about Saddam. He remembered what his father had said about trouble. He felt the stares, the eyes drilling into his back. He kept his own eyes on Mr. MacDonald, but Mac didn't look at him.

"There is a lot of speculation right now," Mr. MacDonald said.

"Well, I still think we should bomb 'em," reiterated Mitch.

Students clapped, louder than they had clapped for Priscilla. Mac signaled the end of the discussion. "I suggest we begin by writing letters," he said.

The class groaned. Writing letters was more work than buying flashlights or gloves. Everyone opened their notebooks.

Mohammed wrote to the students of Public School 89. His letter was short.

> Dear Students,
> I'm sorry for what happened. I hope everyone in your
> family is safe and that you can go back to school soon.
> Sincerely yours,
> Hamed
> Eighth Grade, Pioneer School

Anxious and needing information, Mohammed went home after school. Strange looks followed him on the bus.

At the house he turned on the TV and sat in his father's chair. A fireman with a dirty face and sad eyes was being interviewed. The World Trade Center ruins smoked in the background. The picture switched from New York to Washington, where a military man spoke gravely of a "response."

Then the newscaster spoke about the hijackers. A grainy video appeared on the screen. "These two men were seen yesterday morning clearing airport security at the Portland International Jetport in Maine," said the newscaster. The man in front was wearing a blue shirt, and he carried a small travel bag. The other looked thin. When their names appeared on the screen, Mohammed froze. *His* name was on the screen. One of the hijackers was named Mohammed!

"They are suspected of flying the airplanes into the World Trade Center," continued the newscaster.

Mohammed stared. So it was true. Arab men had done it. Muslim men!

On the TV that afternoon, he learned about the "Osama" Mitch had mentioned in class. He learned that Osama bin Laden was the head of a global terrorist network called al-Qaeda and that he was an Islamic extremist who had declared holy war against Americans. When Osama's picture appeared on the TV, Mohammed moved close to the screen, inches from the image of a bearded face, gray at the temples and shaded by a checkered headdress. Mohammed tried to find something in the man's eyes that spoke to mass murder, but the face he saw looked like any of the dark-skinned and bearded faces he met at their masjid in the city.

At supper that evening he sought to engage his father on the subject. He recounted what he had seen on the news about the hijacker's name—his name.

His father nodded. "I have heard that," he said, putting down his fork.

Mohammed watched his father and mother not eat. "But, Abi, why would this Osama bin Laden order Muslim men to kill people with hijacked planes?"

His father shook his head. "Why men do evil is hidden from us, but I can tell you those who did this are hijackers not only of airplanes. They are hijackers of Islam and the Prophet, peace be upon him." He paused, his face grave. "We should be thankful that we are safe, that we are together, and that we are in America. Those who are guilty will be punished, if not in this life, then in the next."

Mohammed nodded. His father often spoke in these phrases.

"But what did you mean by trouble, Abi? You told Mother there could be trouble."

His father looked at his mother. His mother looked at her plate.

"Son, trouble comes when people are blinded by anger and hate, when they cannot see the good men differently from the bad ones. We are Muslims—peace-loving Muslims—and we are Americans, too. Everything will be all right for us. Trust in Allah."

The oldest of eight boys, Hasan Ahmed was born in a crumbling mud-brick house in the impoverished *baladi* district of Cairo. By age six he worked in his father's business, helping repair motorcycles under the leafy umbrella of a lebbek tree, the smell of gasoline as familiar as the stench of burning garbage carried on the khamsin winds from the City of the Dead.

His father (the grandfather Mohammed would never know) was a gifted mechanic who inspired his son with a dream—a dream to someday repair motorcycles under a roof instead of a lebbek tree. In this dream the Ahmed business would occupy a spacious building with electric lights, a concrete floor, tools on the walls, and a large sign hanging outside. It was a dream Hasan Ahmed would never forget.

At age twelve he learned to weld, working nights to pay for auto shop classes in a state secondary school. At seventeen he was drafted into the Egyptian army. Three years later, he was a tank mechanic on his way to the United States Army's Automotive and Armaments Command at the Rock

Island arsenal in Illinois to learn all there was to know about American-made engines.

If Hasan Ahmed had been sent to the moon, he could not have been more unprepared. Everything he saw astounded him: convenience stores, endless forests, the friendliness of strangers. America was so different from the chaos and clamor of Cairo, so distant from many of his Muslim beliefs. Men drank beer at baseball games. Women showed their legs in public. Children talked back to parents. There were too many freedoms in America, but there was also much tolerance.

A year later he was back in Egypt, finishing his soldier enlistment, hired by John Deere, the tractor company, newly installed in Cairo. At night he read and translated thick maintenance manuals from English to Arabic. During the day he fixed the green combines that harvested cotton in the delta fields. He still helped his father repair motorcycles under the lebbek tree. The old man still talked of the roof, the concrete floor, the tools on the wall, his dream. But his son couldn't stop thinking about America.

The next year, John Deere sent him to Iowa—the Dubuque Works factory—and he saw the Mississippi for the first time. The sight of it filled him with a sense of possibility. In America the promise was clear. Hard work brought welcome and opportunity. Hard work made dreams come true. He joined a mosque, shopped at Walmart. He began to belong.

Then he met Mohammed's mother on his first trip to Chicago. Lisa Sanchez worked as a room maid at the Abbott Hotel on Belmont Avenue. She was dark skinned like him. He spoke to her in Arabic. She answered in bits of English. She said *bueno* many times. They talked with their hands. He asked her name, and when she left, he wrote it on hotel stationary. Back in Dubuque he sent her a letter in care of the Abbott. She wrote back in Spanish. He bought a dictionary. He visited Chicago again—soon every other weekend.

With a month remaining on his work visa, he put his name on a list of candidates looking for American jobs. Each candidate was asked to write a short biographical sketch. Mohammed's father wrote five typewritten, single-spaced pages, his English persuasive. America beckoned, he said.

Two weeks later, a letter came offering him work. He took a Greyhound east, and early one fall morning, from a bus window, he saw Ohio for the first time.

Many things happened after that. He started his job. He worked very hard and spent very little. He brought Mohammed's mother from Chicago and married her. Five years later, he had saved enough money to buy his own garage—one with a steel roof and a concrete floor—in a small town where he could own a house, raise his family, and live an old man's dream—now an American dream.

Norman didn't appear at the bus stop the next morning. "I bet he doesn't show all week," said Merrill, Mohammed's next-best friend. "You know his mom." In middle school Norman's mother was known as a satellite mom—always circling, on alert.

Mohammed boarded the bus. As he moved toward an empty seat, a redheaded high schooler stuck his arm across the aisle, blocking his way. "What's your name, kid?" he asked loudly.

The bus noise turned quiet. Mohammed suspected the redheaded kid already knew his name, but he answered anyway.

The high schooler repeated it slowly. "*Mo-ham-med?* One of those hijackers was Mohammed. I heard it on the news. Are you Arab?"

Everyone looked at him.

"Sit down back there," ordered the bus driver, looking in his mirror. Mohammed leaned against the freckled arm, but the high schooler refused to let him pass.

"Are you?"

"I'm an American," Mohammed replied, remembering his father's words at the supper table. He tried to sound firm, but his legs felt wobbly.

The seatmate of the redheaded kid said, "His mom's a Mexican, Carl."

"Yeah, but his old man is an Arab," countered another high schooler.

Mohammed pushed against the arm. The redheaded kid was big. His arm had curly red hair.

"Leave him alone," said Merrill.

The high schooler shot Merrill a menacing look before he turned back to Mohammed. "You better not be related to that bin Laden guy," he said.

No one laughed. Mohammed said nothing. He realized he was afraid.

The driver said, "If you don't sit down back there, I'm going to…"

The arm lifted. "Rag head," sneered one of the high schooler's friends.

Mohammed hurried to an empty row at the back of the bus. He knew everyone was watching. His face felt hot.

"Jerks," said Merrill, sitting beside him. "You should report them."

Mohammed didn't answer. His heart was thumping, his palms sweaty. The old question was back again, pushing away every other thought: *Why did he have to be so different?*

❖   ❖   ❖

American flags printed on computer paper were taped to the lockers in the corridors. Kids had copied Priscilla, too, many wearing black ribbons pinned to their shirts and blouses. On the blackboard in French class, someone had written *"Vive l'Amérique."*

In social studies they started the chapter on Pilgrims and Puritans. Mr. MacDonald asked several students to read aloud, Mohammed among them. He read about the Mayflower Compact and the landing on Plymouth Rock. After the reading, Mac talked about the foundations of liberty. He talked about religious persecution. He looked sternly at the class as he spoke. "What I have always found troubling," he said, eyeing each of them, "was that many of the first Americans—including the Puritans—who came here to escape the religious intolerance in their own countries eventually became intolerant themselves, persecuting those with religious beliefs different from their own. I am troubled by how soon they forgot." Mohammed sensed that Mac was speaking not just about the first Americans.

At lunch he ate by himself. Merrill had left early to take a make-up test. Mohammed nibbled at his sandwich. His carton of milk grew warm. The morning had been a disaster—the incident on the bus, the heavy air of tragedy in his classes. And Priscilla Smith hadn't smiled at him in the hall.

At the next table, Mitch Redding and his friends talked loudly. Mohammed heard Mitch say, "My dad says all Arabs want to be terrorists."

Performing the *Zuhr* prayer at school was an obligation that Mohammed still felt uneasy about. Special arrangements had been made for him to make his noon prayer in the nurse's office. His father had spoken with Mr. Vander Bogart about making an accommodation. The wall with the vaccination chart aligned conveniently with Mecca, and the school nurse, Mrs. Kirmil, took lunch in the teachers' lounge at that hour. The Vander had given Mohammed permission to use his office restroom for the ritual washing of face, hands, and feet before prayer. "Just don't leave a mess," he had advised.

Mohammed's own preferences were not considered. He would have preferred not to be the only Muslim in middle school. He would have preferred to save his noon prayer for later, double it up with the *Asr* prayer at home. But in Saturday Koran classes, his teacher, Yaseen Haneez—the bearded, bear-size imam whose loud voice and unblinking gaze still made Mohammed tremble—had been clear: Mohammed was old enough to offer a noon prayer no matter where he was. So every day before lunch ended, Mohammed retreated to the Vander's office bathroom to wash—the smell of Old Spice strong inside—then to Mrs. Kirmil's office to pray.

During the first weeks of school, he had kept the purpose of these visits a secret from his friends, though his absence did not pass unnoticed. Mohammed knew he shouldn't be ashamed, but for some reason he was. Once Merrill had asked, "Why are you going to see the nurse so much? Are you sick?"

Mohammed had been ready. "Gotta take a pill." *Yeah, the pill of prayer.*

Then one Friday at lunch, Edgar McHugh choked on a Tater Tot. Teddy White—a member of the Young Engineers' club and a kid Mohammed considered bold beyond his years—jumped up, and just like the man they had watched in the health science video, he performed the Heimlich on Edgar—picture perfect—sending the Tater Tot flying across the cafeteria. Edgar was rushed to the nurse's office for examination, accompanied by Mr. Plante, the assistant principal. In front of the vaccination chart, they stumbled over Mohammed on his knees, touching his head to the floor in private audience with Allah. The moment elicited an expletive from Mr. Plante that would be repeated in lunchroom circles for months after. By the next day everyone in school had heard. "Pill, eh?" Merrill had said, shaking his head.

That afternoon, after escaping Mitch and friends in the lunchroom, Mohammed decided to make his prayer as short as possible. But in the Vander's office, he found the bathroom door locked. Mrs. Cooter, the secretary, appeared behind him. "The toilet is stopped, and the principal is in a meeting," she declared, making this peculiar conjunction sound perfectly normal. "You'll have to use the hall restroom."

He had performed *wudu* in the hall restroom before, when the other had been in use, but this was the first time he had been told the principal's bathroom was out of service.

Inside the hall restroom he stood before one of the sinks, wetting himself swiftly, not wanting to be observed by other boys who entered. The sight of a kid with one foot in the basin always brought stares. And there was another reason for not getting too wet: unlike the principal's bathroom, the boys' restroom had no paper towels. Mohammed dried himself before one of the blow-dryers, holding up one foot then the other to the warm air.

When he reached the nurse's office, Mrs. Kirmil was back from lunch, sitting in her chair. She smelled of cigarette smoke.

"Excuse me," he said, halting at the door. "I didn't know you were here."

Mrs. Kirmil, a curt and unsympathetic woman in the face of student pain, student blood, and student screams, sounded more heartless than usual. "I need the office today," she snapped. "You'll have to find some other place. And tomorrow I have weight checks, so…" She made a motion with her hand, suggesting that tomorrow had come, kids were lined up to be weighed, and Mohammed was in the way.

He retreated to his locker, the skin of his face tight with air-blown dryness. At first he was relieved. He hadn't wanted to pray. But as he waited for the fifth-period bell to ring, a new question troubled him. Had the stopped-up toilet and weight checks been a coincidence?

That afternoon Mohammed walked from the bus stop to Norman's house, where Norman's mother answered the door. She looked surprised to see him. "Mo—ham—med," she said, forcing a smile.

"Hi, Mrs. Hazelton. How's Norm?"

Norman's mother surveyed the street over Mohammed's shoulder. "He's a little better," she said.

"Yeah. He said he felt sick."

Mrs. Hazelton frowned. "What happened—it upset him terribly. It upset all of us."

Mohammed nodded.

"I have a sister in New York. We've been crazy with worry since Tuesday."

Mohammed froze. Had Mrs. Hazelton's sister been in one of the towers? Was she one of the missing, one of the dead? No wonder Norman had missed school. Mohammed could think of nothing to say.

"We didn't hear from her until this morning," continued Mrs. Hazelton. "She works in New Jersey, but she has to go to the city a lot. I won't be surprised if she comes back to Ohio now."

Mohammed nodded, relieved but puzzled. Giving up New York for Ohio? That he would never have done. He waited for Mrs. Hazelton to invite him in, but she remained in the entry, holding the door half closed behind her.

"I brought Norm's assignments."

Mrs. Hazleton continued to look down the street. "You can leave them with me," she said. "Norm's lying down."

Strange, Mohammed thought. Norman's mother always invited him inside. "Sure," he said, slipping off his backpack and dropping to one knee to pull out the assignment sheet and textbook. He handed both to Norman's mother.

"We had a test in math. He's supposed to study those pages."

Mrs. Hazelton backed into the house. "I'll let him know."

"Tell him I hope he feels better," Mohammed said.

But Norman's mother had already closed the door.

The American flag—the one usually flown on the Fourth of July—hung above the front door of the Ahmed house. When Mohammed inquired why it was up, his mother said, "Peoples see we love America, too."

"Father doesn't want trouble, does he?"

"No trouble," she agreed.

While his mother worked in the kitchen, Mohammed lingered nearby, debating whether to confide his own problems. "I had some trouble today," he said finally. Then he told her about the redheaded kid on the bus and what Mitch had said in the lunchroom. He told her about Norman's mother. He did not tell her about missing noon prayer. "I think Mrs. Hazelton doesn't want me around Norm."

Lisa Ahmed wiped her hands with a dishtowel. She lifted her son's chin until his brown eyes met her own. *"La gente van a decir muchas cosas,"* she said. People are going to say lots of things. She continued in Spanish: "You did not fly those airplanes, and neither did your father, but some people are going to hate us because they think we are like those terrible men. One day people will see that we are not, that we love America, and when they do, everything will be all right. Then there will be no trouble."

She hugged him, then whispered in his ear. *"Ignoralos.* No speak. No fight. Remember what your father say. You American, too."

Born in Esperanza, Mexico, the youngest of six girls, Lisa Sanchez was the daughter who always wanted to work. *"Deme trabajo,"* she liked to say when she was old enough to walk and drag a corn broom across the dirt floor of the family's two-room shack. At age five she followed her mother into the fields to scavenge corn and beans to eat. At ten she picked baby squash in wet rows, paid by the pail. As a teen she worked in the produce sheds, boxing cherry tomatoes sent north to feed fair-skinned people called gringos in a place called *América.*

Many people talked of this place. There was work in America, Lisa heard, gringo work that paid in dollars. In one hour she could earn more than she made in a day in Mexico. So she heard. But to get gringo work, she had to jump a fence and outrun the gringo police who tried to keep outsiders from getting in.

Lisa Sanchez did the math and began to dream. For a price there were men who would help her jump the fence and elude the police. They would deliver her to America.

For the next five years, she worked and saved. She labored in the fields through the heat of the day. At night she worked in the packing sheds. By her eighteenth birthday she had saved seven thousand pesos—$300—the fee to reach a place called Sacramento, where work waited, three crossings guaranteed. Her cousin came, joining a group of twenty; everyone else was a stranger. On their first try they were caught in the desert north of Calexico, California. Someone tripped underground sensors, bringing helicopters and the gringo police with dogs. On the second attempt their guide abandoned them. The men in their group took the lead but only got them lost. Water ran out. Their throats grew dry and voiceless. They clung to the narrow shade of thorn scrub until border patrollers on horseback found them.

The third try delivered them to Sacramento after they hid in the nose of a refrigerated trailer, crates of lettuce stacked behind them. They stood tightly packed together, no room to turn, smelling one another for sixteen hours. When the trailer grew cold inside, they shivered. When it grew hot, the smell of lettuce ripening too fast made them sick. Only the dream of work kept Lisa Sanchez on her feet.

For the next year she and her cousin joined the migrant picking circuit, smelling American dirt up close. They harvested grapes in California, walnuts in Oregon, and apples in Washington. Then they traveled to Nevada and found jobs in the casino hotels doing laundry, cleaning rooms, and mopping kitchen floors—no end of work. Lisa never shook the habit of watching for the border police, an ever-present shadow. She knew what the gringo law said: she was unwelcome, illegal. Yet, oddly, no one she met made her feel so. On the contrary, she felt needed, sheltered. She even got advice. "Blend in, Lisa," said one of her bosses. "Blend in, work hard, and America will embrace you."

She and her cousin moved east with the promise of better money and less police trouble. They joined a group headed to Lafayette, Louisiana, for the crayfish season. Six months later, they were picking crabmeat at Safari Seafood in Belhaven, North Carolina. When her cousin decided to return to Mexico, Lisa Sanchez saw no reason to go. She felt the bulge of twenty-dollar bills in her pocket. Already she could order pizza in English. She took a bus to Chicago—she had wanted to go to New York City but had mistakenly understood that Chicago was warmer—and found work at the Abbott Hotel.

The man she met and married, the one for whom she willingly embraced Islam without fully understanding it—except the part about a husband not drinking alcohol, the part about respecting the wife—was like her, not afraid to work, not afraid to dream. Like him, she was thankful for the welcome America had given them.

Students filed into the gymnasium Friday morning. Mr. Vander Bogart stood in the center of the basketball court with the middle school band and chorus marshaled behind him. "Our president has proclaimed today a national day for prayer and remembrance," he announced through a microphone.

It was eight forty-six—the moment the first plane had struck the North Tower. Mr. Vander Bogart asked for a moment of silence.

Everyone looked down, somber, silent. Even the rowdiest students went quiet. Mohammed thought of the doomed passengers, that terrible moment, the mystery of violent death. He had never traveled in an airplane. Now he wasn't sure he wanted to. Their trip to New York City was to be by bus.

Mr. Vander Bogart lifted his head and turned to the music director, who led the band in the national anthem. One of the students walked from the bleachers to lead the school in the Pledge of Allegiance. Then their principal proceeded to talk about the day of infamy. He spoke of the victims. He eulogized the sacrifice of firefighters and the bravery of law enforcement. He talked about heroes and cowards, about good triumphing over evil. He started to talk about the greatness of America when time ran out.

It was three minutes after nine. Another moment of silence was observed for the second plane crashing into the second tower. Again, everyone bowed their heads.

Next the band played "America the Beautiful," and the chorus sang all eight verses. When the song ended, Mr. Plante read Psalm 23. The singing of "Amazing Grace" followed, the entire gymnasium joining in. As girls cried and teachers swayed, Mohammed felt ill at ease. He seemed to be the only one who didn't know the words. He was glad when it was over and Mac took the microphone to read a letter from the Red Cross requesting donations. By then all eyes were on the scoreboard clock, anticipating the third moment of silence for the next plane. When it came at nine thirty-seven, Mohammed bowed his head again, staring at his shirt buttons. He felt other kids watching him.

A musical interlude followed. Kids were allowed to stretch and talk. Everyone spoke in hushed voices. Then a seventh-grader read a poem she had written called "Black Day."

Oh black day,
Bright steel falling,
Lives cut short. Love denied.

Oh black day,
Dark clouds rising,
Dreams downed. Hopes ended.

Oh…

After the third "black day," Mohammed stopped listening.

Mr. Vander Bogart returned to the microphone to introduce the local police chief, who spoke about vigilance. He asked all students to report any suspicious sightings to parents and teachers. Then the plane in Pennsylvania—the one where the passengers had fought back—was remembered at three minutes after ten. During this last moment of silence, Mohammed thought about the passengers and how the plane had flown over Ohio, maybe over his house. The thought of being close to the doomed passengers made him feel strangely sorrowful.

With the band playing and the chorus leading, everyone sang "God Bless America." Mohammed mouthed the words—he knew them by heart—but what he really wanted to do was run home and hide in his room.

The assembly overshadowed the rest of the day. Classes were shortened. Teachers looked somber. In the lunchroom gaiety was sucked from the usually festive Friday by four minutes of silence for the dead.

No announcement was made about weigh-ins at the nurse's office. Mohammed stuck with his plan not to pray at school.

That afternoon the Young Engineers gathered in room 113 with Miss Cutter. Mohammed saw the news on her face before she spoke.

"People, I'm sorry to announce that the school board has suspended all excursions. That means our trip to New York is off."

Several students asked why. Mohammed was not one of them. He knew why.

"Terrorism concerns," said Miss Cutter.

"Postponed or canceled?" asked Teddy White, lawyerlike.

"I think that will depend on future events."

"But isn't that giving in?" asked Priscilla. "Isn't that what terrorists want? To keep us home?"

As usual, everyone turned to look at Priscilla. Mohammed resisted the urge.

"I suppose it is," agreed their adviser. "But right now the board's concern is your safety."

The Young Engineers rolled their eyes. A few shook their heads. Mohammed stared out a window. Silence fell on room 113. Miss Cutter studied their faces. "Considering the circumstances," she said, just above a whisper, "none of us should be surprised by this decision. I know you must be disappointed. I am disappointed. But there are many young people out there, many in New York, who are feeling something other than disappointment today. They have not lost out on a field trip. They have lost a parent…a brother…a sister…a friend. I'm sure you'll agree that disappointment is not the word to describe what they must be feeling." She paused, then added, "Please think of them."

No one spoke. Mohammed stared at his hands. What could you say to that? His dream was dead.

When he entered his house, he heard Mrs. Heath speaking with his mother in the living room. He set his book bag quietly on the kitchen floor.

Mrs. Heath was their neighbor—a widow who had moved from New York City two summers before. She hired him to cut her grass, rake leaves, and shovel snow. He had saved $150 working for Mrs. Heath—money set aside for the Young Engineers' trip to New York. Mrs. Heath was also his friend. She invited him to her kitchen for milk and snacks—cookies, brownies, pie—baked and served with the assurance that Crisco, not lard, was used in the recipes. Mrs. Heath knew Muslims couldn't eat pork. She knew a lot about Muslims, more than most people in their town. She knew Muslims prayed five times a day. She knew about Ramadan, the Koran, and mosques. She knew about all the rules. She also knew that Muslim kids were still kids. At Christmas she gave him and Nura Maryam candy canes. She delivered baskets with chocolate eggs on Easter. And knowing that he and his sister didn't trick-or-treat, she brought them treats the day before Halloween.

To Mohammed, their silver-haired neighbor with the pinched nose, alert blue eyes, and quick smile was the grandmother they never had, the one who spoiled them. She was also the only person he knew who had actually *lived* in New York, the city he wanted so badly to visit.

Now her city had been attacked. The towers lay in ruin. Thousands were dead. And Muslims had done it. Mohammed listened near the kitchen door.

"I've hardly slept since Tuesday," Mrs. Heath told his mother, her voice quiet. "I haven't tried to call anybody. I guess I'm afraid what I might hear if I do. I start to dial then hang up. Bob knew so many people. He worked in the South Tower, eighty-sixth floor—New York State Department of Taxation. I wonder what he would have done."

Bob was the late Mr. Heath. Mohammed had never met him, but he knew Mrs. Heath had moved to Ohio after his death.

"And I have been thinking of Mohammed, too," she said.

Mohammed froze at the door.

"Lisa, you know as well as I do that there are people who do not behave well when something like this happens. They look for scapegoats."

"Scape…goat?" his mother repeated hesitantly.

"Yes. When the goat is blamed, you know, for everybody's sins and is sent off somewhere. The Hebrew people did it."

"*Chivo expiatorio*?" suggested his mother. *Scapegoat* in Spanish.

"Yes, " said Mrs. Heath. "That sounds right. Well, adults look for scapegoats, and sometimes their children imitate them."

"I see."

"Unfortunately, we all know how cruel kids can be. I don't want to see Mohammed hurt at school by what his classmates might say or do."

His mother said, "We talk. I say no fight."

"As long as he knows he can talk to somebody."

"Thank you for your worry."

"I'm afraid there are a lot of people to worry about these days," said Mrs. Heath, "but you, Hasan, and the children are the nearest, so I might as well worry about you. That's why I left New York—to have neighbors to worry about."

Mohammed made noise in the kitchen before he entered the living room.

"Hello there," said Mrs. Heath, smiling faintly. Like his mother, she looked as if she had spent the last days crying. For the first time she looked like a widow. "I'm going to bake a pie tomorrow," she said, her posture improving, her voice jumping from soft to falsely vibrant. "So come in the afternoon. I've got leaves to rake, if you want to work. You're still saving?"

He nodded, unwilling to mention his reason for saving—the club trip—had just been canceled. Now was not the moment.

"Fine," she said, trying to sound cheery. "We're on—as they say."

Mohammed excused himself and went to his room. *What a lady*, he thought as he climbed the stairs. New York had been stabbed in its heart, and she was going to bake a pie.

Food was never simple in the Ahmed household. It needed information. For Mohammed, food was full of decisions.

At middle school the ritual of trading sandwiches and swapping snacks was not an option for him. Who wanted carrot and pickle spread on whole wheat bread? Or mashed beans in a kaiser roll? Mohammed couldn't trade for ham, even turkey ham. Ham was haram—unsafe, unlawful, forbidden for a Muslim to eat. Any food that contained pork, pork products, or pork flavorings was haram. Bologna was haram. Hot dogs. Any sandwich with Kraft cheese. Any filling with Miracle Whip. Any bread with dough conditioners. What was he supposed to say? "Hey, kid, can I see the label on that mayo?"

Then there was the tricky question of what Merrill called the payday sandwiches—the ones everyone wanted to trade for: chicken salad, sliced turkey, roast beef. These were halal, or permitted for Muslims to eat, but there was a catch. Mr. Chicken, Mr. Turkey, and Mr. Steer had to be slaughtered *by* a Muslim according to Islamic rules. When Mohammed explained this to Merrill, his response was, "Stick with tuna, dude." And he was right. There was no way to know who had killed the chicken in Edgar McHugh's grilled chicken sandwich. Poultry at Mohammed's house was bought from Majd Udeen, a butcher who delivered fresh halal meat from animals sacrificed according to the rules. But the payday sandwiches at middle school lunch tables were *mushbooh*—neither halal nor haram, rather in the twilight zone of food—suspect, doubtful. As his father often said, "What was once halal might be haram."

Snacks and sweets only added to Mohammed's dilemma. So many were off-limits: Doritos. Cheetos. Fritos. Four kinds of Ruffles. Twinkies. Keebler cookies. Nabisco crackers. Pepperidge Farm Goldfish. Dolly Madison doughnuts. Marshmallows. Devil Dogs. Milky Ways. Snickers. Skittles. Tootsie Rolls. Most hard candies. Gatorade. Hi-C fruit punch. Even deliverance from bad breath had restrictions. Certs, Clorets, Chiclets, and Life Savers—all were haram. (They had an ingredient made from chicken feathers.) Lack of a portable mouth freshener presented a major mortification for Mohammed. What if Priscilla Smith actually *spoke* to him? He had to be ready.

In such cases he consulted the book: *Halal and Haram in US Supermarkets and Restaurants.* His father had bought it from a Sunni bibliophile who stocked the masjid library every year. In it were all the products in America a Muslim could and could not eat, bathe with, brush with, or wash with—from coast to coast. From cheeses to chewing gum, soups to shampoos, the safe and unsafe ingredients were listed in black and red ink.

The book resided in their kitchen, where Mohammed's mother would ask her son to help translate such unfamiliar items as frozen bagels. Often it went with them to the grocery store, where they could be seen turning its pages as they read product labels. Haram and *mushbooh* usually lurked in fine print. Flavorings and colorings had to be watched carefully. Many contained the most unlawful ingredient in the big book: alcohol.

Alcohol was right up there with pork on the forbidden list. Fermentation was treacherous terrain, and as his father often said, a Muslim didn't have to drink a whole bottle to go to hell. Molecules counted—even *after* they had evaporated from Miss Meringue's Oven-Baked Rum Cake.

Mohammed concerned himself less with rum cake, however, than he did with Raisin Bran. Raisin Bran stared up at him from the breakfast table on cereal mornings while rum cake did not. Such was life in the Ahmed household when all the popular breakfast cereals were *mushbooh*. Froot Loops. Cocoa Puffs. Cocoa Krispies. Trix. Lucky Charms. Cap'n Crunch.

Not surprisingly, Corn Flakes and Special K were halal, but after Raisin Bran who wanted more flakes? Quaker oatmeal was safe, too, but only the old-fashioned original flavor. As Norman said, "Leave it to the Quakers."

Mohammed didn't complain. He would never dare. He knew it was his duty to eat according to the rules, just as it was his duty to dress by them. It was one of the paths to surrender and peace. It was obedience. But in his dreams he sinned, sometimes wishing for a close encounter with haram—a bite of a McDonald's Sausage McMuffin, for example. Just one bite.

Every Friday Mohammed's father drove to the city to attend Salat al-Jumu'ah, the weekly gathering prayer at Masjid Dawoud. In the gathering prayer Muslims prayed as a congregation and listened to a sermon. That evening, after his trip to the city, Hasan Ahmed turned to his son at the supper table. "Something happened today at the masjid," he said soberly. "I want you to hear it."

Mohammed put down his fork. He knew not to speak.

"A man from the street walked in after prayer," his father began. "He had been drinking. Abu Bakr, our concierge, asked him to remove his shoes, but he refused. He said he had come to burn down the masjid. He said other things, too. He was very upset. Some of the brothers asked him to leave. At first he refused, but then he agreed.

"Later, we heard the sound of windows breaking, and then we smelled gasoline. We ran outside. The man who had refused to take off his shoes was pouring gas from a can at the front of the building. When we called to him to stop, he pulled a gun from his coat. He pointed the gun at where the gas had been spilled, and he pulled the trigger, but the gun did not fire. Yaseen Haneez approached the man, asking him to leave. The man pointed the gun at Mr. Haneez and pulled the trigger. Again it did not fire. Then the man ran to the corner, where a car was waiting. The police were called, but the man was not caught."

Mohammed's father studied his son. "*That* was the kind of trouble I was talking about the other day," he concluded.

Mohammed nodded. He pictured the thick-bearded Yaseen Haneez, his bearlike figure standing before the gunman. "Why was Mr. Haneez not afraid?" he asked.

"I don't know," replied his father. "Sometimes it is foolish not to be afraid."

His mother nodded.

"As to trouble, that may not be the last. I am telling you this not to alarm you but to prepare you. Your mother told me you have had some trouble, too."

Mohammed looked at his mother. *She had told him.* "A little," he replied. Fortunately he hadn't mentioned skipping noon prayer. *That* would be trouble.

"She also told you what you should do when there is a problem, and I expect you to obey. No good will come from returning a provocation. Do not be foolish. Walk away."

"Yes, Abi." He stared at the floor. Should he divulge his own disaster? The masjid had escaped destruction, but not his dream. "Miss Cutter canceled the trip to New York today," he said.

His father and mother exchanged glances. His mother seemed to want to console him, but she said nothing.

"It is for the best," his father said. "This is no time to go to New York—or anywhere. I'm sure there will be other opportunities."

Mohammed stared at his fork. He knew his father would say that. His father always said that. And his mother stayed silent. New York was nothing to them.

Back in his room he removed the colored tacks from the Rand McNally map. No dream, no tacks. As he fell asleep that night, he thought about Yaseen Haneez and the nameless gunman. The question returned: *why hadn't the old teacher been afraid?*

Mohammed was seven when his father drove him to Masjid Dawoud for his first Saturday Koran class. Upstairs in the big hallway, he sat with other boys his age, facing a replica mihrab painted on the wall nearest to Mecca. He wore his head covering and held his small, leather-bound Koran just out of the box. Yaseen Haneez had handed a copy to each of them, his voice deeply reverent. "Never mark it. Never let it touch the floor. Never get it wet. Let no other book be above it. And let no day pass without reading it."

But there was to be no reading yet. First came the learning of Arabic letters and vowels with straight-faced Sister Hala Jamal, her crooked fingers tracing letters on the blackboard. Her hands were arthritic, but her long ruler was swift as a bird when she swatted daydreamers between the benches. *Tajwid*, or proper pronunciation, followed with the less severe Sister Meryem Bouhida. Mohammed liked the sounds she was able to draw from the back of his throat, the way his lips learned to embrace soft vowels, how his tongue found new places to go. The painfully slow reading of the Koran began months later—al-Fatiha first, then al-Fatiha again, word by word, line by line, week after week. Sometimes they listened to Saeed Patel, a member of the masjid, recite other chapters of the Koran, obediently repeating them in chorus. Abdul-Wadood, another member, taught them Allah's names and told them stories of the Prophet. Some Saturdays they listened to the poems of Ayesha bin Mahmood. Other Saturdays they colored pictures in *Our Muslim World* coloring books. Students who memorized their supplications were allowed to borrow a book from the children's shelf of the masjid library. This was where Mohammed discovered *Miracle in the Ant,* one of his favorites.

Saturday morning followed Saturday morning. Mohammed turned eight, then nine. He was tall for his age at ten and then thin as a beanpole at eleven, still a permanent fixture in the Koran classes in the upstairs hall. Staying home Saturday mornings was never an option, not even when he was sick. Once he overheard his father tell his mother (when she had suggested he be allowed to sleep in because of a cold) that he did not want his son to lose his "Islamic identity." At the time Mohammed had had no clue what his father meant. Islamic identity? It sounded like some kind of card he was supposed to carry. Now he thought he understood. His father didn't want him to be like any other boy.

He was taught the five duties of every Muslim—declaring allegiance to God, daily prayer, charity to the poor, fasting during Ramadan, and the pilgrimage to Mecca. He was taught how to behave in the masjid, the rules for respecting elders, and how to dress. Eventually he was reading verses from Juz-Amma. And there were always the competitions in which he never excelled: speech forums, writing contests. Who could memorize the most pages of the Koran? Who could recite the longest passage? Unlike most of the boys, Mohammed found no passion for it. He felt guilty about this, and he hoped no one would notice. He especially hoped no one would mention it to his father. He wanted to please his father, to be the boy his father wanted him to be. The dilemma was that Mohammed wasn't sure he wanted to be that boy, that he *could* be that boy, the one his father had told his mother about, the one who carried the card.

The big sign on Highway 32 advertised "AHMED AUTOMOTIVE" in large letters. When crabgrass grew tall around the sign poles, Mohammed was sent to pull it. On weekends he picked up litter on the highway. He set up and took down the signboard that offered "Free Towing." At the gas pumps, he helped Delmar Moffit, the man who worked for his father. While Delmar pumped fuel, Mohammed cleaned windshields, checked tire pressure, ran for additives, and made sure Delmar didn't forgot to tighten the gas caps. Between customers, he swept the service island and listened to Delmar give opinions. This Saturday Delmar had something to say about September 11.

"Russians might be behind it," he said. "Never could trust Communists."

Delmar had worked at the station since Mohammed could remember. Gray-haired and bristle-faced, Delmar wore the same clothes every day and never brought a lunch. His mouth always smelled of cigarettes. His eyes were set in wrinkles like warthog eyes, and his front teeth were gone. But he grinned just the same.

"'Course people are saying other things," he continued. "Lot of talk about Arabs and some long-bearded Jew hater."

"Osama bin Laden," said Mohammed.

"Who?"

"The man who doesn't like Jews."

"Is that his name?"

"He doesn't like Americans, either."

"Give me five minutes with him, and he'll like 'em even less." Delmar chuckled, then coughed. "I already told your old man. I said, 'Hasan, don't be surprised if business drops. Folks are angry, and when they get riled, they do stupid things like try to get even, even if it hurts 'em.'"

"Get even?" Mohammed echoed.

"Yup. If it's Arabs that done it, your old man is advertising for trouble with that sign out there on the highway. He oughta take it down until matters cool off. At any rate, I done my duty telling him. By my reckoning, Mr. Gerhard is going to be getting our business. The Shell station on the east side, too."

Delmar coughed again, then spat. "When the pumping slows down, Hamed, we probably won't be needing your help around here. I've already told your old man I can handle the island myself. I'm staying with him no matter what."

Mohammed studied Delmar's face. He wasn't talking about some stranger trying to burn down a masjid. He was talking about people they knew. "You're saying people won't buy gas because of what happened in New York?"

"Heard talk."

"But that's not fair."

"Lots of things ain't fair." Delmar pulled a rag from his pants and began to wipe the pumps. "Called a boycott. Write it down, lad."

"A boycott?"

"Yup. They'll strike us, Hamed. This here gasoline may come from Arabs—most of it anyhow—but people won't want to buy it if an Arab is pumping it."

That afternoon Mohammed counted the customers. Cars pulled into the station as usual, both sides of the island keeping them busy. Some days were slower than others, but this one seemed no different than most. Convinced that Delmar had been wrong, Mohammed stopped counting cars at twenty. How could people buy their gas elsewhere? His father had the best service in town.

Sunday night the Ahmed family had gathered in the living room to begin the *Isha* prayer, when a succession of loud blasts sounded outside their windows. Mohammed suddenly found himself pushed to the floor, his father on top of him. He closed his eyes, frightened by the alarm in his father's voice as he ordered Mohammed's mother to cover Nura Maryam and stay down.

Then the discharges stopped. Nura Maryam started to cry. His father asked if anyone was hurt. His mother, who had repeatedly invoked the name of God in Spanish, said they were fine. Mohammed said nothing, too squished to speak.

They waited. The sounds of their breathing filled the house. Then another sequence shattered the stillness, louder than the first, too fast for a gun. The next instant his father was off him. The living room went black. "Keep down!" enjoined his voice from the darkness. He had turned off the lights.

From the windows, silvery flashes illuminated the living room. The blasts dropped to sputters and pops. The smell of burned paper reached them. Mohammed heard his father open the front door. "It's all right," he called.

Mohammed sat up and rubbed his eyes. He recognized the burned smell. When the lights came on, dirty yellow smoke floated in the living room. "Firecrackers!" he blurted.

His father held a tube of charred cardboard. "Someone was having fun," he muttered.

"A joke?" suggested his mother, waving away the smoke.

"Probably just kids trying to scare us."

"They scare," agreed his mother.

His father nodded. "Let us resume our prayers," he said. "It is nothing to worry about."

But Mohammed knew this wasn't true. His father's words were a mask. Behind the mask was the man with the gun at the masjid. Trouble was behind his words.

When the phone rang, everyone jumped. His father answered. "Yes, Mrs. Heath," he said. "No, Mrs. Heath, that won't be necessary. We're fine. Thank you. Good night, Mrs. Heath."

His father hung up. "She wanted to call the police."

That night Mohammed woke to the sound of a car speeding down Dana Street, its tires screeching. He heard steps on the creaky wooden floors of their house. Mohammed knew his father was checking.

The next morning Norman stood at the bus stop.

"A lot's been going on," Mohammed said, summing up the week's events.

Norman looked thinner. His book bag hung heavily at his side. He stared at the ground.

"Are you better?"

Norman said, "I was never that sick."

Mohammed remembered what Mrs. Hazelton had said about her sister in New York. "Is your aunt okay?"

Norman nodded.

"Your mom sounded worried."

Another nod.

"Did you get the assignments?"

Norman scuffed the sidewalk. "I just couldn't come down, that's all."

Mohammed studied his friend with the nerdy glasses and neatly parted hair. Norman was quiet but never this quiet. "Are you all right?"

Before Norman could answer, Merrill arrived. He clapped Norman on the back. "Why so serious, girls? Who's dead?"

Mohammed shrugged. "We're just talking."

Then Norman said, "About three thousand dead, Merrill, in case you haven't heard. Mostly New Yorkers." He didn't raise his voice, but his words hit Merrill like a jab. Merrill stepped back, his face crooked. "Jeez, sorry I asked."

Norman shook his head. "Not as sorry as I am. You guys just don't get it."

Mohammed and Merrill exchanged puzzled looks. When the bus arrived, Mohammed remembered the redheaded bully. "There's this high school kid," he began. "He has been saying things about Arabs. The other day he—"

Norman cut him off. "Can we talk later?"

The bus door opened. Mohammed prepared to face his tormentor. "Sure," he muttered.

But the redheaded kid was sitting near a window, busy with friends. The aisle was safe. Mohammed whizzed by. He slid into the seat next to Norman. Both boys set their backpacks on their laps. Mohammed resumed in a hushed tone. "See that red-haired kid over there? He's the one who—"

"Mohammed," interrupted Norman, "I can't talk to you anymore."

Mohammed stared. Norman shifted on the seat. Voices and laughter filled the bus.

"I promised, okay? I'm sorry." Norman dropped his chin to his chest. He played with the zipper on his book bag. "If I didn't promise, she was going to make trouble. And I know my mother. She would."

Mohammed nodded. Of course. Satellite mom. "What trouble?"

"I don't know. Trouble for you. For your family. She only said 'trouble.' She's really worked up. You don't want to be around her when she gets like that."

Mohammed remembered how Norman's mother had watched the street. Had she been thinking about trouble then? "Because of what those hijackers did?"

His friend stared at his hands, answering with silence.

"That's ridiculous, Norman, and you know it. I didn't have anything to do with that. It was bunch of crazy men. Evil men."

"Arab men," Norman interjected.

Mohammed groaned.

"They killed thousands of people, Hamed. Thousands."

"I know that." Mohammed stared out the window.

"It's just so horrible."

"It's horrible, all right," Mohammed said. "And it's horrible what your mother wants you to do. She has it wrong, Norman."

"I promised, okay? It's only for a while, until she gets over it."

"You're talking to me now."

"I'm explaining."

"How's your mother going to know if you talk to me or not? Is she coming to school?"

"I wouldn't put it past her," Norman said. "I shouldn't even be sitting here."

Mohammed motioned toward the empty seats. "Your choice."

Norman didn't move. "Forget it," he mumbled. "We're almost there."

"Yeah."

After the high schoolers got off, the bus stopped at the middle school.

"I got tons of catching up to do," Norman said wearily. "And my mother to thank for it."

They shuffled off the bus.

"You can borrow my notes if you want."

"Thanks, Hamed."

They kept in step, their book bags bumping.

"I've been feeling lousy, too," Mohammed said. "Not sick. Just different."

Norman listened.

"Did you hear one of them was named Mohammed?"

"Yeah. I saw it on the news."

"You can pick your friends but not your name."

"Or your mother."

"I'm so ashamed."

"Me, too," Norman said.

That morning the dilemma of noon prayer followed Mohammed like a shadow. Pray or not pray? He had heard the TV reports: the hijackers had prayed on the planes.

Prayer had been in the air. Friday had been a national day of prayer. The president had asked them to pray. So had Mr. Vander Bogart. Now prayer was in the news.

Mohammed tried to imagine the passengers huddled in the back of the doomed jetliners, praying to God, praying to be saved, praying for life, while in the plane's cockpit the terrorists prayed to God for death and success.

Pray or not pray? He was inclined to pass.

At lunch he met Norman in the cafeteria. They spoke little, both bruised from what had been said on the bus. When they finished, Norman said, "Aren't you going to pray?"

Mohammed explained what had happened on Thursday with Mrs. Kirmil and Mrs. Cooter.

Norman shook his head. "They're in cahoots. Vander doesn't have a clue."

"You think?"

"Ask him. I guarantee he'll let you pray."

Mohammed checked the lunchroom clock. There was still time. "Thanks, Norm," he said, rising from the table.

When he reached the office, he found Mr. Vander Bogart behind his desk, torn between a sandwich and the *Cincinnati Post*. Mrs. Cooter was gone. The principal waved him in. Mohammed knew the Vander didn't like speeches, unless they were his own, so he kept it short. "May I use your bathroom, Mr. Vander Bogart? I mean, before I pray?"

The principal lowered the paper but not his sandwich. Already he was nodding. "Of course, Mohammed. You know you don't have to ask. Go to it."

Norman was right. The Vander didn't have a clue.

"I just wanted to make sure it was fixed, sir."

"Fixed? What was fixed?" He looked puzzled.

"The toilet. It was stopped up. I was going to use the hall restroom, but I thought I'd check—"

"No one told me about a stopped-up toilet," the Vander declared. "And if it was, it isn't now. I just used it. Go. It's yours." He returned to his sandwich.

Mohammed didn't move. "Sir?"

The principal looked up, his face patient. "Yes, Mohammed?"

"Is there a problem with me using Mrs. Kirmil's office to do my prayer?"

The puzzled look returned. "Of course not. Why? Has there been some difficulty?" The Vander lowered his sandwich.

Mohammed shook his head. It was better not to point fingers. "No, sir. No difficulty. I was just wondering, you know—because of everything that happened—if there was a problem with me praying here."

The Vander stiffened. "Certainly not," he snapped. He put his hands flat on his desk and looked intently at Mohammed. "What happened last week had nothing to do with you. If someone in this school is making you feel so—student or teacher—I want to know. That goes for your prayer, too."

His voice had grown loud, as if he were giving a speech. He stood. "Come," he said, moving to the door. Mohammed followed, wishing he hadn't come. In the outer office Mrs. Cooter sat at her desk. Her head was down as they passed. The Vander marched across the hall and entered the nurse's office. Mrs. Kirmil was inside. So was the smell of cigarette smoke. The principal sniffed and grimaced. "Mrs. Kirmil, I have Mohammed here. I just want you to assure him that you don't have a problem with him using this space for his prayer while you are at lunch. I want him to feel comfortable, especially after what has happened. Do you agree?"

Mrs. Kirmil looked at Mr. Vander Bogart but not at Mohammed. "Yes, of course," she replied flatly. "The other day there were supposed to be weigh-ins, but the assembly—"

"Fine," the principal shot back.

"In an emergency," continued Mrs. Kirmil, "I might have to ask him—"

"Yes, yes, of course, an emergency. But we don't have those every day."

The Vander seemed in a hurry to get back to his sandwich. "I want Mohammed to know that we are completely supportive, and that we respect his obligations as a Muslim in this predominately Christian middle school of ours. That's all. I know you're on board, Mrs. Kirmil. Thank you."

Mohammed followed the principal across the hall, trying to keep up. They stopped in the office.

"You see? No problem." He glanced around, his eyes passing over Mrs. Cooter. Then he pointed to the bathroom. "Now go to it. Just don't leave a mess."

Inside, Mohammed performed his *wudu* hastily. When he returned to the nurse's room, Mrs. Kirmil was gone, but not the smell of her cigarette smoke. He faced the vaccination chart, blocking out the corridor sounds. Then he raised his hands and began.

He finished just as the fifth-period bell rang.

In study hall he went to the library room for an Internet pass.

"Class?" barked Mrs. Kapler, somehow in a whisper.

"History," answered Mohammed.

Mrs. Kapler wrote in the pass book. "Topic?"

"The Statue of Liberty."

Mrs. Kapler peered over her glasses. "Again?"

Mohammed nodded. He regularly browsed the Statue of Liberty website. With no Internet at home—his father said it was a waste of money—the only place he could get online was at school.

Mrs. Kapler handed him a pass with the familiar refrain. "Fifteen minutes. No downloads. No e-mail. No chats." He found an empty workstation and sat.

When the browser opened, he typed in the National Park Service address for the Statue of Liberty monument. He found the drop-down for the webcam, then clicked the icon. He might not be going to New York, but at least he could visit electronically.

He waited for the page to load. A message popped up: "Webcam not available." He clicked the Visitors tab. On the screen a notice appeared:

TEMPORARILY CLOSED TO THE PUBLIC

Public safety concerns since September 11, 2001,
have necessitated the closing of the
national parks on Liberty and Ellis Islands.
Ferry service has been suspended indefinitely.
The islands and the monument remain
off-limits to the public until further notice.

NPS

Mohammed closed the browser. *Of course.*

He felt strangely relieved. What was the point of going to New York if he couldn't visit Miss Liberty. No matter. He didn't need the Internet or a webcam to see her. She came to him in his dreams.

The dream was always the same.

It was night. He was alone on Liberty Island, and there was a storm. He was standing next to the granite-clad pedestal, looking up at the statue, rain stabbing his face. Miss Liberty loomed above him like a colossal specter, her torchlight undimmed by the rain. He heard the thunder of an angry sea. A pounding surf shook the ground. The wind tore through his hair. Then he was inside the monument, climbing the open stairway of the pedestal, passing the colonnade, where the wind blew stronger, its voice shrill. Next he found himself on the spiral staircase of the statue. The storm's roar dropped to a muffled moan. The air smelled of tar and the sea. His footfalls echoed ominously in the statue's cavernous interior. Miss Liberty seemed restless. Her copper skin creaked. The iron staircase trembled. When he stood in the crown, the wind drove him back from the observation windows. He ascended a ladder inside the tunnel of her arm. The climb grew steeper. Ahead he made out a door outlined in light. The arm swayed. The iron armature shuddered. If he slipped, he would fall backward into Liberty's shoulder and drop into the cavern of ribs. He fixed his eyes on the light above him. At the end of the tunnel, he opened an overhead door, the light too bright to look at. He pulled himself onto the torch platform, gripping the railing against the wind. Miss Liberty swayed. The city lights shone like diluted stars. He looked down. The rays of Liberty's crown seemed close enough to touch. Her eyes were black. The shaded edge of her nose looked sharp. Seen from above, she was more darkness than light, a shadow draped in green.

The wind tore at his clothes. He tightened his grip on the railing. Miss Liberty moved as if she were alive. Her iron trestle groaned. Her arm rocked. The torch balcony tilted from side to side. Then in one violent gust, he was swept off the platform and into the night. He fell through the darkness toward the sea, the roar of the surf loud. The wind no longer screamed. He closed his eyes and held his breath, waiting for impact, but no jarring blow came. Instead he slipped quietly into the sea like something unnoticed.

Salt water filled his nose and stung his eyes. The waves turned him in somersaults. The island's deadly undertow pulled him down. When he could fight it no more—his clothes heavy, seawater swallowed—he sank, his last breath suddenly flooded, something hard inside him giving way. Into the dark depths he dropped, his body weightless, his head seeming to leave him behind.

In his dream his eyes were closed, yet he made out the shadow of something large looming above him. A diffused yellowish glow lit the sea. He felt buffeted by the current, and then something touched him. The sea slipped by. The yellow glow brightened. In moments he was out of the sea, coughing up salt water and gasping for air. He turned from the light to see what held him—the clasp of fingers, the palm of a large hand. When he looked up, her face was close to his—the face of Miss Liberty. And she was smiling.

Her tunic flapped in the wind. Her tablet lay near her feet. She lowered him to the lawn at the seawall before she picked up the tablet and raised herself onto the pedestal again. The folds of her garment fell into place. Her smile faded. She lifted her torch into the sky and fixed her eyes on the harbor, becoming a statue once more.

The wind died. The sea calmed. Manhattan's lights glistened to the east. Mohammed stood wet, cold—and breathing. Then he lay awake in his bed.

In the morning, before sunrise, with the hour of prayer at hand, the dream remained large in his mind. He wondered what it meant.

The pictures of the nineteen hijackers appeared on the news. All had Arab faces, Arab names. Mohammed the ringleader.

Mohammed, son of the mechanic, acquired new notoriety in school. Kids who knew him only as Hamed made the connection. "Hey, it's Mohammed, like the hijacker."

He avoided Priscilla in the hallways. He didn't look at her in classes. His secret desire was to become invisible. Then came the trouble in PE.

Boys' phys ed had always held awkward moments for Mohammed. Unlike his classmates who sported trim athletic shorts to gym class, he wore baggy Bermudas selected by his father according to a strict interpretation of the Islamic dress code. He was the only boy who didn't remove his shirt in PE—not in the locker room, not when they wrestled, not in the team picking of "shirts" or "skins." Then there was Coach Chamley. Coach C taught middle school PE and coached high school football. He was a flat-faced, beefy man who liked to say "y'all." He called eighth-grade boys "turkeys."

On Tuesday Coach C led them to the soccer field, where he turned them loose with a ball. It was here, as Mohammed dribbled down the sideline, that Ralph Trumbull landed a running block that sent Mohammed tumbling out of bounds. Before Mohammed got to his feet, Ralph pressed his face into the grass. "Smell the weeds, Taliban," he hissed.

The next shot came from Mitch in front of the goal. When it looked as if Mohammed might break away and score, Mitch stepped into him and raised a knee into his groin. "That's for New York," he spat. "For your hijacking cousins."

Coach C's whistle split the air. He waved his hands in disgust. Mohammed lay on the ground, clutching his groin, his face twisted in agony.

"This ain't tackle, y'all," he chided.

"Sorry, Coach," said Mitch, exchanging smiles with Ralph.

Coach C stood over Mohammed. "Are you all right?"

Mohammed rolled onto his side, gulping for air, trying to shrink the pain. Faces stared down at him, but Mohammed saw only shadows against the sky. Everything spun.

Coach C looked at his watch. "Time to hit the showers, turkeys."

The circle of boys dissolved. Mohammed remained on the field.

"I don't want to see anything like that again, y'all," Coach C yelled. He turned to Merrill and Norman. "Help him up."

They lifted him to his feet. "He did it on purpose," Mohammed gasped.

"We know," Merrill said.

Inside the gym he walked on his own. In one of the bathroom stalls, he threw up his lunch. For the rest of the day, his stomach ached.

That night at supper, the nausea lingered. Mohammed nibbled at his food. He said nothing to his parents about the assault or the verbal attacks.

"Funny thing," remarked his father. "We had only two customers today."

He said he would put up an American flag at the station.

In the news there were reports of angry Americans. Protesters outside a masjid in Chicago waved flags, shouting, "USA! USA!" An Arab cab driver in Cincinnati was pulled from his vehicle and assaulted. On the television Mohammed and his parents saw pictures of an Islamic center in Texas damaged by a pipe bomb. They listened to an interview with a Muslim businessman in Maryland whose Arabic bookstore was burned to the ground by a suspicious fire. Two women wearing hijabs—the Muslim headscarves—told a story of being harassed in the street, chased, and spat upon.

Thursday evening, September 20, the Ahmed family watched the president address the nation. Mohammed's father nodded many times during the speech. He clapped when the president said, "The enemy of America is not our many Muslim friends; it is not our many Arab friends. No one should be singled out for unfair treatment or unkind words."

Mohammed sat in silence. His thoughts were on the *Tribute to Heroes* telethon to be broadcast the next night. Middle school was abuzz with the event. Tom Cruise, Sylvester Stallone, and

Will Smith would be manning the phones. Bon Jovi would sing from New York. Mohammed was a secret fan of Bon Jovi—secret at home at least, since his father did not approve of such music.

The next evening, after his father went to bed, he asked his mother if he could stay up. He told her the telethon was to raise money for the victims of the attacks.

"Change to pajamas," she whispered. "I watch, too."

The first hour was better than he expected. They sat together on the couch, the TV volume low. Mohammed identified Bruce Springsteen for his mother. She recognized Enrique Iglesias. Hollywood's biggest stars were taking calls.

Mohammed stared at the toll-free number on the screen. The phones looked busy. Everyone was giving. Couldn't he afford to pledge ten dollars for the victims in New York? It would do more good than that letter he had written to Public School 89. He turned to his mother. "Why don't we call? I have my trip money."

Her eyes darted overhead. Mohammed's father slept above them. "You save, Hamed."

Mohammed shrugged. "Save for what? If I can't go to New York, I might as well help someone who lives there."

His mother studied him. Matters of charity were usually decided by her husband.

"It's only ten dollars, Mom. I want to help."

She glanced at the stairs. "Okay," she agreed. "But no wake your father."

Mohammed jumped from the couch and ran to write down the number. When he returned, Wyclef Jean was singing "Redemption Song." Mohammed wondered which star would take his call. He was about to pick up the phone when he heard footfalls on the stairs. His father entered the room, squinting from the light. "What is this?" he asked.

"Money for the families," answered his mother, sitting up.

His father peered at Wyclef Jean's serpent hair. "We have no money to give to anyone, Lisa. I'm not selling gas."

Mohammed said, "I'm the one who wants to give, Abi. Ten dollars from my savings."

"Son, you won't give anything until I know where it is going and what it is for. We will give our zakat when the time is right and to those we deem needy."

"But, Abi, it's my money."

His father raised one hand to silence him. The other he pointed at Wyclef Jean. "Turn—him—off!"

His mother pressed the remote. Her eyes motioned Mohammed to the stairs.

"To bed," his father said. "You have to help me at the station tomorrow."

Mohammed ascended in silence, holding the paper with the toll-free number. In his room he wadded it up and threw it in the trash. Would his father ever understand?

At Ahmed Automotive the next morning, shattered glass glistened on the asphalt. Mohammed's father stopped to stare at it. "Someone broke in," he muttered to his son.

The plate-glass window of the office was cleanly demolished. Mohammed's father entered through the opening, stepping over glass. He went to the door that led to the garage and tried the knob, finding it locked. "They didn't go for the tools." He checked the metal desk, opening drawers. "Nothing missing," he said, turning to count the cans of oil on the shelves.

Mohammed's foot bumped into something beneath the desk. "Here's what they used," he said, toeing a brick from under the desk.

His father finished counting. "They didn't touch the oil. It must have been vandals."

They gazed at the brick on the floor. His father picked it up. "Expensive brick," he said, handing it to his son. "Put it in the trash and get the broom."

Mohammed held the brick, suddenly remembering that he, too, was in a bad mood—in case his father hadn't noticed. And not because of a broken window. Because of last night. Because of Bon Jovi. Because fourteen-year-olds had rights, too.

He studied the brick, turning it over. On the backside, he read the message. His self-pity evaporated. "Dad!"

Both of them stared at the two words written as one, scrawled in black paint.

GO HOME

"It wasn't vandals was it, Abi?"

"No," replied his father, as softly as Mohammed had ever heard him answer.

Silence hung between them.

"Are you going to call the police?"

"I don't know," he said.

"Police won't do any good," declared Delmar when he arrived. "You gotta catch 'em when they toss it. Otherwise it's hearsay." He eyed the asphalt as Mohammed swept up the last of the glass. "Leastways, there was no fire. Could have torched the place if they'd had a mind to. Just looking to scare you, I reckon."

Mohammed's father frowned. "If I report it, maybe they'll keep an eye on the place."

"Some truth there," agreed Delmar. "Report it then."

Hasan Ahmed climbed into the tow truck and left without dictating his usual list of chores to Mohammed.

Delmar watched him drive off. "I told him there was gonna be trouble." He went to the garage and returned with an empty

Texaco pail. He sat. "Might as well get comfortable. We won't be filling any gas tanks today."

That morning no one pulled in for gas. No one stopped for oil or additives or antifreeze or tire repairs or any repairs. Mohammed leaned on his broom, watching cars pass down the highway. Then the Coca-Cola truck arrived and parked next to the pop machine. "Kind of dead around here," the driver observed, looking around. "But it's been dead everywhere since the eleventh. No one's traveling right now."

Mohammed was mildly encouraged. Maybe people were staying home, using less gasoline. He went to the garage and raised the roll-up doors. What the station needed was to *look* open for business.

Inside, both bays were vacant, no cars on the lifts. Mohammed looked at the workbench. Tools were stored, the compressor hose coiled. Ahmed Automotive looked *out* of business. Delmar wandered in.

"What's going to happen?" Mohammed asked, surveying the empty garage.

"Well, the police won't do nothing. They don't care if we sell gas or not."

"I mean what's going to happen to us?"

"Reckon the place will shut down," replied Delmar. "You and me will be joining the unemployed."

Mohammed stared.

"Being without a job won't be so bad for you," Delmar added. "You're just a kid. I'm gonna have to find another." He started to chuckle, then coughed, spitting yellow phlegm at his feet. "Don't know who'd wanna hire me, though."

Hasan Ahmed returned with two sheets of plywood tied to the tow truck.

"Good move," Delmar said. "Let 'em throw the kitchen sink now."

Mohammed was sent to the garage for a tape measure and a handsaw. When he returned, Delmar was asking, "So is the sheriff hanging anyone by sundown?"

"They promised to watch the place, but I'm not sure they will. I have to file a written complaint."

Delmar thumped the plywood. "I told Hamed the very same. Worthless, the whole lot. Don't care if we sell gas. Don't care if we go under."

"That's enough, Delmar," said Hasan Ahmed.

For the next hour Mohammed ran for tools while the men cut and fit the sheets of plywood to the window frame. Then the drive-through bell dinged at the pumps. A white taxi stopped beside the self-service island. The driver—a thin, delicate man—got out and waved. It was Raja Saleem, a friend of Mohammed's father.

"Haven't seen him for a while," remarked Delmar.

Raja Saleem began to pump his gas. Mohammed approached with his squeegee to wash the windshield. "Not today, boy," said Raja. "Glass not dirty."

Usually the taxi's windshield was bug covered from night fares on Ohio roads. "I'll clean it anyway," he said.

Mr. Saleem kept his hand on the pump handle, watching the numbers on the meter. Mohammed had just wet the glass when he heard the nozzle return to its holder. Raja was reaching for his wallet when Hasan Ahmed and Delmar approached.

"Buying fumes are you?" said Delmar, reading the pump numbers.

Raja Saleem held out three dollars to Mohammed's father. "Business down," he said. "No gas money."

Hasan Ahmed nodded. "We've noticed the same."

Raja Saleem's delicate frame looked thinner than usual. His face was taut and humorless. "This man you see?" he said, touching himself. "Me! Not driving now. Customers tell dispatcher don't send foreign driver. No accents. No business." He pointed to the plywood window. "What happened there, man?"

"Vandals," replied Hasan. He said nothing about the message on the brick.

"Better take down sign," said Raja, pointing to AHMED AUTOMOTIVE. "You advertising trouble, man. No offense, but my wife say I look too Arab."

Delmar nodded. "She's right on that one, but it ain't your doing."

"You know somebody want to buy taxi cheap, let me know."

When Mohammed finished cleaning the windshield, he stood by his father.

"Dirty shame," Delmar croaked.

"Crazy terrorists," Raja said.

"I'm sure it's temporary," said Hasan Ahmed. "We have been slow, too. People aren't traveling, Raja. They're not buying gas. They're not taking cabs. It's affecting all of us. The best we can do is to be patient. Remember, this is America. If you work hard, business always gets better. Have faith. You'll see."

Mohammed looked at his father. These words, or something like them, he had heard many times, mostly at the supper table. Work hard. Have faith. This is America, etc. But now his father's voice sounded different. It sounded unsure.

Raja Saleem shook his head. "You see news, man? People make mistakes. They shoot Pakistanis wearing turbans. They think they Arabs. Last week man from Phoenix kill man from Karachi. I am from Karachi. Another man, he shoot Pakistani, Afghani, and Lebanese in one day. My children cry. Kids at school say bad things. Where will it go?"

"I don't like it, either," said Mohammed's father. "But we must be patient."

"Patience don't pay bills, Hasan."

Mohammed picked up the stool and moved away. He didn't want Raja Saleem to think he was waiting for a tip.

"Boy!" he called, reaching into his pocket.

"That's all right, Mr. Saleem," Mohammed replied. "Like you said, it was already clean."

Raja Saleem nodded. Delmar coughed. His father said nothing. Then the Pakistani cabby got into his taxi and drove away.

For the remainder of the day, Mohammed swept and reswept the station. Delmar repeatedly wiped down the pumps. Hasan Ahmed worked at his desk behind the plywood. The hours passed. Cars zoomed down the highway. None stopped for gas.

For the next Young Engineers' meeting, Mrs. Cutter asked the club members to bring something related to the architecture or engineering of New York—photograph, poster, or souvenir. "If we can't visit the city, then we can pretend to," she said.

Mohammed brought his 3-D puzzle of the Empire State Building mounted on a board. His father gave him a ride to school.

At the club meeting, his presentation was a hit. Even Miss Cutter was impressed. "It looks so realistic," she bubbled.

Mohammed spoke knowledgeably of what was now the tallest building in the city. He recited its precise height (1,453 feet to the tip of the lightning rod), the number of stairs (1,860), how many bricks were mortared in its walls (10 million), how fast the elevator rose (1,200 feet per minute). He informed the club that the Empire State Building didn't sway, not even in a

110-mile-per-hour wind. Everyone admired Mohammed's replica, which was twenty inches tall. Priscilla Smith touched it.

On the bus ride home success went sour. The sight of Mohammed balancing a tall building on a board was impossible for the redheaded high schooler to ignore.

"Will you look at what Taliban is carrying?" he announced, inserting his knee into the aisle. He shook his head, as if he didn't believe what he saw. "What nerve! And after what your kind did—"

Merrill spoke up. "Leave him alone. He's not bothering you."

"Yeah," chimed Norman, not quite so boldly.

"Shut up, twerps!" snapped the redheaded kid, his face dark. One of his friends pointed to the replica. "Hey, Carl, maybe that one should be next."

Mohammed held the puzzle board with both hands.

"Yeah," said someone else.

The redheaded kid delivered a sharp, backhanded blow to the model, sending the top half flying to the floor, where approximately forty stories of replica limestone broke into a hundred puzzle pieces.

The bus went silent. The driver looked in his mirror. "What's going on back there?"

"It was an accident," claimed the redheaded kid.

Merrill and Norman kneeled to retrieve the pieces. Mohammed balanced the decapitated building. Kids backed up in the aisle.

"Hurry," said Norman.

"In your seats!" barked the driver.

"Move along, girls," taunted the redheaded kid.

They moved to the rear and sat. Merrill and Norman emptied their hands of puzzle pieces. "Bad idea," Merrill said. Mohammed nodded, holding back tears.

At home his mother asked what had happened. "It fell," Mohammed answered. In his room he dismantled the model, heaping the pieces in a pile. His tears dropped on the board. *Ground Zero*, he told himself, the phrase coming to him after hearing it repeated on TV news broadcasts for the last three weeks. *Ground Zero. Ground Zero. Ground Zero.*

Mohammed knew he wasn't alone. He knew there were kids in other schools who were having trouble after September 11. The eighth-grade girl from Oklahoma was one of them. Her picture appeared in the *Cincinnati Post* under the headline: "School Says Muslim Girl Can't Return with Head Scarf."

Mohammed read the article. He studied the picture. The girl was dark-skinned and dark-haired. Her face seemed oddly familiar. The newspaper reported that she had been suspended for wearing her hijab to class.

He was not surprised. Hijabs often brought trouble. The girls in his Koran classes had said so. There was no blending in with a hijab, no becoming invisible. Mohammed thought that wearing a hijab was like wearing long pants in PE. You got noticed.

According to the newspaper, the girl had worn her scarf since the beginning of classes. No one had objected. After the attacks, parents began to complain. Then she was assaulted in the restroom, her glasses broken, and her hijab thrown into a toilet. She was told by school officials that she would no longer be allowed to wear the scarf, since the dress code forbade any type of head covering. When the girl showed up the next day wearing her hijab, she was sent home.

Mohammed thanked Allah for not being a girl. Muslim girls had it tougher than Muslim boys.

He returned to the picture, suddenly realizing what was familiar about this girl's face. She *looked* like Nura Maryam—not

Nura Maryam now—but Nura Maryam grown up. He was looking at the face of his teenage sister.

The likeness was weird. It occurred to him that at another time, in another place, his sister could have been this girl from Oklahoma with the broken glasses, the girl sent home from school.

Poor Nura Maryam, he thought. Some day she would have to wear a hijab.

Sunday morning Mohammed found a suspicious-looking plastic bag in their front yard. The bag was full of a dark red liquid that smelled like raw hamburger. As soon as he lifted it, he knew what it was. He dropped it on the grass and ran into the house. The bag contained blood.

His father took it to the kitchen sink, where the family gathered behind him.

"Pig's blood," he said after sticking his finger in the bag and sniffing it.

How his father determined this, Mohammed didn't know. His mother made a face. Nura Maryam asked, "What pig blood, Hamed?"

"Blood from a pig. You know—pig. Haram."

Nura Maryam backed away.

"Probably the same ones who threw the firecrackers," said Hasan Ahmed.

"And the brick," added Mohammed.

His mother sat at the kitchen table, her face worried. "Hasan, what they do next?"

His father emptied the bag down the drain. "I'll talk to the police again," he said.

That same night, the sign at the station was vandalized. Hasan Ahmed spotted the mischief from his truck the next morning.

"DEATH TO MUSLIMS" had been painted in large red letters on both sides of the sign.

When Mohammed biked to the station that afternoon, the sign was propped against the back wall of the station. The twin sign poles stood naked on the highway. His father was gone. Delmar manned the pumps.

"No time to be loud or proud," he said, shaking his head. "They had to bring a ladder to do it. Nothing dumb about 'em."

"And my dad?"

"Down at the police station. Third time already, filling out papers. They're gonna give him the runaround."

They gazed at where "AHMED AUTOMOTIVE" had once occupied a piece of the sky.

"Leastways, it won't hurt business," observed Delmar. "Fact is, may help."

October came. Mitch and his friends continued to harass Mohammed. At lunch they "accidentally" knocked over his milk. In the corridor rush between classes, they pushed him. They mocked his Bermuda shorts in PE. When Mohammed found a sign stuck to his locker with the words "Osama Lives Here," he knew the culprits.

The boycott of Ahmed Automotive continued, even as its owner flew the American flag. At the Ahmed home, the struggle to pay bills began. Mohammed's mother put the family on a budget, economizing at mealtimes. She cooked dinners with beans and bread. Rice became a regular. Lentils. Eggplant. Mohammed hated eggplant.

The first Friday in October, Hasan Ahmed announced that he would be attending late prayer at the masjid. "I would like you to come," he told Mohammed at breakfast. "I will pick you up at school."

Promptly at three, his father pulled into the school parking lot as middle schoolers boarded buses. Worried that his father might arrive wearing his black head covering, Mohammed ran to meet the truck before it arrived at the loading zone. Inside the car the smell of aftershave was strong. His father's beard was neatly trimmed, his clothes pressed. But his head was uncovered.

They rode in silence. Mohammed stared out the window, counting American flags on the highway. At every gas station, he saw cars lined up at the pumps. "Are you going to put up the sign again?" he asked.

"Not yet," his father said.

Mohammed considered this. "Is Mrs. Heath buying gas?"

"Yes."

The whine of the tires filled the silence.

"And Mr. Saleem?"

"I haven't seen Mr. Saleem," his father replied.

Mohammed wondered if Raja Saleem had sold his taxi.

As they entered the city, he spotted a white bedsheet hung on the highway fence. Written on the sheet was a red-lettered message kept to a single word:

Kill 'em

"Look!" he said.

His father glanced at the sign.

"Kill who?" Mohammed wondered aloud, looking over his shoulder. He noticed the white house behind the sign, an American flag flying from the porch.

Hasan Ahmed shook his head before he spoke. "We are on our way to prayer, Son. Let us not talk about killing."

Mohammed recalled the brick thrown through the station glass. Its warning had also been written in red. "Maybe that's who ruined our sign," he said.

His father didn't answer.

Masjid Dawoud stood out in a neighborhood of rundown, graffiti-scrawled buildings. Squeezed between a dry cleaners and a used clothing bazaar, it was a narrow, white clapboard structure with trim green shutters, a curb roof, and a meticulously maintained patch of lawn.

On the street outside Mohammed looked for signs of bullet ricochets left by the would-be arsonist. He saw none, but he did observe a patrol car parked on the corner. Two policemen watched the masjid.

Inside the entrance hall he stepped first with his right foot, saying two *rak'ats* to himself. He removed his shoes and placed them next to others on a rack by the door. The smells of cologne and scented soap filled the hall. Men stood in their socks. All sported dress shirts and trimmed beards—presentable for congregational prayer. They greeted Hasan Ahmed warmly, their voices soft. They shook Mohammed's hand. He recognized many of their faces. Saeed Patel and Abdul-Wadood were teachers in the Saturday morning Koran classes. Next to the prayer clocks stood Majd Udeen, his head already covered. He was the butcher who sold halal meat to his father.

Conversation among the men rang heavy with the word *trouble*. Some spoke of the arsonist.

"There should be more extinguishers," said Izz Al-Busaid, who ran the masjid library.

"Twenty would not be enough," countered Sayf Malik, an elder member.

Other men discussed the attacks in New York and Washington. "The face of terror is not our face," said Majd Udeen, eliciting nods. Others talked of relatives and friends who had been persecuted. Listeners shook their heads, deeply dismayed.

Mohammed overheard a few men talking business. One of them said, "The worst is not over yet. You'll see boycotts."

His father glanced toward the washroom, reminding him to do *wudu*. When he returned, Saeed Patel was reciting the call to prayer. Men moved into the chapel. Mohammed took a spare covering from a table and placed it on his head.

The prayer hall was the largest room in the masjid. It had no furniture. The floor was carpeted to look like individual prayer mats. The walls were decorated with Arabic writings, painted hangings, and photographs of the Great Masjid in Mecca. Mohammed especially liked to look at the photos. The size and complexity of the Great Masjid elicited wonder from the young engineer. One day he would make his hajj there—a pilgrimage every able-bodied Muslim was obliged to make at least once in his lifetime.

Inside the hall the men lined up in straight rows, shoulder to shoulder, facing the mihrab where the imam stood, his back to them. Mohammed recognized the burly figure of Yaseen Haneez—he who had dodged the arsonist's bullet. He would give the sermon.

Taking his place where the boys prayed, Mohammed stood in the last row by himself. His father stood in the middle of the second row with men his age.

"*Allahu Akbar,*" began the imam.

Mohammed listened to the rhythmic chants, repeating each prayer in a low voice. Beyond the imam's voice, he listened for something else, something he half expected to hear at any moment—an interruption. Loud music, or a car honking, or people shouting from the street. Perhaps the man who had refused to remove his shoes would return with friends who would refuse to remove their shoes, too.

Then he remembered the police car parked on the corner.

They recited the statement of peace. Mohammed turned his head first to the right, then to the left. *"As-salamu alaykum,"* he said, sniffing the air for gasoline but smelling only men's cologne.

Yaseen Haneez turned from the mihrab and stepped to the podium. He began his sermon by talking of enlightenment from the eternal torch of Islam. He went on to speak of discouraging evil and fostering brotherhood. Mohammed clamped his mouth shut on a yawn. He looked around the hall. Everyone appeared attentive. There was no noise from the street. No intruder. No sirens.

"Be kind, but also be not afraid," the imam said, his voice loud, unwavering. "To show that you are afraid is to show another that you do not believe in his capacity to make the right choice—the choice to be kind rather than unkind, the choice to do the wise thing instead of the wrong thing."

Yaseen Haneez looked straight at Mohammed. "My brothers, my sons," he said, his voice rising, his beard trembling. "I will finish with this. Please take it with you to your homes, to your neighbors and friends. Listen and remember: life is too short to be afraid. Give others the chance not to be."

Silence. *Why is Yaseen Haneez staring at me?* Mohammed wondered. He tried to make sense of the imam's words. Don't be afraid, yes, but what did he mean by "Give others the chance not to be?"

"Allahu Akbar!" said one of the men. They said it in unison. Mohammed added his voice. Then everybody stood. The service was over.

Outside, the police car hadn't moved. The uniformed occupants watched the exodus of bearded men from the white clapboard building. As Mohammed retreated down the sidewalk, he waved—a sudden impulse. The policemen looked surprised, but neither waved back.

Saturday morning, a story in the Cincinnati paper caught his eye.

French Paraglider Sentenced

French daredevil Thierry Devaux, 41, who flew a
motorized parachute into the Statue of Liberty, was
ordered to pay $7,000 in fines and restitution. He told the
court Friday that he didn't intend to cause harm, but US
Magistrate Judge Douglas Eaton banned Devaux from
flying any similar object anywhere in the United States
for three years and ordered him to pay for the damage
to the statue's gold leaf and copper railing.

Mohammed remembered the incident. It had been in
the papers and broadcast from news helicopters only a week
before the September 11 attacks. He recalled the pictures of
the French stuntman dangling from Miss Liberty, his parasail
snagged on her torch after a failed landing. The police had
come. The National Park Service had evacuated tourists. Then
the firefighters had arrived for the rescue—some of the same
New York firefighters who would climb to their deaths in the
burning towers days later.

The Frenchman had been rescued then arrested. It was not
the first time Monsieur Devaux had flirted with the Statue of
Liberty. He had made other attempts. Some years before he had
been caught spending the night in the statue.

Even now, the story held a special connection for Mohammed,
bringing back the most vivid scenes from his own strange dream,
his own peculiar rescue. *He,* too, had dangled from her torch.
He also had spent the night at the Statue of Liberty.

He still wanted to see her.

Sunday he took lunch to his father and Delmar at the station.

"Slower than a seven-year itch," said the old man when Mohammed asked about business. "Mac bought gas. And that lady teacher. What's her name? Hair gone to seed like a dandelion."

"Miss Cutter?"

"That's her. Always wanting to pump her own gas. Real independent." Delmar shook his head. "Leastways, she ain't boycotting. That gives her an 'A' in my book."

Inside the garage his father worked under the tow truck.

"Something break, Abi?" Mohammed inquired.

"No, just tightening things. I don't want any rattles if I have to sell it."

"Sell it?" repeated Mohammed.

"I may have to, Son."

During lunch, Delmar said, "The honkers drove by again."

"I heard them," replied Hasan Ahmed.

"Honkers?" Mohammed asked.

Delmar chewed on a bean burrito. "A bunch of idiots trying to scare folks. Oughta report 'em, Hasan."

"That won't be necessary, Delmar. It's a free country."

"Too free, I'd say. Keeping an eye on the place, they are. Running off customers."

He swallowed, then coughed, his thin frame doubling over with the effort.

Hasan Ahmed indicated the food still in the container. "Take those home for supper, Delmar."

"I'll do that," he said, reaching for the leftovers.

That afternoon the station's drive-through bell rang once. It was Majd Udeen, the butcher who trucked freshly killed halal to the towns. Mr. Udeen stopped weekly to deliver their meat. After speaking with Mohammed's father in the office, he departed without leaving any white-papered packages.

Mohammed washed and vacuumed the tow truck. When he heard the horn honking, he looked up to see Delmar motioning toward two pickup trucks on the highway. Men stood in the back of one truck, slashing the air with American flags. The second pickup looked empty except for the driver. Then two people in the bed stood up, lifting a sign.

NO GAS FROM ARABS

"Them's the honkers!" shouted Delmar as they drove out of sight.

Mohammed glanced at the office where his father sat behind the plywood, his head buried in a ledger.

"If I was twenty years younger…" Delmar lamented. Then he shook his fist at the pale Ohio sky.

That week Mohammed overheard his parents in the kitchen. They were going over bills.

"I work," his mother said. "Nura Maryam stay with Senora Heath."

"No, you should stay home for the children."

"Then I sell empanadas. People buy. They good."

"Lisa, it won't make a difference. We need to sell gas."

"I help."

"You are helping."

"And the electric bill? The phone?"

Mohammed's parents never argued—they discussed—his mother often disagreeing, his father always prevailing.

"We'll manage," said Hasan Ahmed. "I'm putting a sign on the truck tomorrow. Maybe someone from out of town will buy it. The money should cover the mortgage."

"What of the gas?" his mother asked.

Mohammed heard the rustle of papers in the kitchen. His father said something about fuel allotments and the Delco man.

"I'll have to let Delmar go," he added, his voice low.

Mohammed froze. *Let Delmar go?*

His mother said, "Hasan, what he do?"

Silence. Then, "I don't know. A man his age won't get hired easily. But it should be temporary. Business can't stay like this forever."

"You think?" His mother sighed. "I wish they catch those terrible men before they ever—" Tears overwhelmed his mother's words.

"We all wish that, Lisa."

More silence. The house was quiet. His father said, "I'll talk to him tomorrow."

As he lay in bed, Mohammed thought about Delmar. The old man knew the ax was coming. He had said so, joked about it, but that didn't make it any easier to accept.

Without a job what would he eat? How would he pay his rent? He remembered how Delmar wore the same clothes, how he devoured the Tupperware lunches made by his mother. He saw Delmar's toothless grin, heard his cough. What if he got sick?

Mohammed thought about his parents and all the bills on the kitchen table. Did his father really have a choice? He was looking after family first. Delmar would go. Then the truck. What next?

He turned on the night lamp and went to his desk, removing from a drawer his passbook to the Ohio Savings Bank. He turned its pages until he reached the last deposit, stunned by the date—September 10. Mrs. Heath had paid him for mowing her lawn that weekend. He had given the money to his father to deposit Monday. Then Tuesday had come, and the reason to save was no more. He read the balance: $158.20. Money saved for a dream—three nights in New York City, ferry tickets, subway fares, dinners, souvenirs, memories. But now the dream was dead.

The next morning he brought the passbook to breakfast, handing it to his father.

"Another deposit?" asked Hasan Ahmed.

"No, Abi, a withdrawal."

His father nodded. "How much?"

"All of it. I want to close the account."

Eyebrows lifted. "Close the account?"

"Yes, Abi."

His mother stirred oatmeal on the stove. His father thumbed the pages of the booklet. When he read the balance, he looked up. "That's almost one hundred and sixty dollars, Mohammed." A distant tone of disapproval rang in his father's voice. "May I ask what you are planning to do with this money?"

Mohammed dropped his gaze. "Since I'm not going on the trip, I want you to have it so you can pay for things. You know, bills. I'd also like to give some to Delmar, I mean Mr. Moffit, in case he loses his job."

Silence, except for Nura Maryam banging her cereal bowl.

"What makes you think Mr. Moffit could lose his job?" asked his father.

Mohammed shrugged. "He told me." His mother served the oatmeal, hovering between them. Mohammed waited for his father to ask how he knew there were bills to pay, but that didn't come. Instead he said, "Son, keep your savings. Your mother and I will manage. So will Delmar. It's your money."

Mohammed recalled the night of the heroes telethon when he had wanted to donate ten dollars to the victims, when he had told his father, "It's *my* money." His father hadn't forgotten.

"But I want to help. It could be zakat. Mr. Moffit is not like us. He's poor."

His father stared at his bowl. His mother spoke. "It very good Hamed think of other men. He good boy."

Hasan Ahmed did not look up. "Yes, of course," he said, his voice husky.

Mohammed's mother retreated to the sink. Mohammed didn't look at his father. When Hasan Ahmed spoke again, his voice was normal. He tried to smile. "Thank you Mohammed for thinking of Mr. Moffit and us. God favors those who think of others. You have learned well, Son. If we need to borrow your money, I will let you know. In any case, we would pay you back as soon as possible."

Mohammed felt a great weight lifted. "No problem, Abi. You can keep it." Then he dug his spoon into the oatmeal and ate his breakfast.

Hasan Ahmed borrowed his son's savings. Mohammed heard from his mother that the entire sum went to Delmar on his last day of work. He never knew what day that was, but when his father asked him to come to the station after school to watch the pumps, he knew Delmar was gone.

Small-town Ohio slid into the first frosty nights of autumn. Color painted the trees. One afternoon, as Mohammed biked to the station, Mitch Redding stepped from behind some trees to block his path. "Hey, sand nigger," he said. "Going to pump that Arab gas nobody wants to buy?"

Ralph Trumbull appeared behind him. "If it isn't sheikh boy on his magic carpet."

They laughed. When Mitch reached for the bike's handlebars, Mohammed pulled it back. "Two against one is it?" he said, noticing for the first time how alike they looked. Blue eyes. Square heads. Flattop haircuts. They could have been brothers.

Mitch smirked. "I don't need help to whip a two-pint Arab. I only need this." He held up his fist, then laughed again, a strange, unhappy laugh.

For an instant Mohammed considered the option of escape. He could launch the bike forward, surprise Mitch, hurt him maybe, then pedal away. Or he could ram it rearward and catch Ralph off guard. Then he remembered Yaseen Haneez. He hadn't run. He had walked fearlessly toward a pointed gun. What had the bearded imam said? *Life is too short to be afraid… Give others the chance not to be…Believe in his capacity to make the right choice.* He had said so many things they all ran together. Still the message was clear. Don't be afraid.

He looked at Mitch and wondered if the Mitch behind the fist—the Mitch with the strange laugh—if that Mitch could be afraid of anything. He certainly didn't look it. But why had he brought Ralph Trumbull? Why was he so mad?

Mohammed gave up his plan for escape. As he lowered the bike to the ground, he saw Yaseen Haneez walking toward a faceless gunman. "You want a fight? Is that what you want, Mitch?" His voice sounded detached, belonging to someone else. His legs felt solid. He moved purposefully and without hurry, something Mitch seemed to notice. "You want to smash my face, right?"

This vivid summary seemed to leave Mitch without words. He stopped smirking. Finally he said, "I'm going to do more than that, rag head."

Mohammed moved away from his bike, hands at his sides.

"Jolt him, Mitch," prodded Ralph. "Launch him back to Arab land."

Mitch ignored Ralph. "You don't get it, do you?" he snarled, his jaw hardening. "Kin of terrorists aren't welcome here. What your people did was murder, and there's no pardon for that. You know what we're going to do to your kind in Afghanistan? We're going to wipe you out."

This didn't sound like Mitch talking. This sounded like an angry adult.

Mohammed kept his voice neutral. "I'm not from Afghanistan, Mitch, and I'm not kin to terrorists. I'm in middle school like you."

"Shut up, you Muslim loser!" yelled Ralph.

Mitch moved closer. Ralph remained behind him. Mohammed knew it was coming. So why was Mitch telling him this?

"I guess hitting me is going to pay back all those lives, right? It's going to make everything better?"

"Don't listen to him," Ralph said.

Mitch raised his fists. "No. It's going to make me feel better. Now put 'em up."

Mohammed heard Yaseen Haneez's voice, the words coming back, connecting: *To show that you are afraid is to show another that you do not believe in his capacity to make the right choice—the choice to be kind rather than unkind, the choice to do the wise thing instead of the wrong thing...*

He kept his hands down. "I'm not afraid of you, Mitch. But I'm not going to fight you. I have nothing to fight about, and you don't, either."

Mitch hesitated, as if to make sense of it. He stared at Mohammed.

"Hit him!" screamed Ralph, annoyed by his friend's indecisiveness. "Are you going to hit him or not?"

His voice seemed to travel a great distance before Mitch heard it, before Mitch acted. For a moment Mitch appeared to be deaf. Then the fear and anger in his heart took charge of his hands, and he unleashed a flurry of blows.

It was over in a few seconds. Mitch could have done more, but once his adversary went down, he seemed to lose interest in the contest. He and Ralph left with Mohammed on the ground. Mitch retreated in silence, without taunts or name-calling. Ralph babbled, "Nice hook, but he was down, and you didn't jump him!"

Mohammed sat up. His nose bled. His left eye felt hot. He got to his feet and retook the bike.

When his father saw his face, he didn't ask what happened. Falling off a bicycle wouldn't have explained it.

"I was in a fight," Mohammed volunteered.

His father frowned. "With whom?"

"A kid from school. He has been saying things about Arabs and Muslims." His mouth hurt when he spoke. He tasted his blood. His nose throbbed, and his eye felt large.

"You couldn't ignore him?"

Mohammed shook his head. His father touched his chin, raising his face. "And what did you do to him, Son?"

Suddenly he felt ashamed. "Nothing," he whispered, lowering his gaze. "I didn't want to fight."

"And why was that?"

Mohammed decided to say nothing about Yaseen Haneez and the faceless gunman. Instead he said, "I didn't think it would make a difference, I guess."

His father studied him. Mohammed waited for a rebuke, but none came. When he looked up, his father smiled. "That is a good reason," he said. "But next time, Son, put up your hands at least. It will save blood."

Mohammed nodded, licking his split lip.

"Go wash your face. I want to look at that eye."

"Yes, Abi."

"You're going to have what, in America, they call a shiner, praise Allah."

At the sight of her son, Lisa Ahmed rattled off a litany of *Dios míos* and *pobrecitos*. Supper preparations were suspended. The kitchen was turned into an infirmary, and wet washcloths and ice were mobilized. When Mrs. Heath was called to see if she had eyedrops, she charged over with her entire first-aid kit. Upon seeing Mohammed she wanted to call parents. "They should be ashamed of these kids," she declared.

The next morning his eye was less swollen. The blood beneath the skin was already turning purple. His mother wanted him to stay home from school, but Mohammed knew he couldn't. His father understood. "Let him go," he said.

At the bus stop, Norman was shocked. Merrill was impressed.

"Why didn't you run?" asked Norman.

"Why didn't you fight?" asked Merrill.

To both questions he gave the same answer—"I couldn't"—a response that left his friends shaking their heads.

On the bus the redheaded high schooler grinned when he saw Mohammed's face. "What happened, Taliban? Run into the marines?"

Middle school was abuzz with news of the fight. Ralph Trumbull had seen to that. In homeroom Mitch was the center of a circle of boys, though Ralph did most of the talking. Mitch Redding looked anything but triumphant.

At lunch Mohammed ignored curious stares in the cafeteria just as he pretended not to hear whispers in the hallways. Somehow he felt empowered by his new distinction. He had fought Mitch Redding, fought with his hands at his sides, and he was in school the next day, beaten but walking. In classes he worked as if nothing had happened, raising his hand when he knew the answer, participating in discussions. The one thing he didn't do was look at Priscilla. The less she saw of his face, the better.

When teachers asked what had happened, he replied simply, "I got in a fight." With Mac that answer wasn't enough. "Who started it?" he shot back.

Mohammed had no intention of implicating Mitch. He had stood up to him for all the lies Mitch believed about him. He wasn't going to turn snitch and give Mitch something to say about him that *was* true.

"I'd rather not say," he replied.

Mac nodded thoughtfully. "I see."

That morning Mac led eighth-grade social studies in a discussion of the new republic and America's first government. Mac was intent on making the back row participate. He peppered Mitch and his friends with questions.

"America gives bigotry no sanction, persecution no assistance," he declared. "Who said that, Mitch?"

Mitch stared at his hands. "I don't remember."

"Ralph, can you tell us?"

"Could you repeat the question?" asked Ralph Trumbull.

The next seven days became "the big week," as Mohammed would later remember it. His father sold the truck. Delmar came by the station. Mrs. Heath went to New York. Priscilla spoke to him. And the YEPS held an extraordinary session at Miss Cutter's house.

His father had been right about the tow truck. An out-of-towner did buy it. He was a persimmon farmer from Brown County who saw the "For Sale" sign from the highway, test-drove the truck, and then haggled with Mohammed's father over a fair price. When the two men finally agreed, Mohammed watched the truck leave the station and ramp onto the highway. The sight left him mixed up. He was glad his father had money to pay bills, but he also felt like they had lost a member of the family. At closing time his father walked home from work. Mohammed rode ahead on his bike.

Two days later, Delmar showed up wearing a shirt Mohammed had never seen before. It was a yellow shirt with a full pack of cigarettes bulging in the pocket. The shirt made Delmar look different.

"Don't say nothing," he blurted when he saw Mohammed's stare. "It ain't new. I bought it at Rockdale's for a dollar. Landlady says it makes me look younger." He chuckled then coughed and spat.

Mohammed thought it made Delmar look thinner.

"Figured I oughta slick up," he continued. "Job hunting, you know. Don't wanna look like I just crawled out from under a rock." Delmar had shaved. His thin gray hair was combed tightly against his scalp. He leaned on one of the pumps in a familiar pose. "Thinking about going to Cincinnati," he said.

"Cincinnati?"

"Yep," he answered coolly. "Ain't gonna ask Gerhard to pump gas. Not that Shell station, neither. Not about to ally myself with the enemy. Cincinnati's got plenty of pumps." He touched his shirt pocket then glanced at the "No Smoking" sign above his head. "Manning the fort, are you, Hamed?"

Mohammed nodded. "Yeah, sort of. It's pretty dead."

"And the wrecker?"

"He sold it two days ago."

Delmar nodded gravely. "Worse than I thought," he muttered.

Silence unfolded between them. Mohammed said, "Sorry you had to go, Delmar. I wish you were here instead of me."

"Ain't no one's fault, Hamed. That's business. Things will get better." He looked toward the office. "Gonna go talk to him, get me a recommendation. This job hunting is a tricky business. Used to be a man's word was enough. Nowadays they want to see papers."

He disappeared into the garage. Some time later, Mohammed heard the sounds of a typewriter pecking, a laugh, then a cough.

When Delmar emerged, he waved a white envelope at Mohammed. "Keep your nose clean, kid," he said as he headed to the highway. "And don't forget to check those gas caps."

Mohammed watched him reach into his pocket and pull out the pack of cigarettes. He stopped, bent over a match, then resumed his walk without hurry, smoke in his wake. The yellow shirt hung loosely on his frame, screaming in the sunlight. Mohammed guessed that his money—the trip savings—had bought it. He was glad the old man had spent at least a dollar on something other than cigarettes. He hoped it would help Delmar find work.

Mrs. Heath told them she would be visiting New York for a few days. "I'm afraid I can't stay away any longer," she explained. "There are people I must console."

She had come to give Mohammed the key to her shed. In the shed were the biscuits to feed SoHo, her collie. "Please don't forget to water my plants," she added.

When Mohammed asked if she would be visiting Ground Zero, Mrs. Heath's face saddened. "If I must," she said, resignation in her voice. "Friends have said it is something we should see, but I'm not so sure."

Mrs. Heath knew he wasn't going to New York. Like his father, she had said there would be other opportunities. In a dreamlike moment Mohammed realized this could have been one of them. Suddenly he heard Mrs. Heath turn to his parents and say, "Here's an idea. Why don't you let me take Mohammed along? He can keep me company, bring along his schoolwork. It's just for a few days."

But it was only a dream. Mrs. Heath made no offer. Instead she kissed his mother and Nura Maryam good-bye. Mohammed dropped back to the planet, remembering that he had given away his savings. Besides, who would feed the dog?

Not once had Priscilla Smith spoken to him in middle school—not in class, not in the lunchroom, not in the halls, not in recess, not a single word. Mohammed had corresponded with his own self-effacing silence. In part, this was why he adored her. She was beyond words.

He had no reason to believe their situation would change. He was bashful. She was bold. He was dark. She was fair. She was popular. He was not. She was a common "P. Smith." He was an uncommon "M. bin Hasan Ahmed Al-Fulani." They were from different ends of the galaxy.

So he was more surprised than anyone when Norman and Merrill ran up to him after lunch to announce that Priscilla was looking for him.

"Yeah, right," he replied.

"Seriously," said Norman.

Mohammed shook his head. "This isn't funny."

"Actually it is," said Merrill. "I don't know what she would want with you."

True. Why would Priscilla Smith look for him?

"But you can ask her yourself," he added. "Here she comes."

Priscilla walked down the hall toward them, urgency in her stride. Suddenly she was in front of him. "I've been looking all over for you," she said with motherly sternness.

Mohammed stood speechless. His two best friends stared, mouths open.

"Miss Cutter has called a session of the YEPS," she said. "It is something important. She has asked me to tell everyone."

Mohammed said nothing. His face felt warm. He hoped it wasn't red.

"She wants to meet at her house at four. Do you know where Miss Cutter lives?"

He nodded, touching the Tic Tacs in his pocket. Priscilla was close.

"Can I tell Miss Cutter you will be there?" She tilted her head to one side, her blond hair bouncing pertly against her shoulder.

"Sure," he grunted. He might have replied, "Yes, of course, Priscilla," or "Count on it." Instead, he grunted.

Priscilla seemed to think that was enough. She smiled. "I'll see you at four. And don't forget. It's urgent."

Then she was gone. His friends grinned.

"What a dude!" observed Merrill.

Mohammed shook his head. "It's just a meeting."

But inside he was tingling. Priscilla had spoken to him. They had conversed—sort of. He could still smell her spearmint-gum breath. The whole thing seemed like a dream, as unexpected and extraordinary as the news that Miss Cutter was holding a meeting of the YEPS at her house.

Around her kitchen table, Miss Cutter gave the Young Engineers the astounding news. "I have called you here," she announced, "because the school board has given us permission to go to New York."

Wide-eyed looks of amazement filled the students' faces. Edgar blurted, "All right!" Teddy White leaped from his chair and looked for someone to high-five. Everyone talked at once.

Mohammed sat stunned. They were going to New York. They were going to New York. They were…He said it, not quite believing it. *Allahu Akbar.*

Miss Cutter's voice rose above the commotion. "People. People, please," she urged. "There are some conditions."

The YEPS fell silent.

"First, the trip is not sanctioned by the board as an official school field trip."

Perplexed looks met these words. Teddy White said, "What's that mean?"

"It means that I am taking you to New York. Not the school. It means that I'm responsible for what happens to you. Not the school."

Heads nodded as if to say, "That's good. Miss Cutter's good. Even the conditions are good."

"The school board, and in particular Mr. Vander Bogart, agreed with Priscilla when she said that not going would be exactly what the terrorists wanted. I think her words were 'giving in.' However, the board did not think this was reason enough for the district to sponsor the trip. Nor did they think it was fair for your fund-raising work to be wasted. Which was why they gave me the option to take you in a private capacity. That is why we are meeting at my house, not the school."

Miss Cutter paused. No one spoke.

"So here's the deal. First, your parents have to give you permission to go. Slips will be handed out. Second, both parents need to sign a waiver freeing me and the school of any personal liability in the event of an accident."

Teddy's hand shot up. "Translation, please?"

"It means, Theodore, that if something terrible happens to you on this trip, your parents can't sue me."

Everyone laughed. Teddy White looked sorry he had asked. How could anyone sue Miss Cutter?

"That includes terrorist attacks," amended their adviser dryly.

Laughter stopped.

"Third. We cannot use school transportation, which means we have to pay our way. Since our group is not large enough to charter a bus, we will buy individual tickets. A round-trip fare to New York costs forty-five dollars."

Their adviser stepped to a wall calendar, flipping to November. "We would leave Wednesday evening, the fourteenth, and return Sunday, the eighteenth. I would need the room deposits no later than the first."

All eyes fixed on Miss Cutter. "There is another option," she offered, turning to face them. "Mr. Vander Bogart said, if we wait until spring, the board would reconsider its sponsorship. That means we might not have to pay our own way."

"No, no, no," began the chorus.

"I want to go now," announced Fuzzy Thornton.

Heads nodded. Even Mohammed's. Teddy said, "If we wait until spring, Ground Zero will be cleaned up. We won't get to see any of it."

Miss Cutter dropped a hammerlock gaze on Teddy. "Theodore," she intoned gravely, "that is not our reason for making this trip. We are going to see what man has built, not what he has destroyed."

"I heard there's a viewing platform," volunteered Gary Phettiplace to no response.

Miss Cutter handed out permission slips. She asked Priscilla to pass around itineraries. "You will notice," she said, "that the

World Trade Center has been deleted. Our tour of the Statue of Liberty has been canceled as well. It is closed to the public."

"Gee, all the good stuff is gone," remarked Edgar.

Miss Cutter pretended not to hear. "Both time slots have been left open," she continued. "Perhaps we will see the Flatiron Building or the Verrazano Bridge."

Mohammed wondered if New York without Miss Liberty was a trip worth making. He waited for Priscilla to make eye contact as she handed him an itinerary. But no, not even a smile. They were strangers again.

"If your parents have any questions, have them call me," added Miss Cutter. "We will meet here again on November first. And don't forget to bring the permission slips and your deposits."

Outside, parents waited in cars to pick up their kids. Mohammed headed home on his bike, glad to have the chilly October air hit his face. Miss Cutter's news had left him in a daze. So they were going to New York after all.

He thought of Mrs. Heath. How happy she would be when she heard. Then he remembered he had to feed SoHo. That reminded him that he had promised to water her porch plants. And that gave him the idea to rake the leaves on her front lawn tomorrow afternoon. Maybe he would rake the backyard, too. This led him to calculate how much Mrs. Heath would pay him for both—the going rate was $10—and he was about to add that amount to $158 when Delmar's yellow shirt suddenly popped into his head. He saw it screaming in the sunlight—Delmar on his way to Cincinnati. At that moment Mohammed awoke to the peculiarity of his math, stunned that he had biked—how many blocks?—before the obvious became obvious and the chilly October air knocked him out of his dreamy daze.

Go to New York? How? He had given away his savings!

After feeding SoHo, he watered Mrs. Heath's plants. Then he inspected her leaf-strewn lawn. *What did raking matter now?* he asked himself. Two solid weeks of raking wouldn't make a difference. The unseasonable sum of leaf raking, grass cutting, *and* snow shoveling—Ohio weather miraculously permitting— would not have made a difference. New York was an illusion.

He considered his options. A job was not one of them. Already he was working at the station every weekend and most afternoons. As for his parents, he saw no help coming from them. He had nothing to sell, no friend to borrow from. Winning the Ohio Lottery was impossible. He had no money to buy a ticket.

The October moon rose large as he biked home.

He knew that giving his savings to Delmar had been the right thing to do. But what timing! *At least Miss Liberty is off the itinerary,* he thought. Closed to the public. Gone was the single best reason for going. A small consolation.

In the kitchen his mother asked, "Why so late?"

"A school meeting," he said. He left the trip papers in his book bag.

When his father asked him what was new at school, he said, "Nothing, Abi."

That night he removed the calendar from his wall and flipped ahead to November. With a highlighter he circled November fourteenth, the day of departure. He was about to circle the other days when he stopped to read the small print of moon phases and holidays. *New Moon* on November sixteenth. *Ramadan Begins.*

He closed the calendar. That sealed it! Ramadan began in the middle of the trip! No way could he go! It was the most sacred month of the Muslim year. There was fasting from dawn to sunset. There were frequent visits to the masjid. There were family prayers and long readings of the Koran. Take a school trip during Ramadan? Travel to New York? His father wouldn't allow it—even if he had the money.

He put on his pajamas and slipped into bed without prayer. Then he fell asleep and dreamed of being saved by Miss Liberty.

IMPRISONED LIGHTNING

"Did you have a good trip?"

Mrs. Heath had returned from New York. Mohammed was in her kitchen getting paid.

"I saw the people I had to see and said the things I had to say," she replied. "There was no pleasure in it. And I did not go to Ground Zero. I just couldn't." She handed Mohammed a box. "Open it," she said.

He folded back the box flaps. Inside he found a statue—a statue of a statue—the sculpted figurine of Miss Liberty.

"They sell them with electric lamps, but that seemed a bit much," said Mrs. Heath.

Mohammed held the figurine, admiring its detail. It had the same weathered finish as Liberty's patinated copper. The stone pedestal looked identical. "It's beautiful," he said.

"It's resin," observed Mrs. Heath dryly. "Still, don't drop it."

He touched the torch. "It looks so real."

"As soon as I saw it, I thought about your trip being canceled. I said to myself, 'If Mohammed can't come to Liberty, then I must bring Liberty to Mohammed.'"

"Thanks, Mrs. Heath." He decided not to tell her the trip had been rescheduled. He had yet to tell his parents.

"It will do as a substitute, I suppose, until you get to see the real one someday."

He nodded. *Yes, someday.*

At lunch Merrill said, "Is it true the club is going to New York?"

Mohammed opened his bag of carrot sticks. "Yup."

"Cool," said Norman.

"When are you leaving?"

"I'm not."

His friends stopped eating. "What?" they asked at once.

Mohammed bit a carrot. "No money. And our fasting month starts that week."

"What about the money you saved?"

"I gave it to my dad. He needed it."

Norman and Merrill ate their lunches. They knew about the bad business at the station.

"Can't you sell something?"

Mohammed shrugged. "Like what? What do I have? What do *you* have that we can sell?"

"I have sixteen dollars," offered Norman. Merrill dug into his pocket. "I've got two."

"Thanks, but my dad won't let me go anyway, not during Ramadan."

His friends ate in silence. Mohammed held out the bag. "Carrot, anyone?"

When the bell rang, he dropped them into the trash. Sometimes life was a leftover carrot.

"What the papers?" asked his mother, pointing to the YEPS's trip agenda and permission slips. She had found them in his book bag.

"Club stuff. I was going to tell you. The trip has been rescheduled."

She stopped her dinner preparations to look at him. She smiled. "The club go?"

"Yes."

Her smiled dimmed. "But you money?"

"Yeah, the money." Then he told her about the meeting at Miss Cutter's house, about the school board's decision, and about the club taking the bus in two weeks.

"I sell something," she said, looking around the kitchen.

Mohammed shook his head. "It's not just the money. Ramadan starts that week."

"*Tan pronto?*"

"The week before Thanksgiving. Dad won't let me go anyway."

She gazed at him. "You want I sign?"

With no money, what was the point? Even if she signed, his father wouldn't. There would be an argument, maybe tears. "No, it's not a good time," he said.

His mother nodded. "Put away then. You father be home."

He crumpled the club papers then dropped them into the kitchen trash. He wanted his mother to see he was serious about not going. There could be no looking back.

"What's up, Mohammed?" Miss Cutter asked when he walked into room 113.

Mohammed liked their strong-voiced adviser with the crazy hair. She was easy to talk to. "I won't be going to New York," he said. "I came to let you know."

She stopped shuffling papers at her desk. "Not going?"

He decided not to mention the money. "Ramadan starts that week. I'm going to have to stay and fast."

Miss Cutter's face fluttered with doubt. Her eyes jumped to a desk calendar, where she flipped October out of the away. "Friday the sixteenth," she muttered. "How did I miss that?"

"A lot of people forget. Most, I think."

Miss Cutter looked up. "Yes, unfortunately we focus too much on turkeys and Christmas trees." Her brow furrowed. Her eyes focused on something distant. "What if I talk to your parents and assure them that you would observe the fasting rules? It would only be for two days."

He shook his head. "My dad is pretty strict about Ramadan."

"Yes, of course. It's a special month."

Mohammed felt guilty about not mentioning the money.

Miss Cutter's face suddenly brightened. "What if we were to fast with you—all of us?" She paused, seeming to give the idea a mental walk around. "We could breakfast early and eat supper in the evening. Fasting is from dawn to sunset, correct?"

He nodded.

"You wouldn't have to fast by yourself. And we wouldn't have to worry about snacking in front of you. Group support and all that." She nodded sharp, decisive nods to herself. "It would teach everyone a little self-discipline. What better way to know how the hungry feel every day? That's the point of Ramadan, isn't it?"

Mohammed said it was.

"I like it," she said. "It suits an engineer to be disciplined and hungry. Let's propose it."

"Propose it?"

"Yes, to the club, to your parents. I think we can convince them. What do you think?"

He thought Miss Cutter was a whiz at devising practical solutions to any problem—even a Ramadan problem. "I can go another time," he offered.

"Nonsense. We couldn't go without you. You're our expert. It wouldn't be the same."

Mohammed wished he had written Miss Cutter a note instead of coming.

"I will speak to your father. I can call him tonight."

"That's all right," he replied, certain the idea was not a good one. "I'll talk to him."

Miss Cutter smiled. "Okay. But don't forget." She stood up and clapped her hands. "We shall propose it to the club on Thursday."

Mohammed moved to the door.

"And, Mohammed, don't worry about the hotel deposit. I'll cover it until we work this out. Sixty dollars shouldn't be a problem."

He thanked her, closing the door. *If she only knew.*

Mrs. Heath's gift—the resin figurine of Miss Liberty—stirred the Ahmed household in unexpected directions. Mohammed's mother held the statue with childlike awe. "It like the *fotos*," she mused. She knew what dreams Miss Liberty symbolized. She knew, too, that her own dream had been one of them. "Hamed, we see statue one day. Your father, he see the Mecca."

Mohammed's father regarded the gift with a dour face. He told his wife that she should discourage their neighbor from spoiling children. "These silly souvenirs only give the boy the wrong idea."

The Statue of Liberty—a *silly souvenir*?

For weeks his father had been in a bad mood. Often absent at the breakfast table, he was routinely silent at supper, gloomy in front of the evening news, and indifferent to the playful antics of Nura Maryam. Even his voice sounded different, especially in prayer, where his usually warm and vibrant intonations had grown cold and remote. His father was becoming a stranger.

When Mohammed asked his mother about it, she said, "He worry for the money."

Now Miss Cutter was suggesting he ask permission to go to New York—travel during Ramadan, fast with his club, and spend money they didn't have.

No way.

Thursday afternoon, the first day of November and the last day for permission slips, he skipped the YEPS meeting at Miss Cutter's house. The next morning his name was butchered over the loudspeaker during school announcements. "Mo-ham-ned tin Amen report to Miss Cutter in room 113 after last period."

When he arrived, she stood at the bulletin board taking down the display for "World Rain Forest Week." She smiled. "Come help," she beckoned.

He pulled paper leaves from the forest.

"So," she began. "We missed you yesterday. What happened?"

"I didn't want to go."

"I see," she said.

He waited for more, but she busied herself with dismantling the rain forest.

"I'm not going to New York, Miss Cutter. I'm sorry."

She nodded. "It is a shame because everyone agreed to fast with you when Ramadan starts. Everyone wants you to come."

He stared the bulletin board.

"Did your father say no?"

"I didn't ask."

Miss Cutter looked at him. "Really?"

Mohammed dropped his head. He felt his throat tighten. "I don't have the money, Miss Cutter. That's the real reason. My dad's business has been bad. Nobody buys gas at the station."

She stepped back and sat on her desk. "I'm sorry to hear that. You should have said something, Mohammed."

"I know. I was embarrassed, I guess."

His adviser looked at him. "Well, you shouldn't be."

"My dad says we'll make the trip when he sells gas again. Since the attacks, it has been slow. He had to sell his truck."

Miss Cutter listened.

"And Delmar—you know, the man who helps my dad?—he was let go to pay bills."

Miss Cutter shook her head. "I didn't realize…" she said, her voice trailing off. "I had heard some things, but I never imagined it had come to this. People should be ashamed of themselves."

Mrs. Heath had said the same thing. It occurred to Mohammed that Mrs. Heath and Miss Cutter were alike in at least one way: they were ashamed of other people.

"But your parents are right. Bills first. I just wish…" She looked at him. "I was thinking I might talk to someone. Perhaps we could find a sponsor."

Mohammed removed another leaf from the blackboard. "It's better this way, Miss Cutter. My dad is stressed. I couldn't talk to him about it. I just won't go. It's okay."

She stared at the pictorial remains of the rain forest: orchids, monkeys, bulldozers, tree stumps. "I understand," she said.

Together they removed the remaining tacks. Miss Cutter remarked that it was never as much fun taking down a bulletin board as putting one up. When they finished, Mohammed slung his book bag on his shoulder. Miss Cutter said, "We'll miss you. I want you to know that. Visiting New York won't be the same."

"Thanks, Miss Cutter. I appreciate that," he said. Then he left the room.

At supper his father told him they would be visiting the masjid Saturday morning.

"Who will watch the station?" Mohammed asked.

"I am closing for the day. We will take the bus."

The bus? That sounded fun. But closing the station? That didn't sound good.

Saturday morning they flagged down a Lakefront Lines motor coach on the highway. Hasan Ahmed read his Koran during the ride while his son stared out the window at brown fields and billboards. As he listened to the muffled talk of passengers, he imagined that this was what the trip to New York would be like when the club took the bus.

They walked from the bus terminal ten blocks through old downtown, the smell of secondhand city strong in the air. At Masjid Dawoud bearded men worked outside. Red graffiti defaced the white clapboard facade. Brown splotches stained the siding. On the sidewalk, more graffiti had been sprayed. A man with a water hose washed the clapboard. Another on a ladder painted over the words "Muslims to Hell." Other men swept up glass from broken windows. Near the door the smell of urine made Mohammed wrinkle his nose.

Yaseen Haneez welcomed them into the entrance hall. He gave Mohammed's father a strong embrace. He shook Mohammed's hand. He was not dressed for prayer.

From the upstairs hall came the chants of children and the voice of Sister Meryem Bouhida teaching small tongues new sounds. Koran classes were underway.

"Private security," Saeed Patel was saying. "You can't count on the police anymore."

Talk inside the hall was about the mischief outside. Mohammed lingered near the shoe rack.

"What do you expect from a police chief who says, and I'm quoting, 'These Muslim people ought to be put under surveillance'?"

"A masjid shouldn't have to be protected. It is already protected."

"Do you think the next time they will only urinate and throw excrement?"

Mohammed listened. *So those were the brown splotches!*

"I think the worst is over."

"The worst maybe, but it will never be over."

Next to the wall hangings of Arabic calligraphy, a public service announcement had been posted. "Muslim Community Safety Kit Available in Office." Mohammed read the kit's contents:

- How to Report Suspicious Activity in Your Community
- How to React to Incidents of Anti-Muslim Hate
- How to React to Acts of Discrimination
- Know Your Rights as an Airline Passenger

He wondered if his father would take a kit. He read the instructions written in small print:

If you believe you have been the victim of an anti-Muslim hate crime or discrimination, you should report the incident to your local police station and FBI office IMMEDIATELY. Ask that the incident be treated as a hate crime. Save evidence. Take photographs. Note the presence of witnesses. Decide on an appropriate response. Consider issuing a statement from community leaders, organizing a protest, meeting with officials, or starting a letter-writing campaign. Mobilize community support. Consider contacting a lawyer. Stay on top of the situation.

No, his father wouldn't take a kit.

Mohammed followed the men outside. Soon he found himself with a paintbrush and a pail of white paint, standing in a work line. Stiff wire brushes and gallons of turpentine were sent for. Later, when he looked to the street, he saw his father and Izz Al-Busaid on their knees lifting paint from the sidewalk. The entire facade of Masjid Dawoud was repainted that afternoon, its clapboard left impeccably white. The sidewalk was scrubbed, new glass installed. The smell of urine at the door was masked by quarts of Pine-Sol.

Majd Udeen, the butcher, gave them a ride to the terminal. On the bus they rode in silence until his father said, "Thank you for pitching in, Son." When Mohammed asked if the culprits would be caught, his father said he didn't know.

"Could it be the ones who ruined our sign?"

"I don't know," he said.

Sunday he washed Mrs. Heath's storm windows.

"Has anything been said about that trip of yours?" she asked.

"The club is going again," Mohammed replied. "The week after next."

It was time she knew. Everyone else did—except his father.

Mrs. Heath looked surprise. "So soon? My goodness! Why didn't you tell me?"

"Because I'm not going. We can't afford it."

She stared at him. "Enough windows," she declared. "We must talk."

They sat in the living room, and Mohammed told her about the trouble at the station, the boycott, Delmar leaving, and about his father selling the wrecker. He said his savings were gone.

"That's why I haven't seen the truck," she remarked, shaking her head. "Shame on your mother for not confiding. What does a man trying to make a living have to do with this terrible business?"

"There's another problem," Mohammed added. "Ramadan starts that week."

Mrs. Heath shook her head. "Muslims travel all the time during Ramadan. That's no reason to stay home."

"I suppose," he replied, struck by the defiance in her tone. "But not having money is."

"Are you coming to the meeting?"

Mohammed nearly jumped. Priscilla Smith stood at his locker.

"I can't," he said, fumbling with his jacket zipper. "I have to help my dad."

The YEPS were meeting at Miss Cutter's that afternoon.

"Oh." Her blond curls seemed to droop.

"Tell Miss Cutter for me, would you?"

"Sure."

When he closed his locker, she still stood there. "Miss Cutter told us what happened," she said, her voice different, softer, not like in class. "About you not going on the trip. I'm sorry."

His face warmed. Had Miss Cutter told the club *why* he wasn't going on the trip?

"Everyone liked Miss Cutter's idea," she continued, "about fasting. Everyone but Edgar." She smiled. Edgar's appetite was legend in the middle school.

Mohammed felt something melt inside him. "Edgar fasting would be a first," he agreed.

"Yeah. Scary." She laughed, her spearmint breath in his face. She had a beautiful laugh.

He looked around. The middle school corridor was deserted.

Priscilla touched her hair. "Well, I better go," she said.

Mohammed nodded. Priscilla didn't move.

"I just want you to know, Hamed, that I don't agree with the way some kids have behaved around here. I think it's terrible."

Mohammed stared at his feet. She was standing close.

"It made me feel awful," she added. "Sometimes I've felt like I want to cry."

He bored holes into his shoes. *Sometimes she wanted to cry?*

"No one has the right to blame you. No one. I just don't want you to think that everyone around here is a bigot."

"Thanks," he mumbled. Nothing else came to him.

"See you," she said.

He ran to the station, Priscilla's spearmint breath propelling him. More than ever he wanted to go to New York (even if Miss Liberty was closed). Priscilla had cried for him. She had felt like she wanted to cry. Close enough. He could still hear her laugh. To go to New York with Priscilla Smith…*Allahu Akbar!*

At Ahmed Automotive he promptly came down to earth.

"Son, find me a crescent wrench," called his father. He lay under Raja Saleem's taxi while the Pakistani fumbled through toolboxes.

Mohammed found the wrench.

His father would not have understood about Priscilla Smith. In Koran classes boys were taught separately from girls. Fortunately he hadn't seen how close Priscilla had just stood to him. Allah forbid that his father should see her in gym shorts!

"Bad clutch bearing, Raja," he said from under the taxi. "It'll take a day to fix."

Mohammed listened. At last his father would have some work.

"Whole day?" blurted Raja Saleem, his eyes bulging. "Whole day too much."

"If the bearing seizes, you'll lose more than that."

The Pakistani pressed his thin lips together. "How much?"

His father slid out from under the taxi. Crumbs of burned oil dotted his face. "No charge. You buy the bearing."

Mohammed couldn't believe it. No charge! When his father most needed work, he would do Raja Saleem's job for free?

"Deal," agreed the cab driver. "But half day better, man."

"If Mohammed helps, maybe we can get it out in less."

Raja Saleem flashed his white teeth. "I bring Saturday. I pick you up, eh?" He turned to Mohammed. "Give window some wipe, boy."

Put that way, what choice did he have? He went for the pail and squeegee. No windshields had been washed since Delmar left. When he returned to the garage, he heard Raja Saleem talking. "I tell dispatcher. I say, 'Look. I have accent, but I not Arab. I Pakistani from Karachi.' I say, 'You know where?' 'No,' he say. I say, 'Nowhere near Arabia. You tell customers, okay? I not Arab. I have family like you. I have bills like you. Confusion will ruin me.' That what I say. In few days I get fare. Next day, two more. Some days I get four, five. Not so bad."

Hasan Ahmed said he was glad to hear it. Mohammed washed the glass. Evidence indicated that Raja spoke the truth. The windshield was dirty.

"And you, Hasan, is still dead?" asked the cab driver.

"Slow," responded his father. "Remember, Raja, I am Arab. It is different for me."

"You take down sign. That good."

His father nodded. "The sign did not help. But we have been holding on. Things will pick up soon. Maybe yours is the first of many repairs."

Mohammed drew the last strokes with the squeegee. Raja Saleem examined the windshield, his face close to the glass. "Very good, boy," he said, reaching tentatively into his pocket.

Mohammed waited. Just because his father worked for free didn't mean he had to.

The taxi driver held out a dime. "Still make trip to New York, boy?"

"No, sir," replied Mohammed, taking the tip.

"Good. No safe," said Raja Saleem. Then he climbed into his taxi, backed out, and drove off.

"Get the mats, turkeys," said Coach Chamley in PE.

Mohammed grimaced. He hated wrestling. He hated the contact, the mat burns, the slippery, sweaty groping. He hated wrestling in his shirt.

"Hazelton, you and Julie first," ordered Coach C.

Julie was the coach's name for Jules, though there was nothing Julie about him. Jules was a lion, in size at least. Hazelton was Norman. Norm was a crumb.

Both boys took positions. Norman tossed a forlorn look at Mohammed before Coach C blew his whistle.

The squeaking began but didn't last long. Coach C had taught them the simple moves—the curl, the screwdriver, the bender—but Norman didn't try any of these. Norman tried to escape. Immediately Jules fished him from a corner and rolled him in a ball. Norman's head looked perilously close to his stomach. One, two, three. Coach C slapped the mat, his whistle shrill.

No one cheered. The expected had occurred. A lion had devoured its prey.

Jules lumbered off. Norman unrolled, his head looking smaller after the contortion.

"Okay," said Coach C, surveying Turkeyville with narrowed eyes. "You, Fuzzball, and White."

Eighth-grade PE breathed a collective sigh of relief. It was a fair pairing. The matches that followed were full of squeaks, red marks, and lots of draws. Mitch wrestled. So did Merrill. Soon four boys were left, Mohammed one of them. He assessed the possible matchups. He could take the pimple-faced Phettiplace, probably draw with Currier. Then there was Mitch's friend, Ralph Trumbull, Lieutenant Bully. Mohammed didn't want to think about *that* possibility.

"Fattyplace, you got Currier," announced the coach.

Now Mohammed had no choice but to think about it. He and Ralph were in the final round.

He looked at the gym clock. Ten minutes left in the period. Maybe Gary and Chuck would go the limit. With any luck he wouldn't have to wrestle. When he looked across the mats, he saw Ralph Trumbull smiling at him.

Mohammed watched the match, thinking of a strategy to survive. Seconds ticked. Nothing came to him. Then, as Gary and Chuck grappled toward a finale, their bodies wet with perspiration, he had an idea.

The match came to an abrupt end when Gary locked Chuck's legs and pinned him. *Slap, slap* went Coach C's hand on the mat. "Purty," he muttered, as if it were a sunset. Gary and Chuck had so many red marks on them they looked as if they had tangled with leeches, not each other.

"Mohammed. Ralph." Coach C clapped his hands. "Get a wiggle."

Five minutes remained in the period. Mohammed suspected they were about to become the longest five minutes of his life. He walked to the center of the mats. Ralph did the same. Under his breath, he muttered, "Gonna break something, Taliban. Gonna make you squeal."

"Take positions," called the coach.

Then without a word, Mohammed reached over his shoulders and peeled off his T-shirt, tossing it beyond the mats. Eighth-grade boys exchanged incredulous looks.

"Jesus," said someone.

"Hamed!" blurted Merrill.

Boys stared. None of them had seen Mohammed without his shirt. Most were surprised to see that his torso looked no different than their own.

Ralph smirked. "Tough boy without your shirt," he sneered in a low voice. "Get close. Are you afraid or what?"

"Close the gap, y'all," called Coach C. "This ain't the hokeypokey."

Laughter rose from the perimeter. Mohammed edged closer. Already he was the fool and the match hadn't begun. But he had a plan. Then the whistle blew.

The first move was Ralph's. He grabbed his opponent's arm and dropped to his chest, rolling Mohammed over his back. When Mohammed hit the mat, the impact made everyone flinch. "Ooh," groaned the boys.

His head reverberated from the blow. His back felt on fire. He saw something white overhead—the gymnasium roof. Then Ralph was on top of him, twisting his arm. Mohammed squealed—Ralph had predicted it—the pain shooting to his shoulder. Ralph was trying to make his other prediction come true. He wanted to break something.

Mohammed's back was pressed against the mat. Ralph only needed to "clean the blades." Match over. Pinned in thirty seconds. Ralph and his friends would never let him forget it.

Both boys glistened with sweat. Mohammed began to wiggle. It was why he had removed his shirt, why Ralph's embrace felt perfect. Wet meant slippery.

Suddenly Ralph lost his grip. Then he lost his opponent. Suddenly there were two bodies where there had been one.

Mohammed jiggled and shimmied. He didn't try to escape. There were not enough mats for that. When Ralph embraced him, he squirmed. When Ralph pressed him, he gyrated. He was an undulating eggbeater on whip speed. He was something buttered on ball bearings. When Ralph grabbed his leg, he rolled. When Ralph gripped his arm, he twisted. He jerked. He twitched. He convulsed.

Ralph's smile disappeared. He looked like a T. rex grappling with an earthworm. He was wet with sweat. So were the mats. So was his prey. First he had him, then he didn't. The seconds ticked. Mohammed knew the price would be mat burn for a week. The perimeter was a blur of convulsed faces. He heard their laughter. He heard his name. "Go, Hamed, go!" The sound was like something sweet to drink. Eighth grade was cheering for *him*!

Coach C seemed reluctant to blow the whistle. He stared, mouth open.

Ralph's 170 pounds grew heavy. With each failed embrace, his strength diminished, his quickness ebbed, though his anger never languished. It showed on his face. He knew what a draw meant. It was as good as a loss.

Merrill pointed to the gym clock. "Coach, it's time!" he shouted.

The whistle blew. The boys jumped to their feet and cheered. They lifted Mohammed from the mats. It was over.

Coach C shook his head. "You call that wrestling?"

"No, sir," replied Mohammed happily. "Survival." Mat burn never felt better.

In the locker room, laughter was loud and infectious. When Ralph tried to make trouble, Mitch stepped in. "Chill, Ralph. All he did was wiggle." Ralph left without further threats. Mitch rejoined the locker room celebration. Mohammed enjoyed the moment.

That afternoon his mother said Mrs. Heath had left him an envelope in the kitchen.

Mohammed took it from the counter and opened it. Inside he found a check for $150, made out to Mohammed Ahmed.

His mother watched him. "For the trip," she said.

He stared at the check. "She told you?"

A nod. "She ask if okay she give the moneys. I say you ask your father."

Mohammed dropped into a chair. Of course his father would have to know. He stared at Mrs. Heath's perfect penmanship. One hundred and fifty dollars! Money to make a dream come true. "Do you think he'll let me go?"

His mother smiled. "For me, you go."

"I know. But will *he* let me?"

"*No sé.*"

"Can you talk to him for me?"

She shook her head. "You ask."

He returned the check to the envelope. "Maybe I shouldn't. It doesn't feel right."

"No right? What no right?"

"Taking money to spend on a trip while Dad isn't selling gas. I should help."

She touched his arm. "You help already."

"That was helping Delmar. Anyway, he'll probably want me to give it back."

"Maybe. Maybe he say keep."

"You think?" Instantly he was hopeful again.

"We see."

He gave her the envelope. "Keep it for me please. If he says no, I'll only feel worse."

"Okay."

He surveyed the kitchen. "Do I have time to thank her?"
She nodded.

"What's for dinner?" he asked.

"*Gallina pinta*," she replied, waiting for the grimace—cooked beans and hominy were not his favorite—but Mohammed said, "Great!"

"Don't thank me, Mohammed. Your smile is thanks enough."

"Thanks, Mrs. Heath," he said. Then he hugged her.

The widow started to protest, then let herself be hugged. "Mind you, it's an advance on snow shoveling."

"Okay."

"Also, for digging my flower beds this spring."

"Right."

"And I owed you for helping with the windows."

"Thank you."

"You're more than welcome. What are dreams for, if not to make them come true? Have you spoken to your father?"

Mohammed shook his head. "That's what I'm afraid of."

"You won't know unless you ask. Give him a chance."

He nodded, even as a new worry jumped in the way. "The other day my father heard Mr. Saleem say that New York isn't safe."

Mrs. Heath shook her finger. "New York is probably safer now than it has ever been. The army is everywhere."

"But there's Ramadan, too. He'll want me to stay."

"I told you. People travel during Ramadan."

"Not my dad. He won't think it's right that you pay for it."

The widow's eyes widened. "Mohammed, dear, *you* are paying for it. Tell him that. But don't wait too long. The sooner, the better. Be brave."

At dinner his father said, "One of your teachers stopped by to have her brakes checked. Miss Cutter."

Mohammed looked up from his food. Miss Cutter at the station!

"We had a long chat," continued his father. "She said the trip to New York has been rescheduled. She asked if you had permission to go. I told her you hadn't mentioned it."

An explanation jumped from his mother. "He no speak, Hasan. He had no moneys."

His father nodded. "I see your mother knows."

Mohammed said he had thrown away the papers that explained everything. He said he hadn't asked permission because of the money. And because of Ramadan.

"Yes, I told her our holy month was coming," his father replied. "I also told her you had used your savings."

Mohammed glanced at his mother. Her eyes said, "Speak! Speak!"

"But I have the money now, Abi. Mrs. Heath loaned it to me."

His father paused his fork. "A loan from Mrs. Heath?" Something in his voice didn't like the surprise.

Mohammed rushed to elaborate. "It's an advance for snow shoveling and other work. I'm going to pay her back."

"I see," said his father. "That was very nice."

"Very good lady," interjected his mother. "She very nice."

"Yes, Lisa, I know that." He turned to his son. "So you want to go now, is that it?"

Mohammed stared into his bowl. "Yes, Abi, I do. Very much."

His father resumed eating. "Don't you think you should be with your family during Ramadan? What about your fast and your prayers?"

"I thought I could fast while I was gone. It would be for two days. The other kids would fast, too."

His father frowned. "Yes. Miss Cutter mentioned it. I told her Ramadan is more than fasting. It is about devotion and pursuing our spirituality, not a game to be played with friends."

Mohammed wondered if Miss Cutter and his father had argued.

"She understood my views. Still, she wanted to know if I would let you go. I said I didn't think this was a good time."

"I will do my *tarawih* every night, Abi. And Friday I will go to congregational prayer."

His father shook his head. "It's not the same, Son."

"I will ask at the hotel for directions to a masjid. New York has many. I will pray there." Desperation had worked into his voice. His mother tried to help.

"When Senora Heath bring the moneys, I tell her, 'Mohammed he ask the father.' I tell Mohammed, 'You ask you father. Maybe he say yes. You ask.' Now he got the moneys—"

"Lisa, please," interrupted Hasan Ahmed.

But his wife hadn't finished. "You give Senor Delmar the moneys. You help Senor Delmar. Now Senora Heath give Mohammed the moneys. She help Mohammed."

"And I will pay her back, Abi," Mohammed added. "She has lots of work."

His father shifted in his chair. His voice took on an edge. "No one in this family is traveling who doesn't have to. Something could happen. It isn't safe."

Mohammed knew that was Raja Saleem speaking. He considered countering with Mrs. Heath. *New York is safer now than it has ever been.* But he remained silent. His father had decided.

"Perhaps we will make the trip as a family next summer. I know your mother would like to see New York. Wouldn't you, Lisa?"

His mother nodded reluctantly.

"It's settled," said Hasan Ahmed, pushing back his chair. "And I want no sulking."

Mohammed and his mother looked at each other across the table.

"We have much to be thankful for," continued his father. "We are Muslims. We are together. And we are about to celebrate Ramadan. *Allahu Akbar.*"

"*Allahu Akbar,*" they repeated mechanically.

"Son, I want you to return that money to Mrs. Heath," his father added.

In his room Mohammed considered the option of living somewhere else, with other parents, with another name. What would it be like to live where a boy was allowed to go to New York City with his club, where a father didn't have trouble, where Ramadan wasn't a problem?

How he wished he could run away, start over, and be a boy with no past. But he knew that couldn't happen. Not even the next best thing could happen—to be an ordinary kid like Norman or Merrill or Mitch. Even Ralph, who was a jerk and a bully, probably had a more normal life than he did. Why did he have to be so different? Everything was more complicated. School. Girls. Obligations. Family. His parents were not only foreign to their town. They were foreign to each other—an odd and exotic combination claimed by the American dream. Did that not make him, their son, odder still? Even before the nineteen men from Arabia had crashed airplanes into buildings, he had felt different. But now he felt like a freak.

His father didn't understand. His father would never understand. Give him a chance, Mrs. Heath had advised. But no such formula worked with his father. Faith and denial were all he understood. And surrender. Most of all, surrender.

He lay on his bed staring at the ceiling when his mother knocked.

"I sorry. I no help," she began.

"That's okay," he said. "I don't want to cause trouble."

His mother surveyed the room. "I talk to him. Later."

"It won't do any good. He has made up his mind."

"We see," she replied. She took the statuette of Miss Liberty from his dresser. "So beautiful," she said.

Mohammed told her about the real statue being closed.

"Then she safe now. Safe from bad mens." She sat on the bed.

"I dream about her, you know." He had never told anyone before, but somehow the moment invited divulgence.

His mother said, "Tell me, Hamed."

He told her, narrating each strange occurrence. "It's night, and I am on the island, looking up at the statue. Rain is falling, and I'm wet…" He described the colossal specter of Miss Liberty, the fury of the wind, and the roar of the waves. He told her how he climbed the spiral staircase listening to his own metallic footfalls and the creak of Liberty's copper skin. He took the statuette from his mother and showed her how he ascended the narrow tunnel of Liberty's arm. He pointed to the tiny balcony encircling the torch.

His mother sat riveted. When Mohammed described the sudden rush of wind sweeping him from the torch into the raging night, she let out a cry.

"That is nothing," continued her son.

He described how he fell and was swallowed by the sea, sinking, kicking for his life. "I was drowning," he said.

His mother covered her face with her hands, shaking her head.

Then he spoke of the large shadow darkening the water, the yellow light shining above him. He explained how he was lifted from the water in the palm of a giant hand, then set on the island, gasping for air. When he looked up, her face was near his—the face of Miss Liberty.

"*Gracias a Dios.*" His mother gasped.

"Moments later, she returned to her pedestal. The wind died. The sea calmed. She became a statue. And I was alive."

Lisa Ahmed shivered as if the room had turned cold. "That a bad dream," she said.

"No, Mother. Don't you see? She saved me." He placed the statuette on the dresser.

His mother rose from the bed. "I go. You pray," she said.

Mohammed knew his mother believed prayer was a protection against bad dreams. As she turned to leave, he said, "Will you give Mrs. Heath her check, please?"

Lisa Ahmed smiled. "Not yet."

"But he might ask. He might get—"

She hushed him with a finger. "We see." Then she left.

Friday afternoon his father closed the station to attend prayer in the city. That evening at the supper table, he said, "I was offered a job today."

Mohammed looked up from his plate.

"Mister You-Deen?" asked his mother, no surprise in her voice.

His father nodded. Majd Udeen was the butcher.

"In the city, Abi?"

"Yes, Son, in the city."

Mohammed wondered why Majd Udeen would need his father. "What kind of job, Abi?"

"I would take care of his delivery trucks. Sometimes I would deliver meat."

Mohammed tried to imagine his father driving one of the meat trucks, carrying the clean, white-papered packages to doorsteps. His father's hands seemed better suited to greasy motor parts than ground beef.

His mother remained silent. Mohammed had the impression she had given her opinion. Or silence was her opinion.

"If it is the will of Allah, I will take it," his father said flatly.

"What about the station?" Mohammed asked.

"I would close it, then find someone to buy it."

His mother rose with her plate, retreating to the kitchen. His father's eyes followed her.

Mohammed tried to imagine life without riding his bike to the station. Weekends wouldn't be the same. No more washing windshields. No playing with the hydraulic lift. No sweet smell of gasoline and grease. No free Cokes. The possibility of listening to Delmar at the pumps gone. How different life would be.

Alone with his father at the table, cold food and empty plates between them, he said, "Abi, will I be able to ride along when you deliver meat?"

His father said, "We'll see."

That night he listened to his parents argue downstairs. His father shouted and his mother shouted back. They never argued like this. Mohammed didn't know whether to cover his ears or crack the bedroom door to hear better. Instead he remained in bed, lying perfectly still. Were they arguing about selling the station? The job offer?

They spoke at once, Spanish over English, Arabic over Spanish. His father sounded defensive, his mother defiant. Suddenly their shouts dropped to unintelligible mutterings.

Mohammed tiptoed to the door, cracking it. When he heard his mother's voice, he froze. She had spoken his name. He waited. There it was again, from his father.

He closed the door and backed into bed. He didn't want to listen. He certainly didn't want to be caught listening. He knew what the argument was about. His trip.

He buried his head under a pillow. Not that it would change the outcome. His father would prevail. He always did. His mother would retreat in tears. But she hadn't cried yet.

Sometime later the house turned quiet. The last thing he heard were footfalls on the carpeted stairs, more felt than heard.

At breakfast, silence hung in the kitchen as heavily as the oatmeal that clung to Nura Maryam's spoon. His father read the paper. His mother packed lunches. Mohammed stared at his toast. No one seemed willing to gamble with words.

"Mr. Saleem will pick us up at eight," his father said before rising from the table.

Today they would repair the clutch for free.

Mohammed pushed away the toast, his appetite diminished by the prospect of spending a Saturday with Raja Saleem. When his father left the kitchen, his mother spoke just above a whisper. "We fight in the night. You father mad."

Mohammed wanted to say, "I know," but he only nodded.

"No worry," she said, handing him the lunches. "We talk."

A horn honked from the driveway. His father strode to the back door as if he would leave without speaking. Then he stopped. "Lisa, we'll be home this afternoon."

"We wait," she replied evenly.

Mohammed followed his father out the door.

Outside, the day smelled of rain and burning leaves. "Welcome, welcome," greeted Raja Saleem, waving them into the cab as if they were customers.

The bad clutch screamed as they drove to the station. On the taxi radio, voices fought with static. Inside the garage Raja Saleem checked his watch. "Half day, Hasan. Remember."

It had been weeks since Mohammed's father had repaired an automobile. Mohammed observed the keenness with which his father worked. He seemed hungry for the touch of warm steel.

By noon the bearing was out. Raja Saleem radioed for a replacement part. An hour later a fellow taxi operator delivered the bearing but refused to hand it over until the Pakistani paid. "Everyone want money these days," Raja complained. "No trust."

With the installation underway, he began to relax. He grew chatty. "So, boy, no class today."

Mohammed said it was Saturday.

"Ah, yes." He smiled. "I mean pray class, boy."

"No, sir. I don't go to Koran classes any longer."

"A shame," said Raja Saleem. "No class. No trip. Big shame."

Please not the trip, Mohammed said to himself. But Raja Saleem continued. "Many Indians drive taxis in New York. Bad drivers, you know. Don't get into cab with an Indian. Accident may kill you. Very bad drivers, all. You ask first. You say, 'Are you Indian?' But don't believe them. They lie. They say they from Pakistan. Stranger like you must be careful."

Mohammed said, "I'm not going to New York."

"Good. You too young to have accident. Stay home." He looked around the garage. "All morning dead. Dead and dead. No gas. No breakdown. How you do business, Hasan?"

Mohammed's father answered from under the taxi. "I don't."

"No help. No truck. No sign. Soon you have no pumps. Then what?"

Hasan Ahmed's head appeared. "Actually, I'm thinking of selling and getting a job."

Raja Saleem's eyes widened. "Job? What job?"

"Mechanic. I would work for someone else."

The cabby stared. "Wait. Who fix this car, man?"

"Don't worry, Raja. I'll give you a referral."

"No, no," said the cabby. "I tell you what, Hasan. I talk to drivers. I send business: gas business, tire business, fixing business. Forget job, forget city."

"If you want to send somebody," his father replied, "send a buyer. Someone with money."

Raja Saleem opened his mouth, then quickly shut it. The man fixing his cab free of charge had just mentioned money. "Okay, okay," he muttered. "If anybody wants, I tell him. Maybe you give me commission, eh?" He winked at Mohammed.

Just before two o'clock Hasan Ahmed finished. "Turn it over," he said.

Raja started the motor and pumped the clutch. The taxi radio made more noise than the new bearing.

Outside, rain fell in sheets. Hasan Ahmed asked the cabby to give Mohammed a ride home.

"Yes, yes, of course. Let's go, boy."

"What about you, Abi?"

"I'll be back in a while," his father answered.

On the ride to his house, Raja Saleem said, "Your father too tame, boy. He need to get mad. He need to get mad as wet rooster."

Mohammed sat silent. His mother had said his father was mad. Raja said he wasn't mad enough. Did it really matter who was right?

He retreated to his room and flopped on the bed. Rain beat the roof. He thought about his father walking home. Who would give him a ride? What friend or customer would stop? He gazed at the ceiling. Some Saturday! Rain. Work without pay. Raja Saleem. Rain. No bike riding, nowhere to go, nothing to do. Rain. And his father was going to get soaked.

The room grew dark. The pounding of the rain deafened to no sound at all. He hugged his pillow and slept. In his dream the storm was loud and he clung to the torch of Miss Liberty. The gale tore at his clothes. He fell and sank into the sea, the dark water pressing out his breath with a suffocating embrace.

Voices awakened him. He kicked off the bedcovers and sat up. He heard his father. Others were talking downstairs. He looked out the window. The rain had stopped. A blue sky peeked past the clouds. The car parked in their driveway belonged to Miss Cutter.

He listened. Her voice rose from the living room. Another woman spoke. It sounded like Mrs. Heath.

"I call them," his mother would later explain. "I say, 'Please talk to Hasan.'"

Mohammed would learn that Mrs. Heath had said many things to his father. "Weren't you ever a boy?" she had asked after he refused to reconsider Mohammed's participation in the club trip. "Didn't you dream when you were his age? I can't believe your father didn't let you follow your dreams. My guess is you wouldn't be here if he hadn't…"

His father had said nothing.

Miss Cutter had reiterated the club's intention to fast together when Ramadan began. She had pledged her willingness to make sure Mohammed's daily prayer obligations were met.

His mother had sent them to the station, where they had talked. Later, they had given him a ride home. His father hadn't walked back in the rain.

Now, as Mohammed lay in his bed listening, Nura Maryam knocked on his door. "Daddy say come," she said.

When he walked into the living room, he saw the taut faces of Miss Cutter and Mrs. Heath. Then his father told him he could go.

His mother grinned. Miss Cutter raised a signed permission slip. Mrs. Heath said, "Start packing, Mohammed." Then he knew it was true.

He looked to the ceiling. *"Allahu Akbar!"* he exclaimed before he dropped to his knees and kissed the carpet. Tears welled in his eyes. At last. He was going. He was going. The presence of grandness swept around him, filling him with joy. He wanted to leap from the floor and embrace his father, but dutiful distance held him back. When he looked up, his father smiled. "We will pray for you, Son. We will pray that New York welcomes you and sends you back to us safe and happy. We will pray that you not forget your devotion or duties."

"I won't, Abi," he replied. "I will fast. I will pray. I won't forget, I promise—"

"And one more thing," Hasan Ahmed added, his face suddenly serious. "When you return from your trip, you will have to pay Mrs. Heath the money she has loaned you."

The widow cackled. "Don't worry, Hasan. I'll get it back. They're predicting a long winter, and I just bought a new snow shovel."

Everyone laughed. Mohammed felt warmth in the room, the bonding of good news.

Miss Cutter said, "I guess that leaves me the details. Our final meeting is Monday. Bring your room deposit. We will pay for the tickets at the terminal."

"Does the boy have a suitcase?" inquired Mrs. Heath.

His father said, "I have something he can use." Then his mother related how she had traveled from Las Vegas to Louisiana carrying everything she owned in a JCPenney's shopping bag.

"I think we can do better than that," Hasan Ahmed said, and everyone laughed again, Mohammed the loudest.

So he was going—finally.

Before his mother left him in his room that night, she said, "He good man, you father," and Mohammed knew this was true. At moments he had tried to imagine living another life, a more normal life, exchanging this father for some other, but he knew he didn't want that.

"He love you very much," said his mother.

With the house quiet and a cloudless, star-dusted Ohio sky filling his bedroom window, he let the news sink in. Everything terrible that had happened since September, the weeks of trouble on the bus and in school, all of it slipped away. Had it been a test, part of some design meant to strengthen his faith? His father would have said it was, but Mohammed wasn't sure. The trip, it seemed, was meant to be.

Sunday the family went to Walmart, chauffeured by Raja Saleem in his taxi. Mohammed wondered if his father had called in a favor.

Raja was full of news. "I tell drivers, Hasan. They bring cars. You get business. Be ready. I tell everybody you cheap. Cars coming soon."

At Walmart Mohammed was outfitted with the adolescent trip essentials. His father bought him a watch. "You will need to know the time to pray," he said. Back at the house, Hasan Ahmed gave Mohammed a qibla compass and showed him how to find the direction of Mecca from New York. They performed

Isha together, his father's voice strong and melodic. In one of the prayers he asked the angels to watch over his son.

Monday Mohammed gave his friends the news. Merrill whooped. "I knew the old man would crumble. It happens in the best of homes."

Norman said, "No way would my mother have let me go. Your dad is all right."

That afternoon at the club meeting, Priscilla looked surprised to see him. Teddy White put his arm across his shoulder. "Hamed, glad you showed up." His voice dropped to a whisper. "I was just telling the Fuzz—how about if we sneak out of the hotel Friday night? We'll wait till Cutter beds down then head to the Garden. The Lakers are in town. We can't get tickets, but we can hang out, maybe see some players."

"Gee, I don't know," Mohammed said.

Then Miss Cutter called the meeting to order. Her first announcement was that Mohammed would be joining them. Everyone clapped. Edgar asked, "Does that mean we have to fast?"

Their adviser nodded. "I have promised his parents that he will observe the traditions of Ramadan, including fasting. Please support him on this."

Last-minute instructions were delivered: departure time, dress code, room rules. As they left, Mohammed found himself standing beside Priscilla. "I'm so glad you're coming," she said.

Speech deserted him before he stammered, "Me, too."

On Tuesday, Mac stopped him in the hall. "Miss Cutter gave me the news," he said with his usual zeal. "I'm so glad you're going. Now make sure you visit the Federal Hall National Memorial on Wall Street," Mac added. "In terms of the events that shaped this country, Mohammed, it is *the* most historic site in the city. The Continental Congress met there. The Bill of Rights was signed inside. It was where George Washington was inaugurated. I need not tell you what an opportunity it is to be close to that kind of history."

Mohammed smiled, grateful to have such a caring and supportive teacher. In his own book of heroes, Mac was up there with George Washington.

His mother helped him pack—clothes, Koran, a prayer mat, his Yankees cap. Then he was sent to say good-bye to Mrs. Heath.

As soon as she opened her door, she waved him quiet. "No thank-yous!" she began. "Gratitude gives this old woman no pleasure. It's seeing you go that warms my heart."

On her kitchen table sat a Kodak camera, new in its plastic package. Mrs. Heath handed it to him. "Take pictures for me," she said.

Mohammed held it. "You've done so much already."

"It's not digital," she rejoined. "I don't have time to take it back, and you don't have time to refuse it."

He could think of nothing smart to say, nothing better than, "Thanks, Mrs. Heath."

"Think of it as a gift from Mr. Heath and me," she said, wiping her eyes. She gave him a hug. "I told your father to take the car. I don't want you to have to walk to the bus station. You'll be doing plenty of walking where you're going."

"I'll never forget this." Then he gave their widowed neighbor a kiss on the cheek.

After supper he went upstairs to get ready. Minutes later his father stood in the door. "We should leave shortly."

Mohammed said, "I'm ready."

His father pointed to the bag. "Did you pack your Koran?"

"Yes, Abi."

"Good. When you travel, Son, it's acceptable to combine your prayers if need be. It is better to pray three times well than five with distractions."

"Yes, Abi."

"Where did you put your money?"

Mohammed patted his front pocket, then the back. He had been told to spread it around.

His father surveyed the room. "Remember what Mr. Saleem said. I'm sure he knows what he is talking about."

"I won't forget, Abi."

Silence. Something invisible between them. Words waiting to be said.

"Well, I better get the car." He moved from the door.

"Abi?"

Mohammed watched him hesitate. "I know you may still think it's a bad idea letting me go, but thanks for giving me the chance."

His father smiled. "Actually, Son, what I came to tell you is that I'm happy you are going. I mean, not happy you are leaving us—we'll miss you—but happy you are not afraid to go." He paused. "You are a good son, Mohammed. I have been a distracted father these last weeks. I had forgotten what it was to be young and have a dream, but you have helped me remember. So I am the one who is thankful. Come."

His father opened his arms. Mohammed ran straight into them, wrapping his own around him.

At the bus station, club members arrived with their parents. Mohammed spotted Priscilla holding a travel bag on wheels. She stood with her mother.

"Hamed, dude!" shouted Teddy White from across the terminal. Teddy was rarely encumbered with parents. His father had dropped him off.

"Mom, Dad, this is Teddy White," Mohammed said after Teddy gave him a high five. "Teddy, these are my parents."

Teddy stuck out his hand, a model of manners. "Pleased to meet you, sir." To Mohammed's mother he nodded readily. "A pleasure, ma'am." Teddy knew how to turn it on. His problem was he didn't know when to turn it off. "Don't worry about that Ramadan thing," he told Mohammed's father. "I'll make sure Hamed doesn't stuff his face. I'll tape his mouth."

"Thank you," said his father. "I hope that won't be necessary."

"Hey, what are friends for, right, Hamed?"

Mohammed hated introductions. Already he felt eyes on them, other parents watching. Even in a bus station his folks stood out. "You can leave," he suggested to his father. "I mean, if you want to. Mrs. Heath might need her car for an emergency or something. I'll be all right."

His father smiled. "Don't worry. I told Mrs. Heath I would call if we were delayed. Besides, your mother wants to see you off."

"I see you no sit with *muchacha*," said his mother loudly.

Mohammed heard his name called. At the ticket counter, Miss Cutter and Edgar beckoned. Salvation. "I'll be right back," he said.

Miss Cutter asked for his money then checked him off her list. Edgar said, "Sit with me, Hamed. The seat is open."

Mohammed knew he was cornered. He had paired with no one, and no one had paired with Edgar. Wide Edgar was known as a seat crowder on the school bus.

"Yeah, sure."

"Did you bring snacks or anything? Because if you didn't, I brought some extra chips and ham sandwiches and stuff. We can hit 'em anytime."

Mohammed said, "I'm not supposed to eat that stuff, Edgar."

"Oh. Right."

"I brought a lunch. Don't worry."

Edgar looked relieved. Mohammed looked around. His parents stood by themselves among the middle school families, strangers in a sea of familiarity. Loud laughter and hand-shaking surrounded them, but they were not part of it. Then Priscilla approached his parents with her mother in tow. Mohammed heard her perky voice. "Hi, I'm Priscilla Smith. Are you Mohammed's folks?"

His father nodded. His mother beamed. "Yes, we the folks."

Mohammed rejoined them.

"This is my mom," said Priscilla. "Mom, these are Mohammed's parents. Remember Mohammed, the boy I told you about?"

Priscilla's mother offered a thin-lipped smile. Something in her face suggested she enjoyed these introductions less than her daughter.

"And this is Mohammed," said Priscilla, turning to face him, her smile bright. "Mohammed, my mom."

He tried a Teddy White. "A pleasure, ma'am."

Mrs. Smith nodded, or seemed to nod—it may have been the illusion of a nod—as if this was the deserving amount of recognition for one who conjured such a smile from her daughter.

"I've been telling Mother what an expert you are on New York," continued Priscilla. "He knows everything there is to know about the Statue of Liberty."

Her enthusiasm was met with cold silence. Mrs. Smith's gaze wandered.

"Yes, yes," interjected Mohammed's mother. "He know the Liberty very much."

"He does," agreed Priscilla. "I guess if you know a thing well, you come to love it."

"*Sí, sí*, he love," his mother gushed, dropping into her bilingual comfort zone.

"Well, I'm just glad they closed it."

Everyone looked at Priscilla's mother, who had just spoken.

"That should keep the terrorists out of it," she added wryly.

Silence. A bus horn honked in the distance. Mohammed's father cleared his throat.

"Mother!" admonished Priscilla. "Please."

"Well, it's true," responded the woman coolly. "After what happened? I'm still not convinced this trip is a good idea."

Mohammed stared at his feet. Priscilla glared at her mother. Then Miss Cutter saved them. "To the boarding area, everyone," she announced.

Mrs. Smith moved off. "Nice meeting you," she observed dryly.

Hasan Ahmed gave away nothing. His wife said, "Very nice you."

Mohammed would forever wonder what his mother meant.

The Greyhound's destination sign read "New York City."

Mohammed left his bag with the man loading the luggage compartments. Then he stood with his parents near the curb. The scene with Priscilla's mother replayed in his head. He had just met the reason his father's business was failing. He had heard its angry voice. Would Priscilla speak to him on the bus? Would her mother forbid it, as Norman's mother had done? For a moment the trip seemed not worth making.

Another Greyhound nosed into its parking spot, hot from the highway. The two buses grumbled at each other side by side. Exhaust fumes filled the platform. Someone coughed.

Mohammed turned to look. He recognized the cough. "Delmar!" he exclaimed.

The proper salutation was "Mr. Moffit," but no one noticed, least of all Delmar.

"Hamed, Hasan, well, I'll—" He spotted Mohammed's mother. "Lisa. What the heck are you all doing here?" He had the same toothless grin, the same unshaved stubble. The rest of him looked withered. He wore the yellow shirt.

"I'm going to New York. I'm taking this bus," Mohammed said.

"Well, I'll be." He coughed again, touching his mouth with nicotine-stained fingers. "'Bout time, Hamed. That's what you was saving for."

Mohammed saw the squeegee in his hand. "Are you working here?"

"Yup. Washing bus windows, helping out with errands. The drivers give me tips and such. It ain't a job exactly, but I get all the free coffee I want."

A bus motor revved, and everyone but Delmar waved away the diesel fumes.

"So you're letting him go, Hasan. You got a good boy here. Wants to see the world like you."

His father nodded. "As soon as business picks up, Delmar, I want you back."

Delmar grinned. "By then I'll be as good as Hamed at cleaning windows." He tried to laugh but coughed instead. "Well, I better get to work." He pointed at Mohammed's bus. "Taking precious cargo that one is. Don't want the driver missing the turnoff to New York." He looked at Mohammed's mother. "Lisa, they make Mexican food in that cafeteria there, but it don't smell as good as yours."

Mohammed's mother said, "I make. Hasan bring."

"Don't bother about that, ma'am. Hasan's got his hands full." He turned to Mohammed. "Have a safe one, Hamed. Give Lady Liberty a kiss for me—tell her old Delmar hasn't forgotten her. Nope, not since the SS *America* passed under her nose just back from Hitler's party, all of us Joes looking up at her. Sight for sore eyes, she was. Anyway, good seeing you folks."

Delmar stepped off the curb and shuffled to the New York Greyhound. Miss Cutter's voice rose above the bus rumble. "It's time," she announced.

The line moved. Passengers in transit stared from the bus windows. As Mohammed neared the door, Nura Maryam leaned from her mother's arms and gave him a hug. "Don't go, Hamed," she said.

The driver took his ticket, punched it, then gave it back. His mother kissed him, her free hand pulling his face toward hers, whispering in his ear, "*Que Dios te bendiga.*" Nura Maryam began to cry. His father said, "Remember to pray, Son."

Mohammed bound up the bus steps, not looking back, diving into the warm Greyhound with its people smells and dirty yellow luminescence. He found Edgar at a window, already snacking. Edgar patted what remained of the aisle seat. "Right here, Hamed," he said, his mouth full of Fritos. Mohammed wedged in. Edgar was big but soft. Much of him moved out of the way.

"I think we might stop at McDonald's for breakfast," Edgar conjectured.

Mohammed looked out the glass, lifting himself to see across Edgar. His parents stood close to the bus, trying to find him. Nura Maryam waved blindly at the windows.

He glanced up the aisle. He didn't see Priscilla, but he saw Delmar through the bus windshield, his face close to the glass.

The old man's warthog eyes squinted in the poor light as he zigzagged the squeegee.

Mohammed felt the weight of the lunch bag on his lap: three sandwiches and an apple. He felt the weight of regret. He knew Delmar should never have been here. This withered old man washing bus windshields for tips should have been pumping gas under a clear blue sky. One September morning had changed all that.

"You bring fruit?" he quizzed Edgar.

Edgar nodded, his mouth full. "…anana," he replied.

"Save it for me," Mohammed said, getting up.

The bus door was still open. Mohammed jumped into the step well.

"Hey," blurted the driver.

"Be right back," he said. He squeezed through a crowd to the front of the bus. "Delmar," he called. "It's clean. The glass is clean!"

Delmar said, "Hamed, ain't you supposed to be…?"

Mohammed handed his lunch bag to Delmar. "Gotta go," he said.

The bus motor revved. "Crazy kid," the driver muttered, closing the bus door behind him. When Mohammed slipped into his seat, Edgar asked, "Hey, where'd you go?"

"To say good-bye."

He didn't know if his parents had seen him. It didn't matter. They would understand. He gazed out the window and saw them standing together, Nura Maryam still waving. His mother joined her. Other parents did the same. The middle school engineers cheered. Edgar wagged his Fritos bag. Mohammed watched his father. He stood like a soldier, rigid, not smiling. Before the bus turned the corner, he lifted one arm in a single wave. Then he was gone.

"'Bout time," exhaled Edgar, licking his lips.

Mohammed held his hands in front of him, palms up. He closed his eyes and recited to himself a short *du'a* for starting a journey. When he finished, he passed his palms over his face.

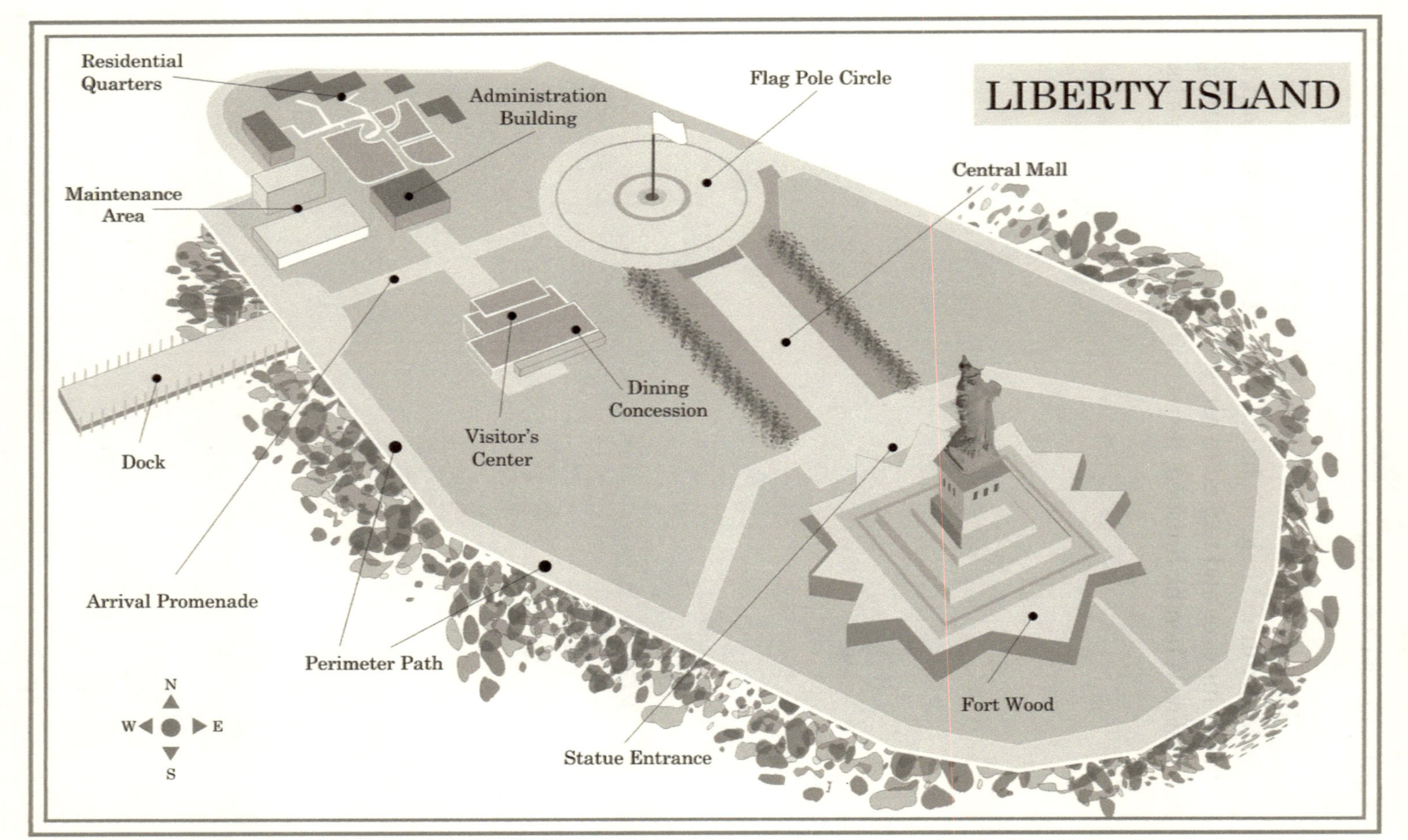

LIBERTY ISLAND
Residential Quarters
Administration Building
Flag Pole Circle
Central Mall
Maintenance Area
Dock
Visitor's Center
Dining Concession
Arrival Promenade
Perimeter Path
Statue Entrance
Fort Wood
N
W E
S

LIBERTY ISLAND

Sunday, November 18, 2001, television morning news shows carried the story of an incident on Liberty Island. A suspected terrorist had been detained near the monument.

A spokesperson for the National Park Service reported that a park policeman on his rounds Saturday night had encountered a young man outside the statue. The suspect—described alternatively as a Middle Eastern male, a young Arab American, and a Muslim male of Arab American descent—had resisted arrest. Heavy rain and gale force winds—from the season's first nor'easter—had hampered police efforts, but the suspect had been apprehended and turned over to the FBI for questioning. His name was not released. A press bulletin from the deputy director of the NPS stated that the incident was under investigation. An FBI spokesman called the report "unconfirmed."

Like many watching the television news that morning, Hasan Ahmed reacted by uttering the universal, "Oh, no." A young Muslim male resisting arrest near the Statue of Liberty? That sounded like a terrorist.

His "Oh, no" was spoken not solely out of concern for the effect this development was sure to have on a failing business. It was spoken out of concern for his son who had departed for

New York four days earlier. Hadn't his club visited the monument just yesterday?

"Lisa, may I see Mohammed's itinerary?" he asked his wife that morning.

Lisa Ahmed removed it from the refrigerator door, where she had consulted it every day. Using the big city references from her Chicago days, she tried to imagine her son in this place or that according to the names on the itinerary.

"It seems they caught a terrorist at the Statue of Liberty."

"Dios mío!" she said. Then she remembered. "But they no go there. No peoples go. It close."

He scanned the itinerary, recalling that he had heard something about the statue's closure. At this hour his son should be on a bus back to Ohio. Miss Cutter had called to say that bad weather had delayed their departure.

"Well, obviously nothing happened," he said, handing the itinerary to his wife, who returned to the kitchen where Nura Maryam sat in her high chair, spooning oatmeal—the only one not fasting that morning.

He opened the *Cincinnati Post*, looking for more news of the incident. He found none. *What a sad business*, he told himself, shaking his head. *Praise Allah the rascal had been caught.*

Six hundred and fifty miles to the east, a National Park Service police officer, now off duty at his home in the Bronx, was also talking to his wife about the incident. He hadn't seen it on the news. He did not scan the Sunday paper for information. He had been there. He had caught the perpetrator.

Officer Bob Slocomb had arrived at his two-story house off Vyse Avenue bone-tired and storm-weary. As he breakfasted in dry clothes, the kitchen quiet—his teenage boys asleep upstairs—the roar of the gale still filled his head. He felt the pelting rain. He heard the wind. Seven years he had worked on the island, seven years patrolling Liberty. He had been a witness to lightning strikes, jumpers, stowaways—he had been on duty the night they caught the French stuntman hiding in a horse chestnut tree—protesters, bomb scares, and blackouts. But he had never seen anything like this.

"Craziest night ever," he told his wife across the table. "The old girl was rocking."

Slocomb had come to the park police after serving in the military. A former marine, he was a big, broad-shouldered man with unshakeable cool and a tough-guy bravado that masked a more caring, sensitive side. He was no newcomer to rain and wind in the coal black of a screaming night. He knew the importance of remaining vigilant, especially now. Vigilance was the backbone of security. And security was what kept America safe. That belief together with his sense of duty had gotten Officer Slocomb through many long watches on Liberty Island.

But now the monument was closed to the public. Ferry service had been suspended and the residential quarters were empty (since September rangers and administrative staff had lodged off-island). With frequent flyovers by the National Guard and patrols by the Coast Guard, policing the island had gotten a whole lot simpler. With that much help, it was easy to drop one's guard on a stormy night—easy to assume that Miss Liberty was safe.

It was raining sheets, the wind at thirty knots, when he and Officer Glovsky came on duty the evening of the seventeenth. Murray, the third in their crew, didn't make the boat, calling in sick. An hour later a second ferry with Murray's replacement was scratched when NOAA radio issued a level-two travel advisory for nonchannel harbor craft.

"So it was just Glov and me," Slocomb told his wife that morning as a third cup of coffee nudged the chill from his bones. "Of course, if the fancy detection hardware had been operational, we would have known we had an intruder—saved all of us some hairy footwork."

Since late September, security contractors had been "wiring" Liberty Island with motion detectors, laser trips, underground sensors, surveillance cameras, even a satellite uplink. Park policing was going high tech, and the rumor at the NPS field office at Floyd Bennett Field was the "new" island was going to cost jobs.

But it wasn't running yet.

Glovsky made the first round, returning forty minutes later to report that "It's wild out there." But Slocomb already knew that. From his post inside a secure, windowless room at the Park Service administration building on the northwest end of the island, he had heard the wind screaming in the large oaks. He had heard the sea.

"Surf's to the south wall," Glovsky said, shedding his wet gear and going to the coffeepot.

"Did you check it out?"

"Heck no. I got a mortgage to pay."

Slocomb had seen it only once. From the terreplein of the old fort, it had been quite a sight—like a trailer on the Weather Channel—the big waves lifting over the sea barrier, rolling across the perimeter path, and crashing onto the fort wall.

"What's the wind?" Glovsky asked.

"About forty."

"It felt stronger."

Slocomb liked the lanky, kinky-haired, prone-to-exaggerate Glovsky. He was dependable, plainspoken, sometimes edgy if life veered from the predictable, but otherwise good company.

"Let Coast know."

Slocomb clipped on a radio and donned his wet-weathers. Before leaving, he joked, "If radar picks up low flying, tell them it's me."

Outside, he leaned into the wind. For once Glovsky hadn't exaggerated. This was no forty-knot blow. This felt like he was standing up in the backseat of a Chrysler convertible doing sixty on the interstate—something he had done once when he was young and foolish.

He looked south, shielding rain from his eyes as he scanned above the trees, searching for the statue's familiar shape. It was why he was there—to make sure Lady Liberty was there, *always* there. No history was going to be made on his watch. No breaking news at ten.

Her figure stood gray in the driving rain—sketched in charcoal—but her torch remained extraordinarily bright. Officer Slocomb was not surprised. He knew that at the very beginning—before she became the symbol for other, loftier ideals—Miss Liberty had served as the upper harbor's first navigational beacon—a lighthouse—one watched over not by a cop, but by a light-keeper, a man who had spent his nights running a steam generator. *Simpler times*, Slocomb told himself. No fear of saboteurs or terrorists then. The job had been making light for ships.

The wind tore at his wet-weathers as he trudged toward the motor pool, rain slipping past his hood ties and running down his back. He thought of his wife and teenage sons, warm and dry in their two-story home back in the Bronx. Probably watching a rented movie and eating microwave popcorn. It was Saturday night.

Inside the motor-pool shed, the jeep sat in a lake of rainwater, still dripping from Glovsky's round. The hood steamed. The windshield wipers stood straight up—evidence that Glovsky had been in a hurry to finish his round. He didn't like these storms.

The engine rolled over on the first turn. Slocomb backed out of the shed, gripping the wheel firmly. The wind wanted to steer. Rain pummeled the jeep's roof. The high beams dissolved into an impenetrable darkness at thirty feet. He turned on the lateral spotlight and guided it to the edge of the arrival promenade before he eased his foot onto the accelerator. *What a night,* he told himself as the jeep began to move.

To his wife sitting across the kitchen table that morning, he said, "I didn't know it then, but I wasn't the only one out there in that gale."

He drove the length of the arrival promenade, spotlighting the empty residential quarters and maintenance buildings, stopping at the flagpole circle to beam past the linden trees. Manhattan through the rain had the glow of a moonrise stalled just below the horizon.

Turning south, he inched along the central mall, lamping toward the harbor, catching sight of the distant breakers, deadly white as they lurched above a roiled sea. Near the monument, the roar of the rain dropped to an audible drilling, its intensity diminished by the massive shelter of a fort, a pedestal, and 150 feet of metal statue. She was a gigantic windbreak, a big umbrella. Slocomb stopped the jeep beside the fort.

At the entrance he angled the spotlight up both stairways, following the balustrade across the open landing to the recessed entryway. He beamed up the fort walls and along the granite stonework of the promenade, wet quartz and mica flecks catching the light. On a clear night the light would have cut cleanly past the pedestal socle, illuminating the balcony parapet and the hem of Liberty's stola. Tonight it lit only slanted lines of rain.

With the spotlight turned off and the window lowered enough to peer out, he checked the torch. It swayed a foot, maybe more. Beyond the din of rain, he heard the creak of Liberty's copper skin and the groan of her stiff iron pylon and dunnage beams flexing in the wind. Amplified by the void of cold air within her, the sound was deep and mournful, like the moan of something monstrous astir. Slocomb had heard it before, but tonight the old girl was really talking.

He lamped the stairways and landing again, lingering on the entry recess. His light caught the uppermost panels of the centennial doors. Nothing stirred. The monument looked secure. He closed the window, touched the accelerator, and turned the jeep up the west side of the central mall. From the arrival promenade he ran the spotlight across the darkened visitors' center and the concession building. At the juncture of the promenade and perimeter paths, he stopped to lamp the pier. White-capped waves crested above the pylons and crashed below the deck. *Not a night for docking,* Slocomb told himself.

Turning south, he hugged the shoulder of the perimeter road, moving past a line of coin-operated binoculars, their flat metal faces looking oddly alien in the rain-driven light. He drew the lamp across an open stretch of side lawn where the cherry trees shook their leafless heads wildly from side to side as if to scold the ground. The thunder of an angry sea was close. Slocomb felt the concussion of waves. He turned the spotlight onto the road ahead, searching for overwash. When sea spray suddenly struck the windshield, Slocomb braked.

Ahead the lamp beam turned foggy—light mixed with surf—but he made out the curling heads of waves rising above the perimeter path, crashing into the darkness. The mad Atlantic had rolled into the Upper Bay, unleashing its wrath on the south shore of Liberty Island. Glovsky had it right. Waves were hitting the fort!

He had come this far to see it—more importantly to say he had seen it—but there was no getting closer. Spray thumped the windshield again, harder this time, with the menacing rap of knuckles. A new prospect occurred to Slocomb—his small jeep taken by a wave. He slipped the gearshift into reverse. The statue wouldn't go into the harbor, but he could. He turned the jeep around and returned to the compound.

Glovsky sat in front of his thirteen-inch TV tuned to a hockey game. "Rangers at Pittsburgh," he reported, his face close to the screen.

"The surf is at the wall," Slocomb reported, unzipping his weathers.

Glovsky turned from the TV. "You went around?"

Slocomb smiled. "Baptized the jeep."

Glovsky shook his head. Slocomb poured himself coffee before he pulled up a chair next to Glovsky. It felt good to be inside. "Watch 'em lose."

"Betcha five."

"You're on."

Gale winds topped seventy-five knots at the NWS station on the southeast tip of the island. Rain pounded the compound with the furor of demonic sledgehammers. The sea thundered. The big oaks howled. The game in Pittsburgh went into overtime.

Neither Officer Slocomb nor Officer Glovsky took the next watch, Murray's watch. When Glovsky stood at the end of regulation, game tied, and said, "Well, I guess I better..." then didn't finish his sentence, it was easy for Slocomb to say, "Wait a bit, Glov. Maybe it'll let up."

The storm roared. The room felt warm. Glovsky said, "Might as well make some coffee then."

Slocomb answered, "Yeah, I could use another cup."

It wasn't just the rain or the wind or the danger of getting washed out to sea that kept both men in the compound. It was also the unspoken, bedrock certainty that they were alone on the island, that nobody else was out there. They could have been camped on the moon. Even the National Guard jets had dropped their flybys. The service radio was quiet. They were alone with a national monument in the middle of a gale on a Saturday night. Nothing would happen. Nothing could happen.

Then shortly before midnight, as Glovsky dozed in his chair, empty coffee cup dangling at his side, and a blurry-eyed Slocomb stared at a postgame show, the noise of the storm was suddenly splintered by an earsplitting screech.

A freight train braked above them, or so it seemed—an enormous freight train. Then the administrative compound shook as if Liberty Island itself had been thumped by a giant fist.

"What the...?" blurted Slocomb, rearing back from the television.

Glovsky's coffee cup slipped from his fingers and fell to the floor. "Whoa!"

Both men leaped from their chairs and looked at each other.

"What was that?"

"Felt like something fell."

"Yeah, something *big*."

They stood motionless, hearing only the storm.

"Maybe it was a quake."

"What?"

"An earthquake."

"We don't have—"

"Storm surge then?"

"You mean a wave?"

"Uh-huh."

Rain hammered the roof. The wind wailed. Slocomb turned off the TV. Glovsky retrieved his cup. The service radio remained quiet. "Should we call?"

"Let me check," said Slocomb. Already the worst-case scenario had occurred to him—history on his watch—but Glovsky was the first to voice it.

"You think it was an attack?"

Slocomb said nothing. Martians could have landed for all he knew. Maybe one of the ferries had hit the seawall. Maybe the dock had broken loose. Maybe one of the residential roofs had blown off. It happened. The island's landfill geology amplified every shock. Had a plane hit the island?

"I'll call," said Slocomb, holding up a radio. As he zipped into his wets, he stopped to feel along his waist, past pepper spray and the cuffs, making sure his Glock was holstered.

"You're not going heavy?" queried Glovsky, motioning toward the gun locker with its Heckler & Koch submachine guns.

"Nope. Just be ready to come."

"Okay."

Slocomb took one of the trigger lamps from its rack and squeezed a bright flash into the room. Before he reached for the door, he stopped long enough to think of how to phrase what needed to be said. "If you lose me, call base."

Glovsky nodded. And that was enough.

He struggled to close the compound door. The wind wanted it. Slocomb leaned every inch of his six-foot-three-inch frame in denial. The rain stabbed like daggers. The gale screamed in his ears. He pushed until the lock caught, and then he clung to the handle, hesitating before he faced the night. What would he see? Would the old girl still command the harbor?

His first thought after the island shook, after coming to his senses, was the gale had moved the statue—that the awful screech had been the sound of copper ripping. The wind had caught her the wrong way, breaking something loose—her torch, her arm—or somehow, against all odds, a rogue wave had hit. He had imagined the worst. Or what he thought could be the worst.

Then Glovsky had mentioned an attack.

In the days immediately after the eleventh—before F-16 jets became a regular fixture over the island, before the contractors came to wire her, before he convinced himself that men bent on terror would have a hard time executing their treachery on the monument—Officer Slocomb had imagined such an event unfolding: an airliner falling steeply from the star-studded sky, roaring into Liberty's broad bosom, driving shattered copper, iron, and stone into the cold sea. He saw the entire island engulfed in a jet-fueled fireball that would light a long night. For weeks the nightmare had shadowed him.

Now, as he stood against the compound door, he wondered if Glovsky could be right.

He shielded his eyes and lifted his face to the cutting rain. She stood—intact and lighted. Her torch still glowed. No airplane had struck. No sabotage had toppled her. He traced the familiar outline to assure himself of her completeness. She looked okay, but what about that screech? What had made the ground shudder? Only something big could have given them such a shake. On Liberty Island there was only one thing that big.

Slocomb set off toward the arrival promenade on foot. He radioed Glovsky. "She looks fine. I'm walking it."

"Copy," crackled the reply.

He set off down the walkway, shouldering the wind. When he reached the promenade, he found the path underwater, not even the curbstones showing. Most of the signage was gone. The boundary hedges lay fitfully on their sides. Several big oaks had been upended, their limbs and roots clawing wildly at the night. *It will be a pretty sight come daylight*, thought Slocomb. He wanted to see the faces of the grounds crew when they stepped off the ferry in the morning.

He triggered the lamp and panned the visitors' center. One of the big maples had dropped on the roof. He swept across the front of the administration building toward the maintenance sheds. Between trees he glimpsed the residential quarters, his lamplight glinting off the jagged edges of broken windows. He pointed the spotlight up the flooded promenade, toward the boat dock, half expecting to see it gone, but the pier remained in place. Waves crashed over its deck.

As he stared, another possibility occurred to him. Had a ship—a ferry maybe—lost its way and slammed into the seawall? He probed the shore with his light, listening beyond the gale for the screech of a steel hull grounded on the rocks. He looked for navigational lights, but only darkness and the slant of the rain met his gaze.

He followed the promenade to the central mall. Only the tops of the boundary hedges showed above the flood. It was the highest water Slocomb had seen on the island. He waded in, lifting the lamp. The surf roared. His light caught breakers battering the fort. He kept to the edge of the mall, the water cold, the dark current pressing him toward the hedges. Halfway up the approach he stopped, the water to his waist. He pointed his light above the pedestal, running it along the statue's base plate and up the left foot where the old entrance had been. He lamped the folds of drapery, lingering for a moment on the offset at the arm. He wasn't sure what he was looking for, something broken, something missing, something moved. But the statue looked whole, immovable, everlasting. And why shouldn't it? He had been in her anchorage. He had seen the massive crossbeams and enormous tension bars that held her down.

Her torch swayed. Her diadem rays nodded. Runoff coursed down her tunic in torrents. Slocomb beamed into her shadows, penetrating the recesses not illuminated by the ground lighting. He noticed her silence. Even as the wind screamed, gone was the creak of copper and the mournful groan of puddle iron he had heard hours before. She was strangely quiet.

At the fort entrance, he checked both stairways before he ascended to the landing and turned his light on the centennial doors. He stepped into the alcove and tried the handles. Secure. He punched his code into the keypad next to the doors, watching the readout on the LCD screen. There had been no power interruptions. The door locks were activated. He examined the decorative bronze panels, tracing with his light the doorjamb and hinges. There were no signs of tool marks. He returned to the keypad. The alarm was on. He tested the handles again and rechecked the screen. Clearly the system was working. The doors hadn't opened. *Still...* He scanned the puddled floor, his own wet tracks, no way to be certain that someone else had stood here dripping. He stepped from the entrance and ran his light up the fort walls, sweeping the twenty-foot granite face. He searched the macadam paving, looking for glints of fallen granite—evidence of an ascent. *Have to be a fool,* he decided. He lifted the radio. "All clear, Glov."

"Roger," came a relieved voice.

"Yeah." *Maybe it was a tremor,* he reflected. An oscillation brought on by the pounding waves. Funny he hadn't felt it before. Then there was that awful screech. He could still hear it.

He waded up the central mall, keeping to the paving stones until the water dropped below his knees. Then he shortcut to the promenade across one of the side lawn paths. When the wind blew the hood off his head, he pulled it on again, holding it down with one hand. He walked faster. *Hot coffee, dry clothes,* he thought. And no more surprises. At least the old girl was safe. But what a scare.

Ahead, the lights of the administration building shimmered through the rain. He gave the promenade one last sweep with the lamp. That's when the beam caught a figure rushing by him like a ghost.

Officer Slocomb's heart skipped a beat, or seemed to. His finger slipped off the lamp trigger. When he squeezed it again, the figure raised his arm to deflect the light's glare. "Freeze!" yelled Slocomb, touching the wet-weathers where his Glock bulged.

The intruder slipped into the darkness as if taken by the wind.

Slocomb blinked. The image of a brown face lingered. "Mother of Christ!" he said. He caught up with his lamp. The figure headed toward the boat dock. Slocomb followed.

They ran in water over their ankles. Slocomb held the intruder in his light. He picked out details—a dark jacket, a fringe of black hair under a cap. The intruder seemed to favor a leg. Was he hurt? When he threw a backward glance, Slocomb glimpsed the white letters on the front of the cap. A Yankees cap! *I've got a terrorist wearing a Yankees cap*, he thought, certain the intruder was a terrorist. Who else? This was no Boy Scout separated from his troop. This was al-Qaeda sneaking around the monument.

He considered the possibility of a bomb. Could this man have explosives under his jacket? Had *he* done something to shake the island?

At the boat dock, an angry sea rose before them. The intruder slacked his pace. Slocomb eased up, switching the lamp to his left hand. He felt for his holster. "Stop or I'll shoot!" he shouted.

When the intruder turned onto the perimeter path and ran toward the statue, Slocomb pulled out his Glock and flicked off the safety. He pulled the trigger once, firing into the sky, the shot sounding small in the immensity of the storm. The intruder didn't look back. Slocomb lowered his weapon and pursued.

They ran past the viewing binoculars, the wind in their teeth. The intruder slipped through the gale like a knife. Slocomb watched the distance between them lengthen. In spite of his leg, the man appeared to be in excellent shape. Lean, athletic—a product of desert training camps, no doubt.

His own heart pounded. His feet felt heavy. He slowed, then stopped, sucking air. He was too far for a wing shot, but he could still take him down. He lifted the Glock, took aim, then hesitated. Should he shoot the intruder in the back? He lifted the Glock slightly and fired twice into the night, both discharges swallowed by the gale. The intruder continued to run.

Slocomb holstered his firearm and fished out the radio. It was time to share the pain. He keyed the mike. "Got an intruder, Glov. Southwest seawall." He gulped air. "Looks Arab."

Later he would wish he had left the last part unsaid. "Arab" would turn a trespasser into a terrorist, a minor incident into Sunday morning news. But at the moment, it seemed important.

Glovsky said, "Copy. On my way."

"Stand by," Slocomb advised. "Call Central. Alert Coast. He may go into the water." There was no point in both of them drowning. The intruder wasn't escaping by boat—not in this surf.

"Copy. Calling now."

Water churned across the road. Ocean spray ran with the rain. Already they had passed the spot where he had reversed the jeep hours before. The intruder became a dim outline at the edge of Slocomb's lamplight. He was rapidly turning back into a ghost.

"Stop, police!" he called, watching him disappear beyond the seawall. Slocomb halted. The storm roared. The pounding surf shook the ground. He cast his beam ahead. The white-toothed waves reared up into the night. *No way*, he thought. Then he spotted the intruder retreating, his dark jacket backlit by the white sea rising behind him.

Slocomb stood. He knew it wasn't a race he could win. There was no time to pull his gun. If the guy carried a bomb, so be it. Demolition was quicker than drowning.

The intruder ran straight to him. Slocomb dropped the lamp and bear-hugged him as they collided, amazed at how thin he was. Then the wave caught them. They clung to each other as they tumbled in a churn of white water that propelled them across the southwest lawn and dropped them dismissively at the fort wall. Slocomb found his feet. He lifted the suspect by his jacket collar and dragged him around the bastion and beyond the next wave. The intruder offered no resistance.

The roar of the sea faded. Slocomb shook the sting of seawater from his eyes. He pulled his gun. "Don't move!" he shouted, pointing the Glock. Beside the fort wall, the intruder looked small, helpless. He appeared to be shivering. Slocomb had no light. His radio was gone. He fished for his cuffs. "Stay down!" In the dim, reflected glow of the statue, Slocomb noticed the baseball cap was still on the man's head. "Hands behind your back!" he barked.

"Excuse me, sir."

"Shut up!" Slocomb cuffed the wrists. He pressed the gun barrel to the suspect's back while he patted him for weapons. He found nothing.

"Please, sir. I won't run."

"No Mister Nice Guy stuff." He pulled the man to his feet and shoved him. "Move!"

They walked, the suspect's limp more pronounced. The rain thinned. The wind no longer screamed. The backside of the statue loomed above them, its green luminescence glinting off the barrel of the Glock and casting Slocomb's shadow upon the thin figure. Overhead, a pair of National Guard fighters dropped out of the clouds, swooping over the island. Slocomb glanced up. When the prisoner turned his head, Slocomb pushed him. "Face forward!" he ordered. "It's over."

In the windowless corner room of the administration building, Glovsky received them with a MP5 from the gun locker. He looked nervous. "I got him," he advised, leveling his weapon at the detainee. When the office lights illuminated the prisoner's face, Glovsky's eyes widened. "What the—?"

He looked at Slocomb. Slocomb looked at the prisoner.

"Damn!" Glovsky blurted. "He's just a kid!"

Slocomb stared.

Thirty minutes had elapsed since Glovsky had informed the National Park Service of the intruder, the *Arab* intruder. An NPS supervisor had notified the FBI, which had alerted the Coast Guard's Maritime Safety and Security Team. The eighty-seven-foot cutter *Ridley*, already patrolling north of Sandy Hook, had been dispatched to ferry federal agents to the island. The mayor's office had put an NYPD helicopter and Atlas operation units on standby. Despite inclement conditions, the New Jersey Air National Guard had scrambled two F-16s. And someone had tipped CNN.

"He's just a kid!" Glovsky repeated, sounding more impressed than astonished.

Officer Slocomb stood speechless, the sea still pounding in his head. "Maybe he's older than he looks," he said. Anything was possible. Some of those hijackers looked young enough.

The prisoner stood handcuffed and shivering. A puddle of water widened at his feet.

"How old are you?" demanded Glovsky.

The prisoner's teeth chattered. "Four...rr...teen, sir."

Slocomb and Glovsky exchanged glances.

"He's lying."

"You got ID?"

The prisoner shook his head.

Slocomb removed his rain gear. He felt old. Was it the fatigue of chasing youth or the aftershock of seeing his catch? "Search him, Glov. I only frisked for fire."

Officer Glovsky slung his weapon. He removed the prisoner's baseball cap, revealing a head of short, curly black hair. "Yankees fan, are we?" He searched the jacket, finding a small, leather-bound book and a strange kind of compass. He placed them on the table before he ran his fingers into the detainee's pockets, extracting wet papers, a wadded ten-dollar bill, pocket change, and a seven-dollar MetroCard. He found no wallet, no watch. How could a terrorist not have a watch? Wasn't terror timed? When he check the prisoner's hands, he saw the cuts. "What happened here?"

"I cut them—on some rocks," the youth stuttered.

Glovsky pursed his lips. "Roll up your pants," he ordered. The prisoner did as he was told, revealing a bloody gash on his shin. When the officer saw it, he shook his head. Had the suspect attempted to scale the wall?

"No ID," he reported. "He has a navigational aid. Cut his leg and hands on the rocks."

Officer Slocomb picked up the leather-bound book, separating the wet pages. He hadn't been to church for years, but he recognized a Bible when he saw one. Then he noticed the strange writing inside. He rechecked the cover. *Holy Koran: Arabic and English Translation.*

"Glov, this isn't good. He's carrying a Koran."

Of course it wasn't good. That made him Muslim. It made him a Muslim with no ID. It made him a young Muslim with no ID, trespassing on government property at night in proximity to a treasured national monument. Hadn't those hijacking pilots recited from the Koran before they hit the towers?

Glovsky examined the wet papers taken from the prisoner's pockets. He flattened them on the table. One had washed-out ink, maybe a phone number. Another had the words "Do It" written in large letters—clearly a directive. A third was a breakfast receipt from Howard Johnson's in Times Square. The 5:25 a.m. time on the receipt caught his eye. A fourteen-year-old eating breakfast at Howard Johnson's at five in the morning? No teenager got up that early.

The last piece of paper came apart at the folds. When Glovsky pieced it together, he read the dates and hours as well as the fragmented names of several prominent New York locations. "Chrysler…uild…" "Brooklyn Brid…" "Unit…Natio…"

"Jesus, this is some kind of plan," he said, looking up in alarm. "It's got landmarks and a schedule. I wonder if they're plotting to attack these places. And he may not be alone. He was at Howard Johnson's at five in the morning—probably meeting someone. Got a number, too, but not legible. There's a note telling him to 'Do It.' Maybe he belongs to one of those sleeper cells."

He turned to the detainee. "Are you Arab, or what?" he demanded. "And don't lie."

The youth shivered. "May I…I…sit?" he asked.

"You're going to stand until you tell us who you are," Slocomb ordered. His eyes picked through the evidence on the table: a pocket Koran, a compass, papers with a scheduled attack on New York. Where were the feds? This was big.

"My name is…Mohammed bin…Hasan…Ahmed," the prisoner said. "From Ohio."

Officers Slocomb and Glovsky exchanged meaningful looks. Mohammed? Mohammed bin…? Silence unfolded in the room.

"Are you Arab?" Glovsky repeated.

The prisoner nodded. "My father."

Officer Glovsky retreated slightly from the prisoner.

Slocomb thought, *So what if he's young? He's Muslim. He's Arab. And he ran. He has to be guilty.* "You're in big trouble, fella," he said, reaching for the radio.

"Big, big," Glovsky echoed. "I bet he cut himself trying to get in."

They stared at the youth standing in the puddle. He looked back miserably. His face began to twist. His lips trembled. The rest of him shook. "Please—please," he stammered. "I just wanted to—to—" Tears started down his face. A plaintive wail carried his next words. "Please don't hurt me. Please, please. I was only looking—" He dropped to his knees and bent to the wet floor. He began to sob, then bawl. "Please," he cried. "I want to go home."

The officers stood motionless, witnesses to the very last thing they expected to see—a terrorist crying. Their eyes met, inquiring, perplexed. *He wants to go home?* They shook their heads. "It's all right," Slocomb said, hearing his voice go unexpectedly soft.

"Yeah, yeah, relax," Glovsky offered.

They were new to this business of fighting terror and protecting America's monuments from foreign attack, but one thing they knew as sure as their own names: terrorists didn't cry.

Outside, the rain had stopped.

Slocomb removed the handcuffs. He wrapped the kid in an army blanket. Glovsky rummaged through the equipment lockers, finding overalls and a pair of field shoes. He gave them to the youth with instructions to change out of his wet clothes. "Wash those hands," he said.

They watched him limp to the bathroom and close the door. Glovsky spoke first. "What do you think?"

Slocomb tapped a finger to his temple. "A little wet upstairs, maybe?" Already he had replayed their mad chase down the perimeter path. Only craziness would explain it.

"You gonna call command?"

"Let's hear what he has to say."

While their detainee changed, Glovsky started another pot of coffee. Then he decided to boil water for tea. A kid wasn't supposed to drink coffee. He mopped the puddle and turned up the heat. Slocomb hung near the radio, gripped by a strange sense of awkwardness. Had he overreacted? This was just a kid. A crazy, crying kid. But how could he have known?

When he emerged from the bathroom, the officers had him hang his wet clothes above a heat register. They gave him hot tea and sat him in a chair. The kid recounted the events of his trip since arriving in New York Thursday morning. He began with the club and Miss Cutter and the bus ride from Ohio. He explained that the paper taken from his pocket was not an attack plan but the club's itinerary. The Chrysler Building and the Brooklyn Bridge were not targets but two of the engineering marvels they had come to visit. He said he had gone to Howard Johnson's at five in the morning because the holy month of Ramadan had begun, and he had to eat breakfast before starting his fast at dawn. The compass was used to find Mecca when he prayed. The washed-out phone number was his teacher's cell. The other paper was from a girl he knew. He said he had ditched the club's visit to Ground Zero, coming instead to see the statue. All he had wanted to do was take pictures.

Officers Slocomb and Glovsky gave each other doubtful looks. Plainspoken truth seemed strange on a night like this. Was this really some kid visiting the city for the first time, some kid who just happened to be a Muslim, a kid who had managed to get on the island?

"Pictures?" Glovsky repeated.

"Where's the camera?" Slocomb asked.

"I lost it," he answered.

"So you knew the statue was closed?"

He nodded.

Glovsky shook his head. "That's called trespassing. You know what trespassing is?"

The kid didn't answer.

"What we want to know is how you got out here," Slocomb said.

"Yeah," chimed Glovsky. "And who helped you?"

Then he told them the rest of his story, ending with his capture at the fort wall. When he finished, he said, "I'm sorry I ran. I was afraid."

Silence followed. Once again the officers of the National Park Police looked at each other. Either the kid was an accomplished liar—an aptitude that didn't agree with his face—or this was one of those stories too unbelievable not to be believed.

Glovsky said, "Some security, eh? Sounds like Newman stayed out of the weather."

Slocomb didn't react. He had heard of freak breaches in security—a visitor separated from his tour group wandering into the West Wing of the White House; an illegal immigrant found asleep in the cockpit of an A-10 at a Tucson airbase. It happened. "Could have been worse," he muttered.

Glovsky nodded, knowing it was true.

"One more question," Officer Slocomb said.

The kid met his gaze.

"You didn't do anything to…" He hesitated, deciding it was too far-fetched. "Did you feel the ground shake when you were out there?"

"Did you hear some god-awful screech?" Glovsky interjected.

"No, sirs, nothing like that," he answered. And even then he was telling the truth.

Jet fighters passed over the island, rattling windows. Slocomb picked up the radio. It was time to send those birds home. "Central, this is Liberty. Intruder apprehended," he said. "Cancel security alert. Hold backup. Intruder is an unarmed minor possibly in need of medical attention. Determining status at this time. Will advise. Over."

Glovsky mopped the floor. Static crackled across the radio.

"Liberty, please repeat. Did you say 'unarmed minor'?"

Slocomb recognized the Texas drawl of National Park Service Police Chief Perez. Had they gotten *him* out of bed? Slocomb drew a breath. "Affirmative."

More static. Then, "Liberty, what in tarnation is a minor doing on—how did he get out there?"

Officer Slocomb stared at the radio. Yeah, it sounded bizarre, but it was the truth. "Apparently he came to take pictures, sir. He's from Ohio, on a school trip. He got on one of the crew boats. Nobody noticed. Then we got weather."

The silence that followed seemed longer than it was. Should he mention the kid was a Muslim?

"Is that you, Slocomb?"

"Yes, sir."

"You've kicked up a lot of dust over an errant sightseer. Coast is on its way. The FBI is patched in, waiting to move. Washington has been notified. Are you saying there is no threat?"

Officer Slocomb glanced at the youth sitting in the oversize overalls. "No threat, sir. We caught a trespasser, not a terrorist."

In the radio background he heard other voices. The words "crew boat" and "crew boat security" were spoken. Then Chief

Perez was back. "I guess that's good news, but it didn't come cheap. How old is the suspect?"

"Fourteen, sir."

Another silence.

"Name?"

Slocomb winced. He motioned to Glovsky for a pencil. "Mohammed bin something, sir. I'll have to spell it." He listened as Chief Perez repeated the name to the parties on the other end. Slocomb heard a buzz of voices. He waited.

"The FBI wants to have a chat with him," Chief Perez said. "They want you to come. We'll ask Coast to drop another crew. Are you going to need medevac?"

Slocomb looked at the youth. His color was back. He wasn't shaking. He sipped tea from a Styrofoam cup. "No, sir. We'll wait for Coast."

Chief Perez said, "They want to know the school, Slocomb. Get the name."

Officer Slocomb beckoned to the boy.

"And the name of someone, a teacher, whoever is in charge. And where they're staying. Anything else? Jesus."

Glovsky found a pencil and paper. He handed them to the youth. Slocomb repeated the request. "Name of school, name of hotel, teacher. Yes, sir."

"Parents' names, address, and phone number. You said Ohio?"

"Yes, sir."

"Fax it."

"Yes, sir."

"Damn craziness. That's it, Slocomb."

Slocomb lowered the handset. Glovsky pointed to the coffeepot. "Better caffeinate."

When the detainee finished answering the questions the man on the radio had asked, he handed the paper to Slocomb.

The officer studied it, sipping coffee. "Miss Cutter. She's the trip leader?"

"Yes, sir."

He pointed to the unpronounceable name. "Your father?"

"Yes, sir."

Glovsky said, "Man, I wouldn't want to be that boat crew come morning." He returned the Heckler & Koch to the gun locker. "Maybe now they'll finish wiring this place."

While they waited, the detainee drank more tea. He declined Glovsky's offer of a cheese and bologna sandwich.

"It's turkey bologna," Glovsky insisted, holding it out. He knew Muslims had rules about food, but he didn't know what they were.

"Thanks. I'm not that hungry," the kid lied.

"What exactly is it you can't eat?" Glovsky asked.

"Pork," Slocomb said. "And pork products, right?" He looked to the boy for confirmation. "If you haven't had enough of the sea, kid, I brought tuna on rye. You're welcome to it."

"Okay."

The youth wolfed the sandwich. His clothes steamed over the register.

"Don't know a whole lot about Muslim people," Glovsky continued. "You got different food and heroes and holidays and everything. But that's okay. I respect that." He swallowed his coffee. "Tolerance is what this country is all about. Isn't it, Slo?"

Officer Slocomb nodded from the fax machine.

The youth sat up in his chair. "How much trouble am I in?" he asked.

Glovsky sucked his teeth. "How about unauthorized boarding of a US Park Police transport, trespassing on federal property, entering a National Park Service monument closed to the public?

Right there you've violated two federal statutes and one state. Then there's resisting arrest. Altogether I'd call that trouble."

"But I didn't resist. I ran."

"If you don't stay still, you're resisting."

Officer Slocomb said, "The men from the FBI want to interview you to make sure this doesn't happen again. You just need to explain how you got here and what you were doing."

"Wouldn't be surprised if it makes the news," Glovsky added. He pointed to the youth's leg. "Let me have a look at that cut."

He disinfected it with iodine and taped a gauze pad over the wound. When he finished, he said, "Better go change. Coast will be here."

The youth shuffled to the bathroom and changed into stiff clothes that smelled of the sea. His sneakers still squished. Outside the bathroom new voices arrived. When he opened the door, he was met by more uniforms—park police and Coast Guard. They observed him with interest, their faces not unfriendly. Officer Slocomb said, "Time to go."

Glovsky returned his money, MetroCard, and compass. "Don't forget this," he said, giving back the Koran. Then he rummaged through one of the desks. "Here, take these, too." He offered a handful of visitor brochures, the top one titled "Welcome to the Statue of Liberty." "Now you have pictures," Glovsky said.

"Thank you."

"Good luck, kid."

Outside, the clouds moved fast. The lights of Manhattan glimmered through the trees. On the promenade Officer Slocomb weaved a path through an archipelago of puddles and fallen limbs. The detainee followed. He wanted to look at the statue, but the Coast Guard men walked close behind him. On the boat he got his chance, glimpsing her monumental night glow one last time. He had done it. It was over.

When the USCG *Ridley* docked at two thirty a.m. Sunday morning, no television cameras or reporters waited at Pier 17. Two FBI agents and Miss Cutter stood at the mooring.

She hugged him, whispering close to his ear. "Are you all right?" He nodded. She looked gaunt, fatigued. Then she asked, "What have you done?"

It was a long story. He summed it into a single sentence. "I got stuck on the island."

Miss Cutter asked if he needed a doctor. "You're limping."

He shook his head. "I banged my shin, that's all."

They were driven in two cars to the FBI office at the Federal Plaza on Lafayette Street. Officer Slocomb rode in one car while Miss Cutter and her student followed in the other. An FBI agent sat between them. At the Federal Building, his pocket Koran was examined then kept by security. So was the compass. Miss Cutter kept the Statue of Liberty pamphlets. They rode the elevator, exiting on the twenty-third floor. Mohammed was surprised to find so many people out of bed and moving within the well-lit corridors at that hour. Miss Cutter and Officer Slocomb were asked to follow one of the agents. Mohammed was left in a room by himself. The room had no windows, only a chair. He sat.

Minutes passed. He fought back a yawn. *No time to sleep,* he told himself. This was too big for sleep. What if his name appeared in the papers? What if Mr. Vander Bogart suspended him from school? What would his father do?

The smell of the sea—his smell—filled the windowless room. He heard the roar of the waves in his head, the awful wail of the wind, the pounding rain. He thought about what had happened, the strange event. It still seemed like a dream.

Then a man in a white shirt opened the door. "Come," he said, no smile.

He was escorted into a conference room. The door closed behind him. Inside the room Miss Cutter and Officer Slocomb sat at a long table with two men. One wore a tie, the other a police uniform with "Chief Alberto Perez" embroidered on the shirtfront. The man with the tie identified himself as the FBI's deputy director of counterterrorism. He asked Mohammed to take a chair and recount the events of the last twelve hours.

Mohammed began with his round-trip on the Staten Island Ferry. He ended with his detection by the officer during the storm. In the conference room, a wall clock ticked loudly.

When Mohammed finished, the deputy director peppered him with questions. Did he recall the name on the jacket of the Port Authority employee watching Pier 11? (He did not.) Was he certain that no crew had been on the Park Police boat when he had boarded? (He was.) Had he seen security personnel guarding the dock when they had tied up at the island? (He had not.) Was he absolutely sure he had seen no park police until Officer Slocomb had found him? (He was absolutely sure.)

The wall clock showed 3:55 a.m. Miss Cutter disguised a yawn. Officer Slocomb sat silent.

"Clearly, it's wake-up call," intoned Chief Perez. There was trouble in the chief's Texas drawl—trouble for someone. "For my part, I guarantee we will tighten ship. ASAP."

The deputy director nodded. He addressed Mohammed directly. His tone hinted doom. Fortunately the security breach had not been terrorist-related, he began. Still, a crime had been committed, several crimes actually, all of them serious. Trespassing on federal property was subject to a $10,000 fine and up to ten years in prison. Violating the emergency closure of a national monument was punishable by a $25,000 fine and up to fifteen years in prison. Unauthorized boarding of a DOT boat at a Port Authority installation was a violation of New York state statutes. The lives of law enforcement personnel, including the officer present, had been unnecessarily jeopardized by a reckless, thoughtless stunt—a stupid stunt. Men had risked their lives navigating aircraft and vessels in gale conditions. Others had been called away from their families on a foul night only to be told that a terrorist alert was an adolescent prank. The mayor had been alerted; so had several high-ranking officials in Washington. And then there was the mortification he had caused his club adviser, Miss Cutter, not to say the inconvenience he had caused the other members of his club.

The FBI deputy director of counterterrorism leveled a stern gaze before he summarized in shotgun bursts. Irresponsible. Selfish. Disrespectful. Lucky to be alive. Under any other circumstances, prosecuted. Thanks to Miss Cutter's intercession, a different ending. No next time. Understood?

Mohammed nodded. Perfectly.

"The world has changed since the eleventh. America is not the same. Remember that—not the same."

Mohammed nodded again. He knew.

The deputy director turned to Miss Cutter. He thanked her for her cooperation. He said a car would take them to their hotel.

Then Chief Perez spoke, his drawl like a slow clock in need of winding. "Miss Cutter, I trust the events of this evening will not be shared by either of you with anyone outside this room—for reasons of national security, you understand. Our intention is to give this incident—this significant breach in security—a low profile. We don't want to give our enemies new ideas. Do I make myself clear?"

Miss Cutter stood. "Chief Perez, I will take that under advisement."

She turned to Officer Slocomb and extended her hand. "I can't thank you enough," she said. "Your efforts averted a tragedy."

Slocomb said it had been nothing, his duty. "The boy meant no harm. The timing wasn't right, that's all."

Miss Cutter fixed Mohammed with a sober stare. "Do you have anything to say to the officer?" she asked.

He tried to think of something bigger than thanks, but nothing came to him. "Thank you, sir," he said. "I'm sorry. I won't forget."

Officer Slocomb nodded. "If the monument opens again— when it opens again—you're welcome to come visit." He smiled. "Maybe it won't be raining next time."

Mohammed said, "Okay."

"Take care."

At the security entrance, his Koran and compass were returned. In the car Miss Cutter suggested he change his clothes at the hotel. "You smell like the sea."

He told her how sorry he was, that he hadn't meant to cause trouble. He hoped she wasn't mad at him. Miss Cutter said she wasn't mad, just disappointed. "I assumed I could trust you, but clearly I was wrong. What a shame the trip had to end this way."

Mohammed wanted to say a debt had been paid to a dream. He wanted to say his pilgrimage had been an American hajj. He wanted to say he had saved her. But some things were simply too big to explain.

"You never intended to go to the mosque, did you?" she asked.

He said he hadn't.

"Shame on you, Mohammed. To lie about prayer."

They rode in silence, Manhattan lights flashing across their faces. Mohammed stared out the window. More than ever, he felt like a stranger in the city.

Miss Cutter cleared her throat. Her voice softened. "But what's important is that you are safe." She reached out and drew him closer. "I'm so thankful for that."

He let himself be hugged, smelling Miss Cutter's day-old hair spray. "Did the FBI call my father?" he asked.

She shook her head. "I told them I would call, but I didn't. There was nothing he could have done in any case. I didn't want to worry him."

"And Mr. Vander Bogart?"

Miss Cutter smiled. "Sleeping soundly, I hope."

More silence, the city passing.

"Are you going to say anything? I mean, are you going to tell them what happened?"

Miss Cutter studied him. "Exactly what *did* happen, Mohammed?" she asked, tilting her head. "As far as I know, you took the ferry, got delayed, got lost, fell and hurt your leg—" She paused. "Or did I leave something out, something you haven't told us?"

"No." Nothing she would believe anyway.

"Then I suppose we should leave it at that," she said.

"Thanks, Miss Cutter. My dad would—well, I'm not sure what he would do."

"Although I'm disappointed in your total disregard for the rules, I think I know why you did it. I understand dreams and the power of wonder. That is why this will stay between us." She opened her purse and took out the Statue of Liberty pamphlets. "Of course you might have a hard time explaining these to the club. I will keep them until we get back."

They left West Twenty-Third Street for Eighth Avenue, passing Madison Square Garden. Mohammed remembered

Teddy White's plan to sneak from the hotel. Not even Teddy had dared, if that was consolation. Miss Cutter told him that a bus for Cincinnati would be leaving the Port Authority terminal at six. She would call parents to notify them that their return had been delayed. "I think we can truthfully claim that bad weather had something to do with this." Then she asked if he had gotten anything to eat.

"One of the officers gave me a sandwich," he said.

"Maybe there will be time to get something before dawn," she suggested. "On top of everything else, I wouldn't want you to break your fast."

He stared at the lights on Eighth Avenue. So far it was the only rule he hadn't broken. When the car passed Forty-Second Street, he asked Miss Cutter how she had found him.

She shook her head wearily. "Believe it or not, not every day is a Mohammed lost in Manhattan," she replied. "Priscilla said you may have taken the ferry—she overhead you, I guess—so the police contacted the ferry company and sent officers to the terminals. The club stayed at the hotel in case you returned, and I accompanied them to Whitehall. When nothing turned up there, the police contacted the local mosques, and they checked hospitals. I made up my mind to call your parents—thinking you may have returned on your own. Then an officer told me that a young man—he called him a young *Arab* man—had breached security on Liberty Island. When the officer asked how Arab you looked, I told him 'enough.' Somehow I knew it was you. It was too much of a coincidence to be anyone else. Then they confirmed it and asked me to accompany the FBI to the pier to meet the boat. I told the club you had been found, that you were okay, but I said nothing about where you had gone. They only know about the ferry."

She paused. "Fortunately, Mohammed, the world proved to be a small place tonight."

The car stopped in front of the hotel. The radio clock read 5:05 a.m. New York City had hosted the visitors from Ohio exactly seventy-two hours—almost to the minute.

"The rest you know," Miss Cutter said, reaching for the car door.

"Do you think it will be on the news?" Mohammed asked. "One of the policemen said it might."

His adviser looked surprised. "Well, let me ask you," she replied. "A Muslim youth is discovered near the Statue of Liberty at night. Is that news?"

"I suppose," he answered. "But I didn't do anything bad."

"Yes," Miss Cutter said, "but that's not what matters anymore."

NYC

<hr>

Between the Ohio and Hudson Rivers, Edgar McHugh consumed three bags of Fritos, two ham sandwiches, a package of powdered gem doughnuts, a Clark bar, a sixteen-ounce Pepsi, and a bottle of Gatorade. Mohammed ate a banana.

The high point of the ride came early, when Bernie Burton threw up on Interstate 70, west of Wheeling. Most of the club nodded off after that, but Mohammed—too excited for sleep—stared out the window at exit signs and interstate gas stations. The grizzled face of Delmar drifted into the glass. His father waved stiffly.

On a trip to the bathroom, he saw Priscilla napping next to Miss Cutter. Resisting an urge to stop and stare, he moved on. Back in his seat, the gentle rock of the Alleghenies overcame him and he dozed. The smell of powdered sugar on Edgar's breath was the last thing he remembered.

Hours later, Miss Cutter spoke. "New York, everybody. To the right."

Mohammed awoke to the sight of the city skyline silhouetted on a gray dawn. Edgar stretched and yawned, the sound of plastic wrappers struggling beneath him. "Where are we?"

"We're there," replied Mohammed meaningfully.

From the New Jersey Turnpike, he tried to identify skyscraper shapes but recognized only the Empire State Building. The missing towers screamed from their hole in the horizon.

They crossed the asphalted marshes of Secaucus. There was a sign to Hoboken—Jon Bon Jovi country—before the exit to Weehawken. Then they stopped at the Lincoln Tunnel toll plaza.

A sign read "No Trucks in Center Tube." Mohammed rose in his seat for a better view of the portal holes. "This is the world's only three-tube underwater tunnel for cars," he told Edgar. His seatmate nodded, a Hostess cupcake in his mouth.

Then they were inside, crossing beneath the Hudson. A military vehicle passed them on the left, alert soldiers with rifles staring up at the bus. Mohammed stared back. When they emerged, someone cheered from the rear. Even Edgar sat up. Mohammed drank in west-side Manhattan, catching his first sight of New Yorkers—two men in thin coats walking fast in the gray light. Then the Greyhound ramped into the Port Authority Bus Terminal.

"Class, stay together," said Miss Cutter above the bustle of unloading.

On the platform Mohammed sniffed Manhattan air. He had readied himself for what news reports had called the "stench of death and destruction," but his first whiff of New York smelled no different than Cincinnati. It smelled of body odor and asphalt, internal combustion and wet sneakers. It also smelled of something edible, possibly deep fried.

Miss Cutter led them to the terminal's ticket plaza, where she delivered the plan: First, to the hotel to leave their bags; then to Grand Central Terminal for breakfast. "We will not be checking in. If you need anything from your luggage, get it before we leave the hotel."

Mohammed unzipped his bag, dug out his Koran, and slipped it into his jacket. He had missed *Isha* on the bus. His sunrise prayer had passed as well. The noon devotion was next. "Remember to pray," his father had said.

They took the underground passageway to the subway station at West Forty-Second Street. Miss Cutter and Priscilla Smith led the way.

"Check out Smith with her Samsonite," scoffed Teddy. "Who does she think she is, Miss American Airlines?"

After buying a pass at a metro machine, the seven YEPS stood on the platform while Miss Cutter promptly took aim at engineering. "Unlike the Lincoln Tunnel, which was dug using the punch-and-sheath technique, most of these train pathways were tunneled with the cut-and-cover method. Does everyone remember the cross sections we looked at?"

Everyone nodded, whether they did or not.

Mohammed took in the rush-hour crowd closing around them. Men in suits held newspapers close to their faces. Well-dressed women talked noiselessly into cell phones. There were students with book bags, workmen with lunch boxes, and Hispanic teenagers joking in Spanish. A ponytailed man played the harmonica. Many of the faces looked gray—like the sky.

At the Fiftieth Street station, they followed Miss Cutter to the street and stood in the gray shadows of a city canyon. "Listen up, people," said their adviser, taking out her map. She pointed to the pavement. "This is Eighth Avenue. That is Fiftieth Street. Uptown is that way. Downtown is that direction. We are here." She put her finger on a crease in the map. "And that is the Worldwide Plaza." She pointed to the redbrick facade of a tall building. "At night you can see an illuminated pyramid at the top."

"How tall is it?" asked Gary Phettiplace.

"Forty stories."

The engineers leaned back to stare.

"Man, that's less than half the towers," someone said.

There was general nodding. Chatter lulled. Mohammed continued to look skyward. *Would every tall building they saw elicit the comparison?* he wondered.

Miss Cutter started down Eighth Avenue, Priscilla beside her. Mohammed fell into step with Edgar. New York faces moved past him. Everyone was going someplace fast amid the chaotic grandeur. He drank in the noise of the traffic—sirens, horns, the shush of buses—and a background roar like a waterfall.

Then they stood on the corner of Forty-Eighth Street waiting to cross. Teddy White spoke to Mohammed in a low voice. "Me, the Fuzz, and Burton are staying in one room. You and pimple-face can have Fatty." Pimple-face was Phettiplace. Fatty was Edgar.

Teddy had a way of making arrangements at his own convenience. Mohammed knew room assignments had just been settled. He and Edgar were together for the trip.

The light changed, and the YEPS crossed Forty-Eighth Street. Ahead, Priscilla Smith walked beside Miss Cutter, pulling her suitcase on wheels. She had forgotten he was on the planet.

At the Days Inn, the club sunk into the lobby sofas while Miss Cutter arranged to store their luggage. Mohammed touched the Koran in his jacket. Should he ask for time to pray?

"This place is dead," observed Fuzzy Thornton, surveying the empty lobby.

"Nine eleven, man," said Teddy. "I bet we have the hotel to ourselves." His voice dropped to a whisper. "Don't forget to bug Cutter about Ground Zero. Maybe she'll let us go."

Mohammed said nothing. To come to New York was to cast oneself in the shadow of its tragedy. He could no more avoid it than he could avoid breathing the city air.

Then Miss Cutter called his name.

At the front desk, she told him the hotel had a small room where he could pray. "I know there are special times. I hope it's not too late."

He followed the desk clerk into a windowless office furnished with a computer desk and chair. The clerk pointed to another door. "You may do your ablutions in there," he said.

Ablutions? Was it a New York word for *wudu*?

He washed then took the compass from his pocket and rotated the needle to the qibla code for New York. The minaret pointer directed him to pray toward the desk. Mecca lay six thousand miles beyond it. When he finished his prayer, he remembered Ramadan was a day away. He offered a *du'a* for the coming month.

O God, bless Mohammad and his household.
Should we go off to one side in this month, set us aright.
Should we swerve, point us straight.

He passed his palms over his face, remaining still for a moment. Already he felt better. Whatever surprises came, whatever disagreeable moments awaited, he was ready. He removed the Koran from his pocket and kissed it.

Back in the lobby the Fuzz gave him a high five. "Prayer's cool," he said, and Mohammed knew Miss Cutter had told them.

They walked to Times Square, turning the corner on Broadway and Forty-Seventh Street. At the sight of Manhattan's most famous crossroads, everyone halted. "Oh, man," gasped Bernie. "It's the core!"

The Ohioans stared, their eyes glazed by the yellow brushstrokes of speeding taxis. Mohammed sucked his breath. The top-heavy chaos of lights seemed to reach above the sky.

"In my old man's business, that's what we call signage," said Teddy, nudging Mohammed. He pointed to the billboard of a scantily clad woman covering her breasts with her hands. "That's Jenna Jameson. Hot stuff, Hamed."

Mohammed couldn't look away. The woman was beautiful, and she was wearing nothing but a spiderweb. He pretended to gaze at the Morgan Stanley Building.

At the Forty-Second Street station, they took the Flushing local to Grand Central, where Miss Cutter handed out pamphlets on the history of the terminal—"Something to digest, people"— before they ate breakfast in the terminal's dining concourse.

Mohammed had a Spanish omelet bagel with orange juice. Edgar had a deluxe big breakfast with extra hash browns, a jumbo cinnamon roll, and a supersized Coke.

"Hey, catch this," said Phettiplace, reading Miss Cutter's pamphlet. "It says here the original Grand Central had a separate waiting room for immigrants, so travelers could avoid associating with them. Can you believe that? A separate room! What a bunch of snobs."

"I believe it," said the Fuzz, wolfing pancakes. "People were more prejudiced then."

Mohammed washed his bagel down with juice, his opinion with it. Everyone believed what they wanted to.

They walked to the Chrysler Building, heading one block north on Lexington Avenue to better view the stainless-steel crown and the famous spire. Miss Cutter passed around her pocket binoculars. Everyone got to see the eagle gargoyles on the fifty-ninth floor. They spied mud flaps, car fenders, and hubcaps. From the corner of First and Forty-Second, they marveled at the Trump World Tower, its narrow, bronze-glassed facade rising above the United Nations complex. Miss Cutter said it was the tallest residential building in the world. "Notice it has no setbacks," she observed. "It is simply an elongated monument, pure and reflective." As they approached the UN, she pointed out what she called the international style of the

Secretariat Building. "Remember our reading, people. Notice the simple geometric form. You will find no historical reference in its design. It is truly a modern building."

At the entrance the YEPS stood in line to be screened by security guards and metal detectors. When Mohammed's turn came, he put his camera, watch, and compass in the tray, but left his Koran in his jacket. "What's in your pocket?" asked the guard, pointing to the bulge.

"A book," he answered. He might have said, "My Koran," but "book" seemed safer.

The guard took it, thumbed through the pages, then told him to proceed.

Inside, they viewed the Foucault pendulum, the moon rocks, and the relics from Hiroshima. According to a sign in the public lobby, the issue being debated that day in the General Assembly was "The Role of Afghan Women in a Post-Taliban Government."

"Now that sounds interesting," remarked Miss Cutter.

Mohammed observed a group of Muslim women wearing hijabs, their faces veiled by niqabs. A few wore burka robes and socks. Had they come from Afghanistan?

Priscilla said, "Did you know that if an Afghan woman was caught wearing nail polish, the Taliban would chop off her fingertips?"

"Yeah, they even made it against the law to fly a kite," added Bernie.

Mohammed looked for something to look at. He had heard enough of the Taliban.

But the discussion continued. Gary said, "We better catch Osama first. He didn't cut off somebody's fingertips. He cut three thousand people into smithereens."

Mohammed stared at the Norman Rockwell mosaic, reading the inscription: "Do unto others as you would have them do unto you." *Please not Osama bin Laden.*

Miss Cutter held up her hands. "This kind of debate is best saved for the classroom. Our purpose here is to know the space and appreciate its design. Let's move on."

Outside, they gazed at the "Let Us Beat Swords into Plowshares" sculpture. Miss Cutter remarked on the significance of landscape gardens as a counterbalance to tall structures. Finally, the words, "Time for lunch," saved them.

In the UN coffee shop, the boys asked her if they would be able to see Ground Zero on Saturday. For the first time, she didn't say no. "We'll see," she answered soberly.

After lunch they took a bus ride through the Queens Midtown Tunnel, Miss Cutter pointing out the ventilated design and the challenges of excavating under the East River. They returned across the Fifty-Ninth Street Bridge so that the Young Engineers could view the cantilever truss structure. Then they boarded the Forty-Second Street crosstown bus to the New York Public Library, where Miss Cutter observed, "At the time of its construction, this was the largest marble structure ever attempted in the United States."

When they returned to the Days Inn that afternoon, the lobby remained empty. No one sat on the sofas. No one checked in. "What did I tell you?" said Teddy as they ascended the elevator. "Nine eleven, man. It killed this place."

Inside their room Mohammed opened the curtains to check the view. Out the window the city was awakening to the night, a million tiny lights filling dark buildings. He tried to look south. Another light was turning on at that moment—the torch of Miss Liberty—adding its dimension to the night—but he could not see it from here.

"What a dump!" exclaimed Edgar from the bathroom. "I had to flush four times. Come look."

Mohammed and Gary Phettiplace entered the bathroom.

"Phew," exhaled Gary. "I don't think four was enough."

"I'm not talking about that. Look!"

Their eyes followed Edgar's finger to the sink. One of the faucet pipes was wrapped in a towel that dripped on the floor.

"That was there already," informed Edgar. "We're down to two towels."

Mohammed shrugged. He had brought his own towel. "Maybe we should call Miss Cutter."

"Call the front desk, that's what I'll do," said Edgar. He went to the phone and pushed the buttons. He waited, surveying the room grimly. "What do you want to bet there's no hot water? Who wants to bet?"

"I don't bet," said Mohammed.

"I don't care," said Gary.

Edgar pressed the phone to his ear. "Yes, this is twelve thirty-four." Edgar's voice attempted baritone in a disgruntled key. "We have a leaky pipe that needs attention. Water is spilling on the floor. Okay, thanks. Oh, can we have more towels? You better hurry on that leak. We're flooded." He hung up, chuckling. "That ought to get them here."

Mohammed checked his watch. He had to catch up on prayer. But first *wudu*. "Guys, I've got to pray."

Inside the bathroom he let the water run, waiting for it to warm. Minutes passed before he realized Edgar would have won his bet. No hot water. He showered anyway. When he emerged, he found the beds stripped to their mattresses. Blankets and pillows lay on the floor. Edgar and Gary held to the opposite ends of a fitted sheet, shaking it like trampoliners gone mad.

"We found pubes!" Edgar declared, pumping his arms wildly.

❖　　❖　　❖

Mohammed consulted his compass, picking the corner with the armchair for his prayer. He removed his mat from the duffel bag and laid it on the carpet. He stood with his eyes closed, listening to his own breathing, trying to feel the pulse of his heart. Behind him the noise of flapping sheets and the voices of Edgar and Gary drifted into the background. He raised his hands to his ears. *"Allahu Akbar,"* he began softly, then recited the first chapter of the Koran in a low voice.

Edgar and Gary ceased sheet shaking to watch their room-mate bow before a corner armchair. At first they exchanged confused looks, each waiting for the other to smile—neither had seen a Muslim pray. Then they stared.

Mohammed moved through the solemn choreograph of prayer postures, his words growing louder. *Alhamdu lillahi rabbil 'alamin.* As he neared the conclusion of his first *rak'at*, a new sound reached him—knuckles on the door. Someone was knocking. He preserved his connection, touching his forehead to the mat. When he heard a man's voice in the room, he hurried to finish. Then a pair of paint-spattered work shoes appeared at his side.

"What in hell's housekeeping are you boys up to?" boomed a gruff voice.

Mohammed didn't like the voice. He remained on his mat. Edgar said, "Oh, this. We're checking the sheets. My friend lost one of his contacts. Didn't you, Gary?"

Silence. Then Gary got it. "Yeah, my lens. Where is it?"

"If you've come to fix the leak, it's in the sink," said Edgar.

It was the maintenance man. Mohammed watched the shoes pivot and move away. His disagreeable voice spoke again. "Is he looking?"

Mohammed sat on his legs, facing the corner.

"Naw," replied Edgar. "He's praying. He's Muslim. They got to do that, you know."

Mohammed saw the man's face in the mirror. It was as coarse and disagreeable as his voice.

"Muslin?" he spat. "Jesus Christ. A leaky pipe *and* a Muslin. Just my luck." The man in the mirror shook his head. His face contorted with revulsion. Mohammed stared at the wall. *Muslin?*

"Well, actually he prayed already," explained Edgar. "Now he's helping us look. Find anything over there, Hamed?"

Mohammed wanted to rise, but he couldn't. The man's look of loathing fixed him to the mat. When the maintenance man retreated to the bathroom, Gary whispered, "You better tell Cutter. He looked funny at you."

"Not Cutter," said Edgar. "She'll make a stink. Go to Teddy's room. We'll watch this guy."

"I'm not staying," replied Gary, his voice low. "How do we know he's not crazy? This is New York. It has all kinds of crackpots."

"What if he rips us off?" Edgar shot back.

Mohammed said, "He's mad at Muslims, I think."

"Duh," said Edgar.

Gary said, "Who cares! Let him fix the sink."

"I'm staying," insisted Edgar.

Metallic clangs came from the bathroom. The maintenance man muttered to himself.

"Stay if you want," said Gary. "Come on, Hamed."

Mohammed hesitated. Should he stay and risk confrontation or leave and avoid trouble? He stooped to fold his prayer rug. What would his father have done?

Gary stood at the door and whispered loudly, "Let's go!"

Mohammed followed. Edgar pointed to the stripped beds. "You have to help me with the sheets, dude."

"Ask *loco* man," said Gary, shutting the door.

❖   ❖   ❖

In the next room, Teddy said, "We got roaches."

"Our sink leaks," countered Gary. "There's a crazy plumber over there fixing it."

Mohammed's thoughts lingered on the maintenance man.

"And Edgar found pubic hairs on the sheets. It made him crazy."

"Oh, gross!"

"Then the plumber guy, he started saying things to Hamed. Hamed was praying, and plumber man talked about leaky pipes and Muslims. The dude is cracked. We got out of there."

"And Edgar?"

"He's with the plumber."

Someone snickered. Gary shrugged. "I told him to come. Didn't I, Hamed?"

Mohammed nodded. The Fuzz asked, "Should we check on him?"

Teddy White smiled malevolently. "No. Give the plumber more time. Edgar won't go down in one flush."

Everyone laughed. Mohammed considered returning to the room. Maybe Edgar shouldn't be alone. Maybe he should face the plumber. Was this the kind of man Yaseen Haneez had confronted on the street in front of the masjid? Now he understood how hard it was to look into hateful eyes. He had felt paralyzed.

There was a knock on the door. Edgar was let into the room. "He's gone."

"Good," Gary said. "I want to take a shower."

"You're gonna help make the beds first."

"No way. It was your idea to take off the sheets. Each makes his own."

Edgar said, "Fine. Come on, Hamed."

Back in the room Mohammed and Edgar untangled the bedsheets. Gary called from the bathroom, "The pipe leaks!"

The boys exchanged glances. Though bold in speech, Edgar was awkward in silence. He fussed over a sheet corner. "I didn't check," he said. "The guy was weird. He didn't shut up. *Muslin* this. *Muslin* that. I couldn't tell if he didn't want to say it right or if he couldn't."

Mohammed recalled the revulsion seen on the man's face. "What else did he say?"

Edgar shrugged. "He had family killed in the towers. I guessed it messed him up."

Mohammed froze. "He lost someone in the attacks?"

"His sister."

He stared at Edgar, but Edgar didn't look back.

"That's what he said. He could have been lying."

Mohammed dropped his gaze, unsure what to say. Suddenly the maintenance man didn't seem so crazy. "That's terrible," he said.

"Yeah, that's what I told him. But I don't think it helped."

That evening at the Big Apple Diner, Edgar ordered fried chicken with onion rings plus a side of mashed potatoes and gravy. Teddy and Bernie had New York strips with a mound of french fries. Fuzzy opted for stuffed pork chops, Gary, meat loaf, while Priscilla and Miss Cutter asked for salads with their meals and ice water to drink. Mohammed ordered the baked scrod with a side of green peas and another of boiled carrots. Edgar said, "Hamed, that's way too many veggies."

Miss Cutter kept the conversation on engineering, revisiting the day's monuments. Teddy countered with Ground Zero, asking again if they could go. Miss Cutter seemed to accede. "It would have to be Saturday afternoon," she said. "I've been thinking about it, and perhaps there is engineering to be learned there, apart from other lessons. We'll see."

It sounded like *yes*.

For dessert she treated the club to ice cream. She reminded everyone that Ramadan began at daybreak. "Don't forget. Tomorrow we fast." She turned to Mohammed and asked if he would like to explain the significance of Ramadan. Mohammed felt vanilla ice cream stick to his throat. He knew Miss Cutter was trying to broaden their horizons, but he didn't want to talk about fasting or Ramadan or anything that had to do with being a Muslim. Not now. Not here. The incident with the maintenance man had left him bruised.

Priscilla broke the silence. "I for one am ready to fast," she said. "It wouldn't be fair to eat in front of Hamed. But I'd like to know why I'm doing it."

Others nodded. Mohammed didn't look at Priscilla. "Okay," he said. Then everyone listened (or pretended to) as he explained about the moon and the Muslim calendar and how the ninth month of the Muslim year is called Ramadan because that was the month the Prophet Muhammad sat alone in the Cave of Hira in the mountains of Arabia receiving the Koran from Allah fourteen centuries before. He explained how during Ramadan all Muslims—except kids, old people, sick people, and pregnant ladies—are not supposed to eat or drink anything from dawn to sunset. "The idea is to feel what the Prophet felt in the cave and also to know how the poor—who never have enough to eat—feel every day. It is a way to know how lucky you are." He said food isn't the only thing off-limits during Ramadan. So is arguing with your parents, fighting with brothers and sisters, gossiping with friends, telling lies, and swearing. "It's also a time to say you're sorry to anyone you've hurt and also to forgive anyone who has hurt you." He added that sharing is important, too, and giving to the poor, but the real work is getting through the day without food. "You have to eat breakfast before there is enough light to tell the difference between a white thread and a black one when they are held up side by side against the sky, which is before dawn. At sunset you break your fast with a small meal—called *iftar*—then eat a big dinner at night. That's what Ramadan is about."

Ice cream melted in bowls. No one spoke. The prospect of an empty stomach sunk in.

"Fascinating," gushed Miss Cutter. "There's so much we don't know."

"So I can't chew gum?" asked Bernie.

Mohammed shook his head. "No gum. No candy. No breath mints."

Gary said, "What about medicine?"

"Medicine is okay, and water to swallow it, but nothing else."

The YEPS exchanged glances. Their faces said that fasting would be as much fun as homework. Miss Cutter spoke. "I promised Mohammed's parents that he would observe Ramadan as if he were at home. So we must support him. No eating on the sly. No sneaking a drink of water. Let's make this a group effort, people. The hours will pass faster than you think."

After dinner, they rode the elevator to the eighty-sixth-floor observatory of the Empire State Building. During the ascent, Mohammed read the brass plate next to the door, recognizing the name: Otis Elevator Company. Miss Liberty had an Otis Elevator. *Soon he would see her.*

He checked his watch, thinking about his family six hundred miles away and a thousand feet down. It was seven thirty on a Thursday evening, the twenty-seventh night of Shaban, the eighth lunar month—the eve of Ramadan. Had his father spotted the new moon yet?

For as long as he could remember, the ritual had been the same. Every year on the eve of Ramadan, his father took him outside in the early evening to check the eastern sky. They stood near the oak tree in their backyard, watching over Mrs. Heath's woods for the first thin crescent of the new moon. When they spotted it, his father shouted joyously into the sky, *"Ramadan Mubarak!"* Later they prayed and read the Koran while his mother worked in the kitchen mixing pancake batter and baking bread for their predawn breakfast.

Mohammed wondered if his father would take Nura Maryam to the oak tree this year. Would he shout, *"Ramadan Mubarak!"* with the same joyous voice? As the elevator rose toward the eighty-sixth floor, other questions came to him. Would his father take the job with Majd Udeen? Would his mother cook only oatmeal for breakfast? Had the redheaded kid noticed he was gone?

The elevator cab bounced. Its doors opened. Suddenly the bedazzling universe that was New York City at night stretched before him. *"Allahu Akbar!"* he gasped.

The club rushed from the indoor viewing area to the outside promenade, their exclamations snatched by the wind. Priscilla began an audio tour while Miss Cutter caught her hat before a gust blew it off her head. Mohammed stopped to stare.

The sight reminded him of a Hubble photograph he had once seen—one taken of so many stars that there was no black between them. New York City at night was like a galaxy of stellar sprawl! He drank in the Chrysler Building and the halogen needle of headlights on Fifth Avenue. He moved east, staring at the infinity of Queens, the black glass of the East River, the bridge lights strung delicately in the night. As he lifted his gaze, he spotted the new moon, his Ramadan moon, a thin, slanted smile rising over Long Island. Something inside him stirred. *"Ramadan Mubarak!"* he shouted. *"Ramadan Mubarak!"*

A sudden roar drowned his exclamations. When Mohammed looked up, he saw two military jets pass overhead, their wing lights blinking as they patrolled the city.

What a place to begin Ramadan, he thought. Then he ran to see the light of Miss Liberty.

From the southwest corner of the observation terrace, he followed the black thread of the Hudson toward the winking shores of Jersey City—his gaze held for a moment by an intense white light near the tip of Manhattan: the flood lamps above Ground Zero. It was not the light he had come to see. *That* light—Miss Liberty's light—was a distant star by comparison, no brighter than a match struck at the edge of a dark sea. Mohammed tingled with excitement.

He loaded quarters into the observatory binoculars, angling them toward the tiny light, pressing close to the cold metal until he found the statue and pedestal rising above the island. The binoculars' optics were terrible. Miss Liberty was a featureless shadow, her outline fuzzy and gray. His hand probed for some magic button that would refine the image and transport him to the island. But there was no zoom, no focus. He strained to improve the magnification by sheer concentration. Then someone touched him on the shoulder. He turned.

"Can you see her?"

Priscilla stood beside him, her hair blown across a smile.

"Sort of," he said, stepping back. He raised his voice above the wind. "Lousy binoculars."

Priscilla moved near. "May I?"

"Sure!" It was a moment he had not imagined—he and Priscilla together at the top of the Empire State Building.

She brushed back her hair and peered into the binoculars. "I can't see anything," she shouted, fondling the metal case.

"Maybe it moved." Mohammed stepped in to sight them. Priscilla drew back. Their heads bumped. Then their gazes locked, the wind stealing nervous laughter. Priscilla eyes sparkled. Mohammed felt something tighten in his chest.

"Would you mind if I borrowed those?" interrupted a woman's voice above the wind.

Miss Cutter stood behind them, one hand holding down her hat, the other pointing to Priscilla's audio player and headphones.

In one step Mohammed attempted to put infinity between himself and Priscilla Smith.

"Are you showing her the statue?"

He nodded. Priscilla handed over the audio tour player.

"We have about twenty minutes," said Miss Cutter. "Don't miss anything!" She slipped on the headphones and moved away.

"I think she's having as much fun as we are!" Priscilla shouted.

Mohammed smiled. His fun was hard to top. He put more coins into the binoculars, adjusted them, and found the fuzzy gray shadow of Miss Liberty. "There. You can sort of see her."

Priscilla squinted. "It doesn't even look like her!" she exclaimed. "What a rip-off!"

"Like I said, lousy binoculars."

She stepped back. "We should take the ferry," she said.

Mohammed gazed at Priscilla's wind-blown hair, lost in the contemplation of her bare neck. "Ferry?" he repeated.

"The Staten Island Ferry!" she shouted, her girl-scented breath washing over him.

Take the ferry to Staten Island?

"On Saturday," she added. "We could take the ferry to see the statue. All of us."

Mohammed gave her a doubtful look. "They want to see Ground Zero."

She turned back to the binoculars. "Then you go!" she yelled. "Ask Miss Cutter."

Ask Miss Cutter to take the ferry?

Priscilla rotated the binoculars toward Brooklyn. "I'll go, too, if you want. Maybe she would say yes if two went."

She would go with him?

His next words were taken by the wind. "I'd like that."

"What?" she shouted, cupping an ear.

He slid the Kodak from his pocket. "Smile!" he shouted. Then he took Priscilla's picture—New York's luminescence reflected on her face.

When they returned to the west terrace, the YEPS were huddled at the suicide fence, their faces pressed to the wire mesh. Everyone strained to see the street below.

"Imagine the ones who jumped!" Bernie yelled.

"Dead before they landed," shouted Edgar. "Never felt a thing. Just blacked out."

Teddy loudly disagreed. "Bull! Didn't you see those pictures? Some were holding hands when they jumped. If you black out, you don't hold hands."

They were talking about the towers. Mohammed stood nearby.

"Some got sucked out," added the Fuzz.

Club members retreated from the fence. No one wanted to be sucked anywhere.

"They say you could hear the plops when the bodies hit."

"I heard the streets were covered with shoes."

"One guy got speared on a flagpole."

Priscilla covered her ears. "Stop it! she yelled. "That's horrible! Horrible!"

The boys exchanged looks of alarm. Eyes darted in search of Miss Cutter.

"How do you think that makes Hamed feel?" Priscilla shrilled.

Mohammed froze.

Teddy said, "Hamed knows we didn't mean anything."

Silence. The wind blew. Priscilla stood apart, her hair wild. "Three thousand people died. Show some respect."

Everyone knew it was true, and everyone hated Priscilla for saying it. Almost everyone. Then Gary Phettiplace sounded the alarm. "Here comes Cutter!"

"*Miss* Cutter," corrected Priscilla.

Mohammed looked at his feet. Sometimes Priscilla confounded him with her sudden vehemence.

"Fascinating tour," exclaimed their adviser. "Absolutely fascinating!" Her hand was on her hat, holding it down. "Are we ready, people?"

Everyone nodded. More than ready.

In the hotel lobby Miss Cutter announced they would depart for breakfast at five the next morning. Faces registered shock.

"Five!"

"In the *morning*?"

Mohammed knew five for the club meant four for him. He had to pray.

Miss Cutter frowned. Priscilla chirped, "I'll get up."

"Thank you, Priscilla," said their adviser. "Anyone who wants breakfast should be in the lobby."

Edgar blurted, "Count me in."

"Me, too," said Gary.

Miss Cutter checked her watch. "I will arrange wake-up calls for four thirty."

Back in the room Mohammed prepared for his evening prayer, washing his feet in the sink. The leaky pipe reminded him of the plumber and his dead sister. Had she jumped from one of the towers? He hoped he would never see him again.

When he came out of the bathroom, the lights were off, Gary was in bed, and Edgar was on the floor watching Jay Leno. "Jay gets nice babes," he said. "The other day he had Shakira."

"Turn it off," groaned Gary from under a pillow. "I wanna sleep."

"So go to sleep," rejoined Edgar.

Mohammed placed his prayer mat in front of the armchair.

"Are you going to pray *again*?" asked Edgar.

Mohammed nodded.

"How many times do you have to do that?"

"Five."

"Turn it off!" insisted Gary.

"Shut up, dink. Five times every day?"

Gary threw back the covers and rolled out of bed.

Edgar said, "I thought I had it bad going to church every Sunday plus Good Friday and Christmas Eve. I'd run out of stuff to pray about if I had to do it five times a day."

Gary turned off the television. Edgar pointed the remote, turning it on again. Gary hit the off button on the console. Edgar pressed the remote, relighting the screen. Gary yanked the plug from the wall. Edgar reconnected it. Gary grabbed the remote and threw it, sending the batteries and cover flying across the room.

"You dink, you!" yelled Edgar, lunging at him.

Gary pushed Edgar backward. Edgar fell on the bed. Gary jumped on him. They locked in an embrace, wrestling in their underwear. Mohammed began his prayer in the dark.

Between grunts and panting and intermittent crescendos of Jay Leno, it was difficult to concentrate, but eventually he focused on his Ramadan prayers. Somewhere between his second and final *rak'at*, the room went quiet. When he rose, the television sound was muted, and the antagonists were asleep, sprawled in the same bed.

Under the covers Mohammed listened to the city through the open window—traffic sounds and that waterfall roar. He thought of Priscilla in her room down the hall. Was she asleep? Or was she staring at the same unfamiliar hotel shadows, listening to the city? He saw her face, her sparkling eyes.

He replayed the idea—her idea—the not-so-crazy idea to see Miss Liberty from the ferry. It made so much sense he wondered why he hadn't thought of it. What better way to see her—with the club or without it, Priscilla at his side. But would Miss Cutter agree?

Neither Edgar nor Gary stirred when Mohammed's watch alarm went off at three forty-five. Cool concrete air wafted through the window. Mohammed shut it noiselessly, making *wudu* and his morning prayer in the dark. He knew how important a good start was to a successful Ramadan. Fasting and prayer. Self-denial and devotion. Saturday Koran classes had drilled in the moral dimension. So had his father. "There are many people who get nothing from fasting but hunger and thirst," he said when Ramadan began. Starting today, no less than total forgiveness of sins was in the balance: a clean wipe of the big blackboard where all bad deeds were written. It was a deal Mohammed knew he could use. He made an extra long prayer, then chanted his dhikr one hundred times. *Alhamdulillah, Alhamdulillah, Alhamdulillah.* He was on a roll.

When the wake-up call hit their phone at four thirty, Edgar stirred. "Just five more, Ma," he implored dreamily.

Mohammed descended to the lobby, the first to arrive. He stood near the windows facing the street, watching the streak of headlights on Eighth Avenue. He studied his reflection in the plate glass—his prominent nose and bushy eyebrows, his gangly frame and loose-fitting clothes—struck by how much he looked like his father.

Then the elevator doors opened, and Miss Cutter emerged, engineers in tow. "Mohammed," she announced, stepping briskly into the lobby. "The troops are ready for breakfast."

YEPS stumbled drowsily from the elevator. Gary and Bernie headed for the sofas, where they dropped. Teddy drifted in a circle. "Hamed, I don't know how you do this for a whole month." Only Priscilla looked crisp. She smiled brightly at Mohammed, at the lobby, at life.

That morning Miss Cutter regaled them about the monuments of New York engineering. At Carnegie Hall she said they were looking at the last large building in New York to be built entirely of masonry, no steel frame. At Rockefeller Center she praised the seventy-story GE Building. "Unlike other art deco towers built during the 1930s, this one was constructed solely as a slab with a flat roof. Simple yet forceful." At the corner of Fifty-Sixth Street, they stared up at Trump Tower. "This building was the tallest concrete-framed tower in the city at the time of its completion," Miss Cutter informed them. "Notice the vertical stepping of the base. Observe how the setbacks are landscaped. Both are brilliantly executed."

"Imagine being The Donald," whispered Teddy.

Inside the lobby of Trump Tower, they gawked at the atrium's seven-story waterfall. They crisscrossed on escalators between the upper and lower retail floors. They visited the outdoor terraces. From beyond polished pink marble came the culinary waftings of Med Grill's bistro. Their noses lifted in unison. Gazes grew distant. When Edgar blurted, "I smell food court," Mohammed knew the struggle had begun.

Noon the first day was Ramadan's toughest hurdle. At breakfast they had picked at plates of eggs and pancakes, sides of bacon and hash browns. There had been complaints that it was too early to eat. Now everyone wished they had forked in more.

Mohammed savored the bistro's smells. He felt the first hot gastric emptiness creep into his stomach. But his face remained a mask. He remembered his father's advice for Ramadan afternoons. "When the urge comes to eat, remember the poor and ask for strength." Good advice, but not the kind he could give to the club members.

"Willpower, Edgar!" cheered Miss Cutter. She pointed them down the escalator. "Let's head to Central Park. There are some wonderful bridges and arches we must see, and the smells of grass and trees will take our minds off lunch."

At Central Park South and Fifth Avenue, she assembled them. "People, we are about to enter one of the urban wonders of the world," she began. "This was the first major park in this country intended entirely for public use. What you must remember as you walk in its eight-hundred-plus acres is that no matter how natural Central Park may look, it has been engineered."

Eyes darted to a nearby food cart: Gilly's Hot Dogs—Manhattan's Finest. Someone groaned. Miss Cutter didn't seem to notice. "The park was constructed when the horse was man's principle means of transportation. To accommodate the carriageways and bridle paths, more than forty bridges and arches were designed and built, most by Mr. Vaux. These are what we shall see today."

"All forty?" bleated Edgar.

"No," answered Miss Cutter. "But enough to keep everyone's thoughts off hot dogs."

Without another word she set off at a brisk pace toward the equestrian statue at the north end of the plaza, Priscilla in step. An hour later they took a restroom break near the zoo.

"I am trusting all of you not to eat or drink while you are out of my sight," said their adviser before disappearing into the ladies' room.

When Mohammed returned from the lavatory, the boys were benched at the north end of Wien Walk waiting for Priscilla and Miss Cutter. Their eyes lingered on a sign advertising the Leaping Frog Café, with its menu of burgers, fries, sandwiches, and wraps.

"Even one bite of that spinach wrap," Edgar moaned. "And I hate spinach."

"All you're doing is making it worse," said Gary.

"Shut up, dink," countered Edgar. "Maybe you want to share those sugar packets you pocketed off the table at HoJo's this morning?"

Everyone looked at Gary.

"You stole sugar?" quizzed the Fuzz.

Gary shrugged, looking guilty. "I give them to the old lady for her Tupperware parties." The bulge in Gary's pocket screamed contraband.

"Share the wealth, dude," said Teddy, extending his hand.

"Yeah, I could use a rush," added the Fuzz. "Might get me to dinner."

Mohammed watched Gary dig into his pocket, remove a fistful of sugar packets, and pass them around. When his turn came, he said, "I can't."

The tearing of packets stopped.

"Come on, Hamed. It's just sugar."

"Yeah, Hamed, be cool."

Mohammed knew he couldn't be cool. He could only be hungry. That was the point. "Sorry. The rule says nothing swallowed. I can't."

Hands hesitated with half-opened sugar packets held in limbo.

"But you guys go ahead," he added. "The rules are for Muslims, anyway."

Edgar said, "Hamed's right. He has to because of his church. But I'm Methodist."

"Yeah," agreed the Fuzz. "Sugar is practically energy, right?"

Tearing resumed. Envelopes moved to lips. "Quick. Before Cutter comes."

Mohammed avoided looking at the Leaping Frog menu. He felt better. He had separated himself without trouble, without sounding like a nerd or a sermonizing stiff. They could suck sugar, he could fast, and everyone remained friends. Different, but friends.

"What are you eating?"

Mohammed immediately recognized Priscilla's voice.

"Are you guys—? Is that—?"

White envelopes jerked from lips. Sugar sprinkled on the walkway. Priscilla put her hands on her hips. "How low can you get? If you guys don't throw those away, I'm telling."

Teddy held his packet aloft so Priscilla could see it was full. He made a point of folding the tear before pitching it into a trash can. Others followed. Edgar said, "Mohammed is okay with it."

Priscilla looked at Mohammed, then at the malefactors. "I thought we were fasting as a club to support Mohammed during Ramadan."

"Stop trying to sound like Miss Cutter," Edgar vented.

"What?"

"I said—oh, forget it." Edgar had spied their adviser. His packet went into the can.

Miss Cutter smiled as she approached. "Everyone ready?" she sang, still walking briskly on a predawn breakfast. "Good. On to Denesmouth Arch then." She didn't notice the sound her shoes made as she crossed the sugar-sprinkled walkway.

As they moved north through the central garden, Edgar whispered, "Hey, any of you drink water in the restroom?"

Lips were licked, but no one answered. Eyes darted to the Sixty-Fifth Street transverse.

"I didn't," said Gary after a hesitation.

"Bull," snapped Edgar. "Your sleeve is wet. Are you saying you peed on it?"

Silence. "Okay, I drank. But just a sip."

"Me, too," said the Fuzz. Bernie nodded his guilt. Then Teddy said, "I drank about a gallon."

The Young Engineers snickered. Edgar put his hands on his hips Priscilla style, his voice falsetto. "Teddy, if you don't throw up that water this instant, I'm telling Miss Cutter."

Eyes went to the only one who hadn't admitted to drinking water in the restroom.

"I rinsed but didn't swallow," admitted Mohammed. "It's allowed."

While his face said it was true, Edgar blurted, "Bull!"

As for engineering, no one went hungry that afternoon. Miss Cutter saw to that. After elaborating upon keystones, springers, and voussoirs, she filled empty stomachs with a full-course repast of arches: rustic arches, brick arches, small stone arches, large stone arches. They examined arches built from Maine granite and Manhattan schist, archways of Westchester gneiss and New Brunswick sandstone. Then came the bridges—stone bridges quarried from mountain graywacke, cross-timbered bridges, bridges with curved walkways. They learned about spandrels, spans, and abutments. They crossed one of the oldest cast-iron bridges in America—Bow Bridge. They gazed dizzily at an endless parade of fountains, statues, and monuments, their adolescent feet dragging on the leaf-littered walkways, the afternoon stretching before them like a desert.

Temptation trekked at their side. The smells of coffee, pastries, and focaccia sandwiches followed them all the way from Merchants' Gate. At every turn, they ran into food. A crepe cart. Warm pretzels. A vendor selling tacos. Even Miss Cutter sensed a digestive crisis. "People, let us head to the bridge," she announced. The Brooklyn Bridge. Their last stop.

Mohammed's head felt airy, his legs hollow. After repeatedly swallowing saliva, his tongue seemed small enough to swallow, too. Everything inside him felt shriveled to the size of a raisin. He had fasted enough times to know that the true seat of hunger lay not in an empty stomach, but in the suggestive powers of the mind. The nose was a coconspirator. So was an undisciplined eye. He had learned that success in fasting came from being able to disconnect the outside from the inside. No nose. A dead eye to food. Prayer was training for that. Inevitably, fasting became a struggle not with hunger, but with oneself.

He checked his watch. Two fifty-five. The spin of the planet had slowed. From now until sunset, the afternoon would run straight uphill. There was also the wind. It gusted down Central Park South, inflating jackets, blowing off caps, and visiting an exceptionally bad hair day on Miss Cutter. Everyone worked to walk. As low gray clouds darkened a dirty Manhattan sky, their adviser offered them the bright side. "At least it's not raining," she said.

Behind her back, Edgar beckoned to the heavens with uplifted arms. "Please, please rain," he whimpered. "I want to go to the hotel."

But no rain fell. Mohammed made a *du'a* that it wouldn't, not today, not tomorrow. Rain could give Miss Cutter a reason to nix his plan—that ride on the Staten Island Ferry.

They took the Lexington Avenue Express then walked to the footbridge entrance across from City Hall Park. The gray day was fading fast, the wind openly quarrelsome. Miss Cutter's step was brisk, but none complained. The end was near.

Mohammed was psyched; hungry, but psyched. This was the Brooklyn Bridge. He was about to cross the most famous monument of steel suspension in the world.

The boys were discussing the movie *Godzilla*, the final scene on the bridge.

"Remember when he jumped on it?"

"Yeah."

"The cables ripped out."

Their voices faded as Mohammed halted on the promenade, looking skyward at the soaring wire ropes looped in graceful catenary curves. The gothic granite arches of the Manhattan tower rose above him like a cathedral turned inside out. The club moved ahead. He lingered, gazing up, entranced by the wirework of the diagonal and vertical stays. When he ran to catch up, the club had moved onto the land span, marching into the dusky shadow of the Manhattan pier. Suddenly a voice snagged him. "Halt!" it barked. "You there, halt!"

Immediately he obeyed. *Halt* was a police word—larger than *stop*. He saw two soldiers run toward him on the pedestrian walk. "Halt," repeated one of them. Both soldiers carried rifles.

Mohammed stood very still. He knew why soldiers were on the bridge—for the same reason they were everywhere in New York. But why had they stopped him?

The soldier in front motioned for the other to fall back. "May I see some identification?" he blurted.

"Excuse me?" Mohammed said.

"Under the emergency provisions of the Federal Safety Transportation Act, we are authorized to inspect pedestrian and vehicular traffic at random checkpoints on public thoroughfares. May I see some ID, please."

The soldier in charge looked nervous. A uniform and helmet were not enough to disguise his youth. Behind him, the watching soldier kept his hands on his gun.

Between gaps in the trusses, Mohammed made out other khaki uniforms on the roadway. "I don't have one," he said. "But that lady over there can identify me." He pointed toward the retreating figure of Miss Cutter.

The soldier's eyes didn't follow. They remained focused. "Please unzip your jacket," he said.

His jacket? He touched the bulges of the Koran and the camera in his pockets. "Sure."

As soon as he unzipped it, the wind grabbed the jacket flaps, spreading them like wings. His buttoned shirtfront ballooned, exposing his white underwear. The soldier stared. His helmet nodded. "Now, if you will provide some identification, please."

Mohammed straightened his shirt and zipped his jacket, realizing that he had just been checked for a bomb. This soldier was making certain he wasn't a terrorist! Was it because he had stood by himself, staring at the bridge towers?

Pedestrians turned to look. Bicycle riders stared. A brown-skinned youth stopped by a soldier was getting noticed. He searched for Miss Cutter. "I'm sorry. I don't have an ID."

The soldier looked doubtful. "No driver's license?"

"I don't drive. I'm fourteen."

He expected the soldier to recognize his mistake, but the soldier's face remained a mask. "You look nervous," he said.

Mohammed shook his head—too quickly. He was nervous. Then he heard Miss Cutter, her voice sharp like the wind.

"Mohammed, is there a problem?" He saw the club stop behind her.

"I think so," he said.

"May I ask what is going on, Corporal?" inquired their adviser. That she identified the soldier as a corporal surprised no one. This was the kind of manly business the practical Miss Cutter knew about.

The soldier asked, "Is this young man with you?"

"He is my student."

The corporal blinked. "Student, ma'am?"

"Yes, one of our group." Miss Cutter's arms stayed straight at her sides.

The soldier took in the group. "Your name, ma'am?"

"Valerie Cutter. I'm a teacher at Pioneer Middle School in Ohio, and these are my students. Now what is the problem, Corporal?"

The soldier's bearing seemed to wilt. He retreated to familiar ground. "Under emergency provisions of the Federal Safety Transportation Act, we are authorized to inspect pedestrian and—"

"Yes. I know," interjected Miss Cutter. "But what did he do?"

The corporal exchanged glances with his backup. The wind invaded an awkward silence. "He was staring at the bridge, ma'am. It looked suspicious."

Miss Cutter's eyebrows arched. "I suppose hundreds of tourists stop to stare at this bridge every day. It was made to stare at, don't you think, Corporal?"

"Yes, ma'am."

"So I fail to see why he was stopped."

The soldier looked from Mohammed to the other adolescents. "The boy is tall for his age, ma'am. We thought he was older."

Miss Cutter pursed her lips. Her expression said soldiers were more tiring than teenagers. "Are you all right?" she asked Mohammed.

Mohammed was about to reply, "Yes, ma'am," then caught himself, nodding instead. Daylight thinned. The Brooklyn tower was dissolving into the gray sky. On the roadway, headlights had come on. Yes, he was all right, but they were missing the bridge.

Miss Cutter read his mind. "Corporal, you have significantly delayed our tour. Our intention had been to walk the length of this bridge before sundown. Thanks to your overzealous intervention, the monument was spared from a fourteen-year-old tourist while the rest of us were spared the pleasure of fully enjoying it. If we had time, I would ask to speak to your superior. I don't like what I'm seeing here. You were profiling this young man, and that is illegal. I suggest you be more careful next time."

"Just doing our duty, ma'am."

"Yes, I suppose. If that is the duty this country requires, may heaven help us. Good afternoon, Corporal." And with that, she started across the bridge.

At midspan, with a light rain starting to fall, Miss Cutter turned them around. The bridge lights had just switched on.

"Thank God," gasped Edgar, new life invigorating his legs. "I thought she might go all the way."

Gary pointed out the irony of fasting the whole day among restaurants and street vendors only to have it end over the East River—a half mile from the nearest food.

Footsteps lightened. Gloominess lifted into the descending night. They had fasted—with complaint, with clandestine swallows of restroom water—but they had survived.

Mohammed had hoped to glimpse Miss Liberty from the bridge, but the low gray sky had swallowed her. Instead he sighted the clunky nautical profile of a Staten Island Ferry departing Whitehall Terminal. Tonight he would ask Miss Cutter.

Before them, the silhouette of Lower Manhattan edged a pale charcoal sky. No one remarked on the towerless horizon or their proximity to Ground Zero. The YEPS nudged one another as they passed other soldiers on the walkway. Priscilla simply glared. "I can't believe they did that!" she told Miss Cutter. Mohammed ignored them.

From the hotel they walked to Beefsteak Charlie's. Even the streets seemed hungry—cavernous in the wet shadows of tall buildings. On three tables set end-to-end, the club demolished sirloin strips, pork ribs, chopped steak, and double cheeseburgers. Mohammed had the coconut shrimp. By dessert, the agony of fasting seemed like ancient history—read about but not lived. Even Miss Cutter looked satisfied. A mellow afterglow flushed her face.

Priscilla nudged Mohammed with her eyes. The time was right.

With no more preamble than, "Miss Cutter, what if we…" he proposed they take the Staten Island Ferry to see Miss Liberty instead of using their last afternoon to visit Ground Zero.

Dessert spoons halted. Dissent descended like lightning.

"No way," blurted Edgar, a chocolate éclair in his mouth. "I'm seeing Ground Zero."

Gary, who almost never agreed with Edgar, agreed. "Yeah, I want to see it, too. That's what we came for."

It was one sentence too much, and even Edgar distanced himself. "No, that's not why we came. But since we're here, we ought to see it."

Teddy jumped in. "We can see the Statue of Liberty anytime. But Ground Zero isn't going to be Ground Zero forever."

Heads nodded.

"I would prefer to see the statue," Priscilla declared.

Someone muttered, "You would."

"I think it would be more educational and less morbid," she continued. "Seeing the Statue of Liberty was on the first itinerary, so I say we stay with it."

Their adviser remained silent. Was she letting democracy take its course?

Teddy said, "If we're going to see the statue from a boat, we might as well buy a postcard."

"Still, it's an opportunity," countered Priscilla. Her eyes darted to Mohammed.

He knew it was his turn, but what could he say that would make a difference? Ground Zero versus a ferry ride? In terms of rubbing elbows with tragedy, it wasn't a contest.

"I say Ground Zero," said Edgar.

"Me, too."

"Yeah, Ground Zero."

It sounded like a vote. Priscilla stared at Mohammed, waiting for him to speak.

He said, "It was just an idea." He started to shrug, then thought better of it. More than anything he wanted to see Miss Liberty. Everyone knew that. What they didn't know was the other reason he had for wanting to take the ferry. "I just can't see Ground Zero," he admitted. "Because of who did it and what everyone thinks about them."

No one spoke. Miss Cutter studied them from the end of the table. "Under the circumstances, I understand why Mohammed doesn't want to go," she said.

Nods. Dessert spoons on hold.

"I am not looking forward to it myself," she continued, her face somber, "yet I think it's fair to those who want to see the World Trade Center site to have that opportunity—if not for engineering's sake, then for history's."

"Mohammed doesn't have to go if he doesn't want to," offered Teddy.

"Why can't he go on the ferry?" said the Fuzz.

"Yeah. While we go to Ground Zero."

Mohammed said nothing. Miss Cutter shook her head. "I'm afraid I can't allow that. If Mohammed chooses not to join us—and I think we should respect his decision—then he would have to wait at the hotel."

"What if he wasn't to go on his own?" Priscilla asked. "What if one of us volunteered to go with him?"

Everyone looked at Miss Cutter. The intervening silence offered an opportunity for someone to volunteer, but no one spoke. Under the table Mohammed felt a nudge from Teddy.

"Definitely not an option," said their adviser.

Priscilla started to explain, "I just thought—"

Amusement lighted Miss Cutter's face. "Are you the one who wishes to keep Mohammed company while he rides to Staten Island?" she asked.

If the ferry itself had barreled into the restaurant, Mohammed could not have looked more shocked. The playful insinuation in Miss Cutter's voice left no doubt. She knew.

"You-who-who-ooooo," sung Teddy White, nudging him again.

Everyone looked at Priscilla—everyone except Mohammed, his face hot.

She touched her chest dramatically, looking incredulous. "Me?" Her nervous laugh echoed Miss Cutter's amusement. "I wasn't suggesting that *I* go. Goodness no! I get seasick."

"I've got a plastic bag," offered Teddy as laughter broke into the open.

"Well, I *do* get seasick," insisted Priscilla. "All I'm saying is that two is safer than one. I don't want to see Ground Zero, either, but I'll go if that's what everyone else wants."

Miss Cutter's smile faded. "I think it is admirable for a friend to look out for another, but as I said, I will not allow individual members to go off on their own—or in pairs."

Mohammed lifted his voice above the table noise. "Hey, it's okay," he said. "I'll wait in the hotel. It's no big deal. Really." He wanted to sound dismissive. Priscilla had tried. And Miss Cutter had tried to be fair. There should be no reason for the club to suspect he had another plan. A *new* plan.

"Then it's settled," said Teddy.

"Yeah, Ground Zero." Dessert spooning resumed.

"A reminder, people. We fast again tomorrow."

Groans were mellowed by full stomachs.

"How do we know Hamed won't eat while we're gone?" asked Edgar, trying to be funny.

Miss Cutter motioned for the checks. "Because," she replied, "I trust him."

The club took the New York night bus tour—narrated, not guided—down Broadway, through the Village, SoHo, and Little Italy. After Chinatown, the bus headed uptown under an ashen sky. Somewhere between the Manhattan and Williamsburg Bridges, rain found them for the second time that day. Wet city lights glistened through the bus windows. Tires sizzled on the glassy pavement. The taped narrator—a peppy Manhattanite—pointed everyone left, to the gleaming spire of the Chrysler Building. Mohammed looked right, at Queens and the East River. He thought about the plan—the *new* plan.

It was simple: Saturday afternoon when Miss Cutter took the club to Ground Zero, he would leave the hotel, take the Seventh Avenue local to South Ferry station, walk to Whitehall Terminal, take the ferry to Staten Island, see Miss Liberty, return to Manhattan, retrace his route to the hotel, and be back in the lobby when the club arrived. A quick trip to Staten Island and back—in pursuit of a dream. It was almost too simple. The ferry was free. His MetroCard covered the subway. Already he had calculated the time. The Staten Island Ferry ran every thirty minutes; the boat ride took another thirty. At most a round-trip to St. George and back would take an hour and a half. Add another hour on the subway. That left him three hours out of the hotel. The waiter at Beefsteak Charlie's had told Miss Cutter there was a three- to four-hour wait—just the wait—at Ground Zero's viewing platform on Fulton Street. *Longer on weekends.* "The line moves slow," he had said. "It's not a place people want to see in a hurry."

The club would never know he had been gone.

The bus sped past Queensboro Bridge. Rivulets of rain swept across the windows. The narrator pointed out Roosevelt Island. Mohammed's thoughts were elsewhere. He replayed the steps—subway, Whitehall, Staten Island, and back. A quick commute.

Now if he could only get permission to leave the hotel.

He stared at the glistening streets, weighing his options. What he needed was an excuse, no, an obligation—a bona fide obligation. Then it came to him—made to fit—the very best reason a Muslim boy needed to leave his hotel. He would ask to visit a masjid! To pray. For Ramadan!

Prayer was perfect.

Mohammed started to praise Allah, then caught himself. First, he would have to find a masjid near the hotel. Then he would ask Miss Cutter. How could she refuse?

He knew that using prayer as an excuse to do something other than prayer was worse than not praying at all. Worse still was misusing prayer in the holy month of Ramadan. That was like stealing at Christmas—more chalk marks on the blackboard of sin. And if he was counting sins, he might as well include dishonesty, disobedience, and the violation of adult trust. Already Miss Cutter had been clear: no ferry ride. Was there really any question what a good Muslim boy—a mostly devout, usually obedient, and basically honest Muslim boy—should do?

The tour bus stopped at a light. Rain rivulets ran vertical on the windows, no longer flattened by the wind. Mohammed stared at his reflection in the wet glass. The Koran in his jacket had the answer. So did the words of the Prophet. *"When something bothers your conscience, give it up!"* His father's voice echoed them. Resist temptation!

But this was not about temptation. This was about pursuing a dream, an old dream. How long had it been?

Since the first day he had seen Miss Liberty's picture on the cover of his second-grade reader, *Welcome to America's Shores*, she had struck him as something magical taken from a bedtime story—a giant metal statue erected on an island at the edge of the sea, a statue with a stairway inside, a ladder in the arm, a place to stand in her hand! His first drawing from school had been of her—a squiggled figure colored green outside the lines, his mother calling her "The most beautiful woman in the world." He had learned her story, made a scrapbook. He had dreamed of seeing her—the power of his imagination bringing him close. How many nights had she come to him? How many times had she saved him? This was no ordinary dream.

Tomorrow was his last day in New York. She was a thirty-minute ferry ride away. Was there not a debt to be paid? He remembered her face as she lifted him from the stormy sea, her smile. How could he not go? For years she had beckoned. For years he had waited.

The bus headed south on Fifth Avenue, the narrator pointing out Museum Mile. Mohammed peered into the shadows of

Central Park. Did there have to be a choice between obedience and a dream?

He knew Teddy, Edgar, and the others struggled with disobedience and deception the same way they struggled with fasting. They struggled at the surface and with the obvious—getting by or getting caught. But he couldn't help but feel the weight of something heavier, something holding him down like rocks in his pockets. Is that what his father had meant by his Islamic identity?

Outside, the rain thinned. As Friday-night crowds returned to midtown streets, the narrator announced their approach to Times Square. Teddy let out a peal of glee. The boys nudged one another in anticipation.

In the end, was the choice his? "Tie your camel and put your trust in God," his father was fond of saying. And perhaps that was the answer.

From Times Square Jenna Jameson in her spiderweb stared at the bus. Out the window Mohammed stared back.

At the hotel the boys hit a nearby food mart before Miss Cutter sent them to their rooms. Teddy and the Fuzz bought ice cream, Bernie and Gary sandwiches, while Edgar filled a grocery bag with the makings of an all-night blowout. Mohammed bought Pringles—one of the doubtful foods. Tonight he wasn't worrying about the rules.

In the elevator he eyed Priscilla. Since leaving Beefsteak Charlie's she had avoided his gaze. Not once had she smiled. Was she mad about what had happened at dinner? Or mad because *they* couldn't go on the ferry and *she* had to go to Ground Zero? He needed to talk to her.

In the room Edgar emptied his grocery bag on the bed. "Want some?" he offered, holding out a bag of pink marshmallows. With their artificial coloring and flavoring, they were forbidden for sure. Mohammed took three—rule breaking on a roll. What were *mushbooh* potato chips and haram marshmallows compared to an unauthorized excursion on the Staten Island Ferry?

Edgar surfed TV channels, popping marshmallows and Pringles into his mouth. Mohammed opened the phone book.

"Who do you want to call?" asked Edgar.

When Mohammed explained about finding a masjid near the hotel, Edgar said, "Oh, I thought you wanted to order pizza." He sounded disappointed. "Call the front desk. They'll know."

Mohammed gazed at the phone with its array of hotel extensions.

"Dial zero one," said Edgar. "Try not to sound like a kid. Otherwise they'll blow you off. This is New York."

Mohammed hesitated. He couldn't afford to be blown off. "How about if you call?" he suggested, holding out the handset. Edgar's worldly grasp of hotel protocol was hard to ignore. His brusque baritone impersonation was unbeatable. And with a mouthful of Pringles—Mohammed's Pringles—Edgar couldn't refuse. He took the phone. "All right. What do you want to know?"

Mohammed explained the functions of a mosque. Edgar listened.

"Okay, so it's like a church. You pray and have potlucks."

"Close enough," Mohammed said.

Edgar dialed. "Yes, McHugh here. Twelve thirty-four." His voice sounded deeper after Pringles. "Yes, I have a Muslim associate visiting from Ohio, and he needs to pray. In fact, he may have to pray tonight." Edgar paused to swig some Orange Crush. "You know that Muslims have to pray every day rain or shine, sleet or snow. They can't miss—or else. So we need to know where the nearest mosque is for praying. Yes, the nearest one. What? No. Just the address. Yes. One Riverside Drive. Two blocks west of Broadway."

Mohammed wrote on his hand.

"Can you repeat that? What center? Oh, Islamic Center… okay…Islamic Cultural Center of Manhattan. Got it. Are you sure he can pray there? I mean, it's a mosque, right? I don't want my friend walking into a gay bar for Muslims."

Edgar winked. Mohammed cringed. The desk clerk must have laughed because Edgar snickered, too. "Yeah, right. Okay. I just wanted to be sure. Thanks. I'll tell him to pray for us. Bye." He hung up then dropped on the bed among his goodies. "Desk clerks, they're bananas. All that coffee. The guy actually thought I was trying to be funny." He motioned to Mohammed for the Pringles. "Is that close enough for you?"

Mohammed didn't need a map to know it was. The masjid was one metro stop from the hotel! "It's perfect," he said.

He rose from the bed. This couldn't wait until morning. "I've got to ask Miss Cutter something," he told Edgar.

The twelfth-floor corridor was empty when he closed the door behind him. Florescent lighting pulsated above an acrylic ceiling. An ice machine hummed eerily from the stairwell. As he padded down the hallway in his socks, an unsettling possibility arose. What if the maintenance man lived in the hotel? What if he suddenly appeared and recognized the "Muslin" kid? Mohammed moved briskly toward Miss Cutter's room.

At 1238 he rapped twice. Inside, someone pressed close to the peephole, the sound of clothes brushing the door. Chain jingling followed, then unlocking. When the door opened, Priscilla stood wearing a tartan flannel nightgown. "Mohammed, what are you doing?" she asked in a voice that became a whisper before the question was completed.

He said he had to talk to Miss Cutter.

Priscilla turned a wary gaze into the room. "I don't think so. She's in the shower."

The sound of running water reached the hallway. "I need to ask her about tomorrow. It's important."

Priscilla's damp hair hung loosely about her shoulders. Her complexion shined. He noticed her bare feet peeking from beneath the hem of her nightgown.

"I shouldn't let you in," she said. "What if Miss Cutter comes out in her underwear?"

Mohammed was drinking in the scents of Priscilla's shampoo when *underwear* hit him.

"Or she might think you and I were up to something."

He tried hard not to imagine Miss Cutter in her underwear. Priscilla was going too fast for his quiet devotion. Already they were *up to something*. And she hadn't meant plotting to overthrow the government. He stepped back. It had seemed like the perfect chance to speak to her alone. Now he wasn't so sure. "I'll wait here," he said.

She closed the door to the width of her face. "Are you really going to stay here while we go to Ground Zero?" she whispered.

He began to nod, then stopped. This business of lying was new. It required quick thinking. "That's why I want to see Miss Cutter," he said. "To get permission to visit a mosque while the club is out."

Priscilla made a face. "Mosque? You're not taking the ferry? That's what I'd do!"

Mohammed shrugged, evasive. "It's not as easy as it sounds."

Priscilla looked at her feet. "I tried harder than you did at dinner. I practically told everyone I would go with you. They thought I was doing it to be with you when I was doing it so you could go. Now I have to stand in line to see a place where three thousand people were crushed to smithereens. At least you get out of that."

When he heard the disappointment in her voice, he moved to the door. He wanted to touch her hand, but his own wouldn't move. How could he not trust her when the idea had been hers? "I'm sorry," he said. "I should have told them I wanted you to go. But I am going to do it. I want you to know that. I am taking the ferry tomorrow. I am going to see her. That's the truth."

Priscilla looked up. "Really?"

"Yeah. I wasn't sure I should tell you. If you didn't know, you wouldn't have to lie."

"I won't tell anyone," she promised, glancing over her shoulder. The sound of running water had stopped.

"I don't feel good about doing this to Miss Cutter, but the only way I can get out of the hotel is if she gives me permission to visit the mosque. That way, everything else—going on the ferry, seeing the statue—will be because I was out with her permission."

Priscilla nodded. "Sort of like telling her you are going to do it without telling her."

"I guess."

She smiled. "I'm so glad. I'm so happy!" Her eyes sparkled. Her next words were whispered with an urgent breathlessness that made Mohammed's heart stop. "Kiss me, Mohammed. Quick. Before Miss Cutter comes. Kiss me for luck."

She opened the door and stepped into the hall. Suddenly her face was near his, her eyes closed. Mohammed wanted to say that Muslims didn't believe in luck, that they believed only in God's will. He started to step back, remembering the old rules about girls, but her breathless, tiptoe hush made him pause. *Come,* it said. *Surrender.* He closed his eyes and leaned toward her.

As soon as they kissed, she backed into the room. Mohammed stood with his lips on fire, his heart pounding. The rest of him tingled. Then Miss Cutter's voice broke the silence. "Priscilla! Who's at the door?"

Mohammed averted his gaze, not risking a glimpse of Miss Cutter in her underwear.

"It's Hamed," she replied. "He wants to see you."

"Well, have him come in."

He entered. His face felt hot. The scent of Priscilla's shampoo circled him. A new taste clung to his lips, something fresh and minty. Toothpaste. Priscilla's toothpaste! He licked his lips again.

Miss Cutter stood in pink pajamas, a towel wrapped around her head. She gave him a solicitous once-over. "Is there something wrong?" she asked. "You look flushed." She marched up to him and touched his forehead with a cool hand that smelled of soap. "Do you feel all right?"

Mohammed said, "I'm not sick. I came to ask you something."

"A problem in the room?"

He shook his head. He saw Priscilla open a book.

Miss Cutter said, "If this is about the ferry, Mohammed, the answer is still no."

He pushed past the taste of Priscilla's lips. "I found a masjid," he began. "I mean, a mosque, near the hotel, and I wanted to know if I could visit it tomorrow when the club goes to Ground Zero. It's only one subway stop from the hotel, just off Broadway, on Riverside Drive. It's called the Islamic Cultural Center of Manhattan. We called the front desk, Edgar and I."

"I see," said Miss Cutter, her face noncommittal. Priscilla continued to read.

"If it's all right with you, I would go there and make my Ramadan prayers."

Miss Cutter studied him. "Where did you say it is?"

He showed her his hand where he had written the name and address. After reading it, she went to the phone and dialed.

"This is Valerie Cutter," she said. "One of my students wishes to pray at a mosque tomorrow. Do you know of one that is close by?"

Mohammed remained hopeful. Corroboration was good. Corroboration meant maybe. So what if the desk clerk had gotten two calls in one hour from guests on the same floor inquiring about the nearest mosque. This was New York. Coincidence was eight million people living on three hundred square miles of the planet. Anything was possible.

He glanced at Priscilla. She looked up from her book, their timing perfect. A silent anticipation telegraphed between them. So far, so good, their faces agreed. Mohammed had to catch himself from licking his lips. After so many licks the taste was fading.

"Yes, that is close," Miss Cutter was saying. "Do you happen to have their phone number? Yes, of course, not at this hour. Okay. Thank you just the same. Good night."

She hung up and looked at her watch. Mohammed didn't move, awaiting the verdict.

"I would have preferred to call them," she said, almost to herself, "but that may not be possible considering our early rise and the busy morning we have scheduled." She paused to look at Mohammed, her expression doubtful. "My first impulse is to say no, for the same reasons I gave when you asked to take the ferry. But I did promise your father that your Ramadan obligations would be met, and I did say I trusted you. Since it is for the purpose of prayer and the mosque is close, I am tentatively going to say yes. Tentatively."

Mohammed checked a celebratory grin. It was, after all, prayer.

"With two conditions," she added, lifting a finger. "First, you must promise to go only to the mosque. I don't want you going anywhere else. Is that understood?"

A nod of assent. Better for his head to deceive than his voice.

"Second, I want you back in the lobby by the time we return. No later than six."

"Yes, ma'am." That was already the plan. "Thank you, Miss Cutter."

"Now off to bed."

He went to the door, permission granted, plan in motion, not daring a last glance at Priscilla. Already she had brought him luck. "Good night," he said.

In the room he found Edgar asleep in a pile of junk food and Gary sacked out in his briefs. He took a shower, then prayed near the armchair, thanking God for giving him the strength to fast on the first day of Ramadan. There was more to be thankful for—especially in the last hour—but there was also much to repent. Deceit. Disobedience. Marshmallows. In bed he listened to the wet sneer of tires and the splash of trounced puddles twelve floors below. He hoped Allah would give him dry skies tomorrow.

He licked his lips one last time, the taste of mint gone. Even if it was for luck, even if it never happened again, he had done it, kissed a girl—and not just any girl. He had kissed Priscilla Smith. It was the one dream he had never expected to come true.

Roused by the four-thirty ring of their wake-up call, Mohammed leaped from his bed as if it were on fire. He had overslept! He had missed his prayer! A bad start. He said a quick *du'a* in the privacy of the bathroom. *There is no God but you. Glory to You.*

Indeed I am a sinner. He was about to say another when Edgar banged on the door.

"Jesus, I've got the runs."

Gary was awake when Mohammed emerged. "No wonder," he said, pointing to the empty marshmallow bag on the floor.

"Oh God," whimpered Edgar from the bathroom as the toilet flushed repeatedly.

In the lobby everyone waited for Edgar. Miss Cutter tapped her shoe. "What did he eat last night?" she asked.

Mohammed wasn't getting Edgar into trouble. Edgar had helped him find a masjid. "I'm not sure," he said.

"A whole bag of marshmallows," Gary declared.

The club members tittered. The elevator doors opened. Edgar staggered into the lobby, his hand over his stomach.

"Are you all right?" asked Miss Cutter.

Edgar forged a weak smile. "I'm just not used to fasting, that's all." He dropped onto one of the sofas. "Would it be okay if I stay in the room?"

"No," said Miss Cutter, concern gone, the folly of marshmallows surrendering to the practicality of breakfast. "You should eat something." She noticed the bulge in Edgar's pants pocket. "What do you have there?" she asked.

Edgar feinted to his empty pocket.

"No, the other one."

Miss Cutter held out her hand as Edgar dug out a pocketful of Milky Way miniatures. She dropped them into her purse. "If you can eat these, you can eat breakfast. I hope you weren't planning to cheat on your fast."

"It was in case I felt better this afternoon," Edgar interjected lamely.

"Because dishonesty is one thing I won't tolerate. I assume everyone here can be trusted to keep their promises."

Heads nodded, Mohammed's, too. Edgar said, "But what if I get the runs again?"

Miss Cutter replied, "Edgar, there are over one thousand public restrooms in this city, not all of them clean, not all of them safe, but you will always be near one of them."

Edgar grunted miserably.

Mohammed wondered if he really was sick or just looking for an excuse not to fast. Either way, Edgar better not complicate his plan.

Outside, the predawn sky clung to low, gunmetal clouds. The city smelled of something unearthed—like a damp cellar. The rain had stopped, but the wind refused to slacken. It tugged at Mohammed's Yankees cap and billowed Priscilla's raincoat. Everyone trudged head down. Edgar backed up Eighth Avenue with both hands on his stomach. "I think I'm gonna puke," he said. But inside the warm orange and brown decor of Howard Johnson's, he finished a bowl of apple oatmeal and two slices of toast with jam.

The club had divided into window booths. Mohammed sat with the boys. Priscilla, Edgar, and the Fuzz sat with Miss Cutter. The arrangement suited Mohammed. He could not have sat across from Priscilla Smith, not now, not without staring. She had winked at him in the lobby.

Teddy nudged Mohammed. "So what's the plan?" he whispered. "You had it fixed with the Pris, but Cutter shot that down. Where are you headed?"

"I'm going to visit a masjid near the hotel."

Teddy's eyes widened. "You're kidding?"

"Not kidding."

"A masjid? That's where they give massages, right?"

Mohammed swallowed his Corn Pops. "No, it's a mosque. I'm going there to pray."

"Oh," Teddy replied, looking disappointed. "I suppose it's better than waiting in the lobby."

Mohammed nodded, careful with his words. "We'll see," he said.

From their window booths the club watched early morning New Yorkers holding to their hats and skirt fronts in the windy canyon of Times Square.

"I'm afraid it's supposed to be like this all day," observed Miss Cutter. "If we're lucky it won't rain until tonight." She looked at her watch then out the window at the streetlight melting into daylight. "It's time," she said, sliding out of the booth. "We have much to see, and we must be back at the hotel by one to check out of our rooms."

They began with what Miss Cutter described as her favorite building, the city's oldest skyscraper: the Flatiron Building. "Isn't it simply dramatic?" she declared as they stopped to behold its narrow end and acutely angled corners. "Like the prow of a tall ship." She went on to describe how the construction of the Flatiron Building had provided New Yorkers with their first opportunity to view the erection of a steel-framed skyscraper and how many people had kept their distance, thinking it might topple over. "Don't you just love the energetic mix of Gothic and Renaissance styles?" she gushed.

As the club gazed at the limestone facade, Edgar suddenly cried, "Miss Cutter, I gotta go!"

Their adviser quickly disappeared inside the Flatiron Building in search of a restroom, tight-legged Edgar in tow. Left on the sidewalk, the club members stared after them.

"Now, *that's* dramatic," offered Gary simply.

Fuzzy Thornton observed, "I wonder if it will still be her favorite building when they come out."

And so it went that morning. Engineering interrupted by Edgar. At Madison Square Garden (where Miss Cutter elaborated on the unique roof design while Teddy scouted for Knicks players), Edgar tossed his oatmeal, toast, and jam. At Penn Station (where everyone gawked at Amtrak Metroliners as Miss Cutter described the *old* Penn Station and tunnel digging under the Hudson), Edgar bolted to the lavatory in the baggage area. When they took the Eighth Avenue Express to 181st Street, they had to make an emergency step-off at Columbus Circle so Edgar could find a restroom. By then it wasn't funny anymore, and not even Teddy made jokes. No one spoke of food. No one complained of hunger. Edgar's ordeal had upstaged fasting.

By eleven o'clock the club sat on the benches in Fort Washington Park gazing up at the latticed towers and the gleaming curves of the George Washington Bridge. Edgar lay limp on a bench, his eyes closed, as Miss Cutter expounded upon the bridge.

"First, people, notice the location," she began, pointing toward New Jersey. "The Palisades cliffs over there, Manhattan's highest ground here, the river at its narrowest. This combination allowed clearance for tall ships without costly approaches—an important consideration for the engineer who would build the first bridge across the Hudson."

"Ugh," groaned Edgar from his bench.

Mohammed stared at the river. In a few hours he would see this same gray water from the ferry.

"Does anyone remember the name of engineer?" asked Miss Cutter.

"That would be Othmar Ammann," answered Priscilla.

Their adviser nodded. "The father of twentieth-century American bridge design."

"Ooh…" moaned Edgar.

"Mr. Ammann," continued Miss Cutter, "brought a number of engineering innovations to this bridge. He decided the dead-weight of the deck and main cables was enough to resist sway in high winds. Then he eliminated the stiffening trusses. You see the result—a slender profile, pleasing to the eye. In short, a beautiful bridge—"

"Owheoooo."

Edgar had curled into a fetal position and was hugging himself.

"Are you all right?" Miss Cutter asked.

"Yeah."

She moved to the bench and knelt, touching his forehead.

"I didn't know marshmallows could do that," remarked the Fuzz.

"He's faking," said Teddy. "He wants Cutter to leave him back at the hotel."

Everyone stared at Edgar. Bernie said, "At least Hamed won't have to stay by himself."

"Yeah, Hamed, have fun."

Miss Cutter returned to the group. "I think it's time to return to the hotel," she said.

Edgar rose from the bench and walked to the 181st station under his own power. Back at the hotel Bernie was sent for bottled water. Miss Cutter took Mohammed aside in the lobby. "I'm afraid you'll have to stay with him," she said. "I don't feel right leaving him alone."

Mohammed nodded.

"I'm sorry about the mosque. I'll make it up to you somehow."

He replied, "No problem, Miss Cutter." And there was no problem. He hadn't planned to visit the mosque anyway. Edgar may have been willing to give up Ground Zero for the hotel, but he was not ready to give up Miss Liberty for Edgar.

When the YEPS departed for Lower Manhattan at 1:10 p.m., Mohammed was left with two pieces of paper: one from Miss Cutter with her cell phone number, the other a folded note from Priscilla. The latter had been slipped secretly into his hand during the bustle of checkout. It remained unread inside his Koran. While he waited for the club to get a head start—twenty minutes or so—he fingered the note between the pages. Nearby Edgar lay on one of the sofas.

"You got to read that every day?" he asked.

Already his voice suggested digestion was on the mend.

"Supposed to."

"Which means you don't."

Mohammed rose from the sofa. "I'm going to the restroom," he said.

"Not getting the runs, are you?" asked Edgar, sounding hopeful.

Mohammed locked himself in a restroom stall, opened his Koran, and fished out Priscilla's note. He examined it, turning it over, looking for—what was he looking for? Smudges of lip balm? The notebook paper was spotless. His neck hair tingled as he unfolded it. Two words were written inside, both in capitals. *DO IT.*

Mohammed stared. He turned the paper over. Was that it? What about last night?

The restroom door opened. "You all right in there?" It was Edgar.

Mohammed flushed. "I'm fine."

The door closed. *Do it?* Mohammed refolded the paper and put it in his pocket. At least she had written something—even if it wasn't warm, fuzzy, and coated with lip balm. Was it an attempt to inspire him? Did she think he would stay in the hotel?

The plan to see Miss Liberty was set. Time to roll the dice. But first, Edgar.

Edgar slouched on the sofa, chin on his chest. "Maybe I should eat something," he remarked feebly.

Mohammed checked his watch. One twenty. Miss Cutter would return after six. There was time to get Edgar food (wasn't the return of Edgar's appetite the one best sign he could be left alone?), but he should hurry.

"I'm staying away from junk food," Edgar was saying. "And I'm tired of burgers."

"How about soup?" suggested Mohammed.

"Naw. Maybe something from that deli down the street, something with meat. Turkey. Pastrami. Ham sounds good, too. And cheese. Swiss maybe."

This sounded like total remission. "Are you sure?"

Edgar dug into his pocket and pulled out money. "Yeah. A sandwich is what I need. With chips. Or fries." He handed Mohammed a fistful of bills. "You want something? It's on me."

Mohammed said, "I'm fasting."

"Oh, right." Edgar tried to look guilty. "Don't bring me anything to drink," he added. "I got water."

Mohammed let Edgar know the plan. "After I get your sandwich, I'm going to go visit the mosque, okay? The one you called about last night. Remember?"

Edgar relaxed. "Yeah, I remember. The Muslim place. You're gonna pray, right?"

He nodded.

Edgar reached for his bottled water. "Pray for my stomach."

Mohammed wanted to make sure Edgar had it right. "It'll take a few hours, washing and praying. So you know."

"Sure. I heard you the other night." Edgar sipped his water. "Does Cutter know?"

"I told her."

"Cool," said Edgar, sinking into the sofa.

Hanging from a ceiling crowded with sausages, netted hams, and a three-foot plastic pickle, the menu board at Bernstein's Deli offered omelets, salads, soups, sandwiches, sides, combos, and cold cuts. His first time in a delicatessen, Mohammed felt like a Martian at Starbucks. He took in the narrow, congested confines and wondered how so much food could fit into so little space. As he navigated the menu in search of turkey and Swiss, he lingered on oddities. Sturgeon. Gefilte fish. Potato knishes. Latkes. Why hadn't Edgar asked for a burger?

"Orda, please," said a white-aproned youth behind the counter.

Mohammed hesitated. "A sandwich," he began. "Something with turkey."

The youth waited, serious but not surly. Mohammed noticed he was dark featured like himself. Bushy brows. Black hair. Could he be Arab? Mexican maybe? His name was embroidered on his apron: Menachem. That wasn't Arab. Definitely not Mexican. Menachem? What kind of name was that? Mohammed stared at the menu board, trying not to look lost.

The youth said, "Overwhelming, isn't it?" He pointed to the board. "My father keeps half that stuff up there because he says it wouldn't be kosher otherwise. You know fathers." He rolled his eyes. Mohammed nodded. Fathers, yes, he knew. But *kosher*? He had heard the word before.

"Try the Woody Allen," offered Menachem, friendly now. "Your choice of three meats with Swiss, American, or muenster on white, wheat, pumpernickel, or sourdough."

Mohammed felt less like a Martian. "Then make that turkey, pastrami, and ham. With Swiss. On white. And some chips."

Menachem hit the cash register keys, calling "HTP Pistol" to a dim figure in the back. Was it his father? Mohammed pulled Edgar's money from his pocket and paid.

"Horseradish on that?" asked the youth.

"Sure." Add horseradish, whatever that was. Add it to sturgeon, kosher, and everything else that sounded foreign. Add it to Menachem.

When the youth disappeared into the back, Mohammed checked his watch. One thirty-three. Precious minutes—all for Edgar. He surveyed the sausages and hams. *A lot of forbidden foods here,* he thought. Plenty that were doubtful, too. But all of them smelled good.

His gaze lit on the back of the cash register. Taped there was a photo of the World Trade Center taken on a cloudless day, sunlight glinting off the steel towers. "God Bless America" read the large print below the picture. Mohammed stared. The sky was so blue, the steel so bright. *Would God bless America?* he wondered. He checked his watch again. The club should be arriving at Ground Zero, getting in line to see what was left. No blue sky today.

He turned to the street front, his eyes wandering over jars of tiny headless fish and an illuminated pretzel. Then he spotted something familiar—a bust of Miss Liberty, shoe box size, facing the window. She was green and plastic, like the three-foot pickle. Mohammed was cheered by finding her in this unexpected corner. Amid so many oddities, in such crowded confines, she could easily have been overlooked.

The youth returned. He handed over a warm brown paper bag. "Supposed to rain again," he said, nodding toward the gray street.

"I hope not," Mohammed replied.

Menachem nodded. "Me, too. As the old ones say, bad weather makes bad business."

It sounded like something Delmar would say. Mohammed thanked him, then left, thinking, "Funny guy, but nice."

Edgar perked up at the sight of lunch. "I feel almost hungry," he said, licking his lips.

Mohammed handed over the bag, no qualms now about leaving Edgar alone. The miraculous recovery had occurred. "Remember. I'll be out three hours or so, okay?"

"Yeah, yeah. Have a good pray." Edgar unwrapped the Woody Allen, sniffing closely. "Horseradish? Oh man! I love horseradish!"

On the street Mohammed glanced at the sky. The gray scudding clouds were so low they seemed to graze the building tops. The cold wind felt wet but no drops fell. *Just three hours,* he told himself, not daring to make it sound like a supplication. *Just hold for three hours.*

He was on his own now, his dream the only compass. He turned south on Eighth Avenue, walking briskly at first, then running with the wind, his camera and Koran jumping in his jacket. By Times Square he was energized, his reservations fading. He was doing it. At the Forty-Second Street station, the Broadway local to Whitehall pulled in just as he ran onto the platform, the opening of its doors synchronizing perfectly with his arrival. Luck seemed to be with him.

THE SAVING OF
MISS LIBERTY

Until that afternoon the closest Mohammed had been to the sea was the Maviri beach in Topolobampo, Mexico, where his mother had let him wet his feet in the blue-green water of the Sea of Cortez. He had been four at the time. He had never boarded a boat, never ridden a ferry. So when he departed on the *Alice Austen* from slip number four at the Whitehall Terminal, Mohammed felt an exhilaration so sudden and overwhelming that he wanted to drop to his knees and praise Allah on the spot. He was sure the biggest adventure of his life had begun. Any misgivings about leaving Edgar, about disobeying Miss Cutter, about mocking the promise of prayer were swept overboard at a salty sixteen knots. He took a window seat on the main deck, Jersey side, and got out his Kodak to check the film counter. He had saved half the roll for this.

On the bench behind him two men talked, their words spilling over.

"And the thing is, when they do it again, they're not going to use airplanes. I mean, these guys aren't dumb. They'll come up with something new."

"Like sink a ferry?"

"Exactly. Remember that one in the Baltic? What was it's name? One of those satellite countries. Estonia? Yeah, it was the *Estonia*. Like nine hundred went down. One ferry."

"But that wasn't a bomb."

"No, the stupid door came off. Still, we're talking a major loss of life here. Ferries carry more passengers than airplanes. All I'm saying is there should be more security."

Mohammed stared out the window, remembering the sign he had seen at the terminal entrance: "Vehicles Prohibited on Ferry Until Further Notice."

"You know the Coast Guard says a ferry attack is not that unlikely. It could be modeled after one of those suicide bombings, the kind the Palestinians do on Israeli buses."

Mohammed looked around for another window seat. Did he really want to hear this on his way to see Miss Liberty?

"On a day like today, for example, when the windows are closed. Lethal combo, man. The explosive pressure from those shock waves tear things up."

"I've heard."

"Then you've got shrapnel, fire, kids, a bunch of injured overboard who can't swim. Terrorists know these things. Even if she doesn't sink, you've got serious numbers."

Mohammed listened.

"I could be sitting here with twenty pounds of explosives under my coat, and they would never know it. I wait until we're in the harbor. I look around. I smile—a suicide bomber always smiles, you know, just before he detonates. It's the smile of joy at impending martyrdom or something. Then I activate my bomb. *Boom!*"

"Jesus!"

Mohammed stood, having spied the stairway to the upper deck. It was time for some fresh air, a better view. As he turned, he noticed the men's white shirts and ties peeping above the collars of their top coats; hands on briefcases, briefcases on laps. *Commuters*, thought Mohammed. *Nervous commuters.*

On the upper deck he stood by the railing, the only passenger outside. No one else seemed willing to brave a raw November wind and the possibility of rain. For Mohammed it was perfect. He had Miss Liberty to himself. Already his eyes had jumped ahead, skipping Ellis Island, locking on her distant silhouette. The low clouds appeared to lift as they passed her. He felt a rush of excitement. This was it.

Stray raindrops splotched his jacket and hands. His gaze dropped to the sea. It was gray like the day, like the sky, like the leaden waterfront of Brooklyn and the abandoned shores of Governors Island. Everything was gray. Everything but the ferry. The ferry was orange—a vibrant, municipal orange. Mohammed remembered why. Years before, on another gray November morning, the fog had not lifted from the Upper Bay when the *American Legion* returned from St. George, motoring in poor visibility. The pilot steered the ferry north, unaware that he was drifting west of the channel toward the Jersey shore. He motored blindly, confident in his navigational aids, until he brought the ferry crashing into the seawall of Liberty Island south of the boat dock. The impact—at full-service speed—sent shock waves through the island. National Park Service employees on the ground and tourists in the crown reported that Miss Liberty shuddered, then swayed. Scores on the boat were injured; an inquiry was held, recommendations were made. There had been other incidents—collisions with docks and freighters. That year all Staten Island Ferries had been painted orange.

Mohammed looked ahead, trying to imagine the *Alice Austen* running into Liberty Island at full speed. Would the impact shake the statue? Had Bartholdi considered the possibility? Had Eiffel engineered for it? And who was Alice Austen?

He checked his watch Two twenty. On schedule. He thumbed the winder sprocket on his camera. Ready. When he looked up, the *Alice Austen* was turning south. *How odd*, he thought. He watched Liberty Island veer off their heading. The ferry angled away. The distance between the island and the boat suddenly widened. He squinted, picking out the tiny figures of men moving across the monument's lawns. They couldn't be visitors. Who were they? He pressed his eye to the camera's viewfinder, but the lens only made everything appear farther away.

The statue receded. In moments she was a hazy silhouette—something tall rising from a heap of gray stone—falling behind them at sixteen knots. The *Alice Austen* returned to the main channel, aligning itself east of Robbins Reef Light Station.

Mohammed stared at where Liberty's gray figure joined the gray sky to the gray water. He had not snapped a single picture.

He gazed at a container ship trimming its wide bulk into the tidal strait of Kill Van Kull. Had he just taken a ferry ride for nothing? Was there any reason to believe the return leg would offer a better view?

He checked his watch. No delays. No rain. Perfect—except for the view. If he had gone with the club to Ground Zero, at least he would have *seen* something.

When the ferry docked, he abandoned the hurricane deck for a window-side bench, where he sat on the return leg, his face close to the glass. As the island came into view again, he shielded his eyes from the florescent glare overhead, watching her distant figure take shape. Just as the ferry seemed headed for her, it steered away.

"You need *binocolo*," said a voice.

Across from him sat a tiny man dressed in a topcoat. A bow tie peeked out at his collar. On his head sat a tweed fedora.

Mohammed nodded. Binoculars would have been good. *Binocolo,* too. He remembered the pair Miss Cutter carried in her purse. "I thought it got closer," he said.

The tiny man smiled. "Used to get close, but no more. Since September you can't see her eyes."

Mohammed turned back to the window. The statue remained a shadowy silhouette. Would this be his last look?

"I see her first time in 1933," continued the little man. "Very close. Ship get close so everybody could see. My father held me up. Everybody pushing. Everybody smell. Twenty days from Napoli. *Che barba!* I remember the smell. But I saw her very close. She looked like a *gigante.* I was ten. I remember my mother cried. I thought she was afraid. The statue too big and we small. Later I knew why she cried." He nodded to himself. "But ships don't get close now. Everybody afraid."

Mohammed made out the men on the monument lawns. He pointed. "Mister, do you know who they are, the men on the island?"

The passenger stared beyond the glass. Mohammed wondered if he could see that far.

"Them? Men working. I see every day, trying to keep secret."

Mohammed gave him a puzzled look. "Are they police?"

The hat bobbed. "Them, too. Everybody working. Big secret, but everybody know. I know." He shrugged his bony shoulders as if to say it couldn't possibly be a secret if he knew. "My son-in-law tell me. He Coast Guard lieutenant. He say they fixing for torrists."

"Tourists?"

"*Terroristi* who took planes, killed the people."

"Terrorists."

"Yes, them. What if they blow up statue, eh? My son-in-law tell me. He Coast Guard. The men put wires and guns, make safe."

Mohammed nodded. The next question came easily. "Do you know how they get out there?"

"Boats," replied the man. "Crew boats or something. Men coming, going. I see every day."

Mohammed gazed at the gray water. Of course, boats. He pulled the camera from his pocket. "The thing is, I wanted to get pictures. That's why I took the ferry. But tonight I have to go back to Ohio, so I don't know when I'll have a chance to get them again."

"Ohio?" said the tiny man. "You lucky you live there. Clean sky."

His watch said three twenty. Out the window Mohammed took in the fading day. It was a crazy idea. Maybe a stupid idea. Still, there was time. "If I went to one of those boats," he asked, "do you think they would let me ride out to the island and back? To take my pictures?"

The little man shrugged. "You ask," he chirped. "Maybe yes. Maybe no. Always coming, going. You look like good boy."

Good? Well, mostly. He checked his watch again. Ten minutes to Whitehall. Twenty to the hotel. That left two hours. "Do you know where the boats leave from?" he asked.

"*Naturalmente!*" replied the old man. "I see every day coming, going. See everything—boats, dirty sky. I see planes hit towers. Everything." He shook his head. "*Terrible.* You see?"

"On the television," Mohammed answered.

"How I cry. Like my mother when she see the statue, I cry. I afraid, too."

Mohammed said nothing. What could he say? What could anyone say?

"So you visit New York?"

"Yes, sir."

The tiny man nodded. "You polite boy. Kids no polite now. My father make me polite. *Si, signore. No, signore.* I no forget."

"My father is very strict."

"Good. Best father strict. What your name?"

When Mohammed gave his name, the little man's eyes brightened. "Ah, nice name."

"My mother is Mexican."

"Ah, *Messicano!* I am Fred. Frederico. My mother dead. She from Salerno. You know *Italia*?"

Mohammed shook his head.

"Okay, no problem," he said, sitting straighter. "You listen, Mohammed *il Messicano*. For boats you go to Pier 11."

"Pier 11?"

"Yes. You know?"

"I think so. The crew boats leave there?"

"*Buono.* South Street, *si*? You walk. Son-in-law tell me. He Coast Guard."

"Okay."

"Ohio boy. Maybe you lucky."

"I hope so."

The old man placed a shriveled hand on his arm. "Everybody coming to cry, to see mess. You come to see statue. That good."

"Thank you. *Gracias*," he replied, his Spanish slipping in.

"*Ah, grazie si. Un messicano da Ohio.* Very good. You know my brothers, they make *la statua*?"

"Your brothers made the Statue of Liberty?"

He shook his head. "No, no. They help make. Men from *Italia*."

Mohammed nodded, remembering that he had read about the Italian immigrants who had built the pedestal.

The little man leaned in, his bony shoulder rubbing Mohammed's arm. "Get close. See her eyes." His own glistened as he smiled.

"I'll try," Mohammed said.

At Pier 11, ferries departed for Hoboken, Belford, Port Liberte, and Port Imperial. Schedule boards announced water taxis leaving for Paulus Hook, Red Hook, the Brooklyn Army Terminal, and Hunter's Point. Mohammed stared at the bustle. Where were the crew boats to Liberty Island? He asked two strangers. Neither knew. He inquired at a ticket booth. The girl behind the glass shrugged.

The more thought he gave it, the crazier the idea seemed. Even if he found a crew boat, what business did he have asking for a ride? The monument was closed. He was a kid. No way would they agree.

Near the entrance he spotted a man with "Port Authority" on his jacket. Should he ask him? Mohammed recalled the soldiers on the bridge. Did he want to risk that again?

Do you want to see Miss Liberty?

His watch said three fifty-five. He pushed the Kodak into his pocket and approached.

"Sure," replied the Port Authority man after Mohammed asked if this was where the crew boats departed for Liberty Island. "It's the *USPP* docked at the end."

No questions. No funny stare. Mohammed wondered if his looks made him appear old enough to be one of the crew. "Thank you, sir," he said.

At the end of the pier, he found the boat moored by itself. It was bus-size craft with a frowning pilothouse and sooty smokestacks. A rusted derrick rose above the cargo of wooden crates, metal drums, and spools of wire.

Mohammed saw no one on deck. He straightened his Yankees cap and walked the length of the boat, stopping even with the stern. He listened. The mooring lines stretched as the *USPP* shifted in the wind. *What an odd name for a boat*, he thought.

He stepped onto the deck. Derrick chains jinked. The boat creaked. "Hello!" he called. His watch said four ten. He waited, but no one appeared.

Adjacent to the pilothouse stood a long windowless room with swing doors at the end. He nudged one door open. "Hello?" Inside the room were rows of wooden benches—enough to seat several dozen men—the crew part of the crew boat. A stairway rose steeply through an opening in the roof. Mohammed moved past the benches and peered into the opening. He saw a room with controls and electronic equipment. "Hello." When no one answered, he returned to the deck.

He waited. Had the boat just returned from the island? Had the crew gone home? He listened. Shouldn't there be somebody on duty?

"Hello!"

A clanging noise answered. Mohammed cocked his head. The sound came from beneath him. Then it sounded it again.

He edged past the cargo of crates and drums to the back of the boat. At the stern stairway, he stopped to peer down the steps. The smell of diesel rose from below. A wave of warmth washed over him. This was the engine room.

"Hello!"

The clanging resumed, loud now. It was a sound Mohammed recognized: man striking metal.

"Hello down there!"

Whoever was banging probably couldn't hear him. Emboldened by this conjecture, he took a step down. The stairs were steep. His eyes adjusted to the engine room's dim light. "Hello!"

Clang, clang, clang.

He took another step. The smell of fuel and lubricants—familiar scents from Ahmed Automotive—filled his nostrils. He shifted uneasily. This was not the same as standing on the deck. He was inside the *USPP,* out of sight. What was the name for someone who hid in a boat?

Something emptied from his legs. Was it boldness? His knees felt wobbly. A dream might be a fine excuse for daring, but it was dark down here. The clanging sounded angry.

"Is anyone here?" he yelled.

He felt the corrugated ridges of the stairway steps. Near his head, pipes hissed. He peered into the engine room's dimly lit confines. He saw no one. The clanging continued, its cadence measured. It sounded less like someone hammering and more like *something* hammering.

"Hello!"

When he started to back up the steps, the clanging stopped. He paused, the silence loud, the clang still echoing. Then the motor started—its low diesel rumble abruptly becoming a loud combustion roar. The steps shook. Engine exhaust vented up the stairwell. Suddenly the boat lurched, and Mohammed fell backward, his footing lost. He slid down the steep steps and into the engine room, the roar of the motor filling his head.

His thoughts raced. *I'm on a boat; the boat is moving. I'm on a boat; the boat is…*

He had landed on the lowest step, his legs outstretched. Nothing hurt. The stairway rose behind him. He scrambled to his feet and grabbed the railing. The boat rolled.

I'm on a…

He ascended the steps, slipping twice. When he reached the top, he hesitated. The pier was too far to jump. He looked at the choppy water, debating a plunge. He could swim it, but that was only the beginning. The pier was high. He saw no ladders. How would he get out of the water?

Heartbeats passed. He ducked back into the stairway. *Allah save me.* What should he do? The roar of the engine wouldn't let him think. The boat sped up. His first urge was to make himself known. They were close enough to turn back. He started up the stairway, then stopped. Would they call the police? He held his breath, trying to think. What if he was arrested? Suddenly the word came to him—that name for someone who hid in a boat, what he had become—a stowaway! Weren't stowaways arrested?

For a moment he wished he was back at the hotel lobby with Edgar or praying in the little room behind the front desk, dutifully mindful of Ramadan and fasting, devotion, and self-denial. But he wasn't at the hotel. He was a stowaway on a boat called *USPP.*

He waited. *Maybe they wouldn't find me,* he thought. *Maybe they wouldn't even look. Maybe they would stay busy driving the boat.*

Surely the *USPP* would return to the dock. It had to. It was a crew boat. *Always coming, going.* Still, what if he was found?

The roll of the boat grew more pronounced. The motor roar filled the stairway. He lifted his head above deck and peeked beyond the stern. The East River water churned white behind them. Between crates and wire spools, he glimpsed the low gray tip of Manhattan. No going back now. He sank back into the stairway and waited. The smell of diesel was strong. The fumes burned his throat. He waved at them with his cap. His stomach felt strange, his head light. Was it the roll of the boat? He lifted his head again to gulp air, suddenly nauseous. But there was nothing to throw up from a fasting stomach. Almost nothing. He heaved a guttural groan, regurgitating a dribble of something yellowish and runny. It hung from his lips before dropping onto his sneaker. He remembered Edgar tossing his breakfast at Madison Square Garden that morning. They were inseparable even in sickness.

He listened for voices. Caution was necessary but escape was imperative. The stairway had become a stowaway hell. He felt another heave coming. His head swam. The diesel fumes stung his eyes. He staggered out of the stairway and into the open. Adjacent to the engine-room door stood a pyramid of stacked metal barrels. Edging himself sideways between two barrels, he found a space wide enough to sit, a narrow den. He drew his feet beneath him, making himself small. He lifted his face, letting the cold, sea-scented wind wash over him, waiting for the nausea to pass. Had he been spotted? The boat hadn't stopped. The only sounds he heard were the engine hum, the splash of waves, and the wind. It whistled through the drums, drawing a strangely sepulchral resonation from the containers—the baritone song of drums keeping his secret.

The deck of *USPP* rolled beneath him. His stomach settled. His head cleared. If only he had something to wash the yellow runny stomach flavor from his mouth. He stared at a small piece of sky above the drums, watching for a head to appear, a pair of eyes peeking down from the top of the pyramid. But only gray clouds hovered above him. The overcast sky seemed full of Ohio and home—dreary days, a cloudy future. He reminded himself that today was Saturday. The second day of fasting was almost over. His mother would be preparing supper. His father would be closing the station, heading home to make his Ramadan prayers. What a shock it would be if they knew that their only son was a stowaway on a crew boat motoring through the choppy waters of New York Harbor on its way to Liberty Island, miles from Miss Cutter and the club.

They would never understand.

He sat perfectly still. His legs grew numb. The gray afternoon grew grayer. He checked his watch. Four thirty. How long had they been motoring? Fifteen minutes? The trip shouldn't take more than twenty—unless the *USPP* wasn't going to Liberty Island, a possibility that had not occurred to him until now. What would he do if the boat docked somewhere else?

He peered between the containers, searching for a landmark, seeing only the sea. The wind whistled through the drums. The minutes passed. He checked his watch again. Four thirty-five. Soon enough he would know. He unknotted his legs and stood, the numbness replaced by the prick of needles as blood rushed into his feet. He waited. Four forty. No sight of land. Then abruptly the sound of the motor shifted. The *USPP* throttled back.

Mohammed heard the crash and hiss of waves. The boat began to pitch and yaw. Drums clanged against one another. The motor revved, then throttled, then revved again. Someone shouted—the first voice he had heard on the boat. The *USPP* heaved—as though to elude the grasp of men—then settled and suddenly became still. The engine went quiet.

Minutes passed. Nothing stirred. Mohammed listened to the swash of waves. Were they on Liberty Island?

He heard no voices. He surveyed the wedge of boat deck visible between the drums. Beyond it he saw only gray sky. No one was in sight. Had the crew left? Or were they in the pilothouse? What if they unloaded the cargo and discovered him? He edged through the gap, casting a quick look at the horizon before he darted into the stairway of the engine room. Diesel fumes hit him—stowaway hell again—but he didn't care. *He had seen her.* He had glimpsed Miss Liberty above the trees. He was here.

Something electric raced through him. *Yes!*

From the engine room rose the thermal murmurs of hot metal cooling. Still no voices. Was the dock deserted? His watch said four fifty-five. He felt the bulge of the camera in his pocket. Five o'clock was quitting time. Had the *USPP* come to pick up the men he had seen on the lawns?

He pulled the camera from his jacket and checked the frame counter. Twelve shots left. But he didn't have to take all of them. He climbed the stairway and stepped around the cargo, lifting the Kodak. There she was, so tall. He brought the viewfinder to his eye, click, wind, click again. Back in the stairway, he let out his breath. He had them. Two pictures of Miss Liberty from the rear! Two photos of her *backside*!

The wind seemed to laugh. *What do you expect?* he told himself. *You're at the boat dock.*

He peered above the stairwell. Still no sign of a crew. He saw the dock and the arrival promenade. No one approached. Should he settle for two shots of Miss Liberty's backside?

He turned his gaze to the seawall extending along the southwestern shore. The best spot to take pictures was from the pedestal lawn, just beyond the trees. It meant getting off the boat. It meant leaving the dock.

He checked his watch. Five ten. Quitting time and then some. Men should appear at any moment. He watched the promenade. Nothing. Unless they quit at six.

The pilothouse door stood ajar. A beacon flashed on the derrick. Someone was around. But where were the workers he had seen? If they quit at six, he would not arrive at the hotel before seven—after the club returned. Miss Cutter would be waiting. Something better than prayer would have to explain his absence. He eyeballed the distance to the pedestal lawn. *If...*he were to take more pictures he would have to drop to the rocks, advance along the seawall, snap a few shots, then hurry back.

He surveyed the empty promenade and the vacant lawns beyond the leafless cherry trees. *Strange.* Liberty Island looked deserted.

Five twenty. Precious minutes wasted. To think his father had bought him a watch to check prayer times. He waited, listening to the wind. Five twenty-five. A voice in his head said, *Okay. Be timid. Don't take a chance.* Was it the goading whisper of a jinni, one of the hidden thought speakers?

No one moved on the dock. The boat seemed to hold its breath. Daylight was fading. Stray drops of rain hit his face and hands. He knew it was now or never. Sit tight or gamble. Take regret—or take photos—back to Ohio. He checked the grounds again. This must be a sign. Was Miss Liberty inviting him to come? Did dreams have that kind of power?

Allah is greater, he told himself as he slipped the camera into his jacket. He left the stairway and strode across the deck. In one jump he was on the dock.

No voice hailed him. No siren sounded. *Go,* said a voice. *Go!*

He left the dock, rounded the railing, then dropped from the seawall to the apron of rocks below. He stopped long enough to push his Koran and the camera deep into their pockets. Then he began hopping rocks, keeping close to the wall, moving toward the pedestal lawn.

The rocks were large, sea-stopping rocks, and he was glad they were dry. A slip meant trouble. To his left he saw Miss Liberty soaring above the island—bigger than her pictures, colossal and cloud scraping. Everything in her pose suggested steel sturdiness and an unbending strength.

The wind pressed him forward. Where the seawall turned east, he stopped to balance on a rock, glancing back at the dock. It was empty, the *USPP* a ghost ship. Five minutes. Five and back to the boat. Then he would pray. He jumped to the next rock, then another, keeping close to the wall, his thoughts jumping, too. Edgar at the hotel. The club at Ground Zero. A tartan flannel nightgown. *"Kiss me, Mohammed. Kiss me for luck."*

Then his foot missed a rock, his shin finding the sharp edge of it, white pain shooting up his leg. When he reached out to break his fall, his hands met the razor-edged shell stubble encrusting the rocks. He bit a cry out of the air, yanking himself off the needle-sharp shells. He got to his feet and looked at his hands. They were crisscrossed with tiny cuts. *No, no, no...* He wanted them to disappear. He looked down at his leg. Blood seeped through his torn pants. *Allah forgive!* He raised the cuff. A bright red gash grinned across his shin. Not deep enough for stitches, but what did it matter? He pulled up his sock top, letting it press on the gash. Cut hands, ripped pants. What would he tell Miss Cutter?

He lifted himself back onto the rocks, feeling for the camera and Koran in their pockets. He looked toward the dock and the *USPP.* Both were deserted. There was time if he hurried.

He jumped one rock, balancing carefully before jumping to the next. His shin throbbed. His palms felt hot. Already he had passed the fort's first bastion. Raindrops spattered his cap and jacket. In another fifty feet he would be clear of the trees and standing beside her. *"See her eyes,"* the tiny man had said.

He focused on the rocks, blocking out the wind and the sea. No more slips. He let everything fall away—his cut hands, his bleeding shin, a pounding heart, his hurried breath. As he leaped from rock to rock, time itself seemed to drop away. Then the trees were gone, and he was standing at the edge of the seawall, nothing obstructing his view. His gaze followed the battered walls of the fort upward past the granite facade of the pedestal to the figure towering above him. Finally she filled the sky.

The sight of her stole his breath. Not even in his dreams—not when he had climbed inside her, not when he had clung to the swaying platform of her torch—had he imagined such an imposing height. She was immense. She was commanding. She looked unassailable. Like a pilgrim before a shrine, he stared awestruck, reverent, drinking her in, a statue himself. Rain hit his face. The wind whistled. *"See her eyes."*

To see them he would have to move closer. He scanned the dock. Empty. No one moved on the *USPP*. As long as he didn't lose sight of the boat. As long as he hurried. He advanced across the rocks. Miss Liberty stood in profile now. He made out the darkened observation windows in her crown, the straight line of her nose. But her eyes remained in shadow.

The rain fell harder. He hesitated. Wasn't this far enough for a prayerless kid from Ohio? Shouldn't he take his pictures and turn back? He leaped to the next rock, paused, then leaped once more, the last. He balanced in the wind and gazed skyward. Finally he saw her eyes.

He knew the tiny man was right. There was something in those eyes, something behind the stern look of cold command. He had seen it in his dream. For a moment the gray day fell away and he was alone with her again, the rain and the wind real. He stood wet and dripping, freshly saved from the sea. It was night, and he was standing where she had put him down, her face near his, her lips smiling, her eyes looking into his own.

He lifted his camera. This was it, what he had come for, what had brought him to her feet. Connection. He clicked off shot after shot, some with the camera turned on its end—the statue filling the frames—snapshots of moment as much as place. He turned to survey the pier and boat—both deserted—and when he looked back, something happened. Their eyes *met.*

Somehow she was looking down, looking straight at him—or so it seemed. He blinked and shook himself. When he looked again, Miss Liberty's gaze commanded the harbor once more. The gray clouds shifted. The wind tugged at his cap. He stared, bewildered by the moment. Had fasting made him light-headed? Had the rain altered appearances?

When he checked the pier, he saw men approaching the *USPP*.

He hurried, jumping from rock to rock, the wall of the perimeter path his cover. Men boarded the *USPP*. Others moved along the dock. Mohammed's thoughts raced like his heart. How would he slip unseen past so many? What should he do if the boat started to leave? Why hadn't he thought of this before?

The rain thickened. The fort and monument disappeared; only rocks were ahead. With each jump came hesitation. Stealth and haste balanced on the edge of slippery granite. The *USPP* became a boat behind frosted glass. The crew were shadows in the teeming rain. Mohammed followed the perimeter path to his right, guided by the barrier wall. Half a soccer field to go, maybe less. With luck—no, with the help of Allah—anyone who saw him now might mistake him for another wet worker running to catch the boat. He just had to get there.

Something dark billowed above the *USPP*—a shadow rising from a shadow. Mohammed teetered on a rock. Then he heard the roar—a sound stuck in his head from an hour before. The *USPP*'s engine had started. The shadow above the boat was smoke.

The cries of men were delivered on the wind. Gray figures scurried on the deck. Smoke blended into rain. The *USPP* was departing. Mohammed stared, but only for an instant, panic propelling him forward. No way was he going to be left behind. *No way.*

He scrambled to the barrier wall and lifted himself over. No need for stealth now. He needed to be seen. The next moment he was on the perimeter path, running in the open toward the dock, frantically waving his hands over his head.

The pain in his shin didn't slow him. "Stop! Please stop!" he shouted with everything in his throat. "Turn back!" When he reached the arrival promenade, he wheeled onto the dock. The *USPP* continued to motor. "Stop! Stop!" Several men moved on the deck—one near the stern paused as if to listen, but he didn't look back. Mohammed turned his wild waves into terrorized jumping jacks. "Please come back!" he shouted, but the wind and pounding rain hammered his words out of the air. The *USPP* slipped from view—first a gray silhouette, then a pale ghost. Finally, like a breath in the fog, she was gone.

Rain fell in sheets. The Jersey shore evaporated. So did the harbor. He stood motionless, his voice emptied of panic and shouting. "Come back," he whispered. "Turn around."

Please…

He shouldn't have lingered on the rocks. He shouldn't have left the *USPP*. He shouldn't have boarded her in the first place. He shouldn't have missed prayer.

The dream had turned into a nightmare, and the nightmare was suddenly as large and frightening as the storm. What to do now? Where to go? How to get back? Stranded had never been part of the plan.

He wiped his watch. Six after six. Within the hour the club would return to the hotel. He needed a miracle. He needed a Jet Ski with keys, a full tank of gas, and instructions on how to drive a Jet Ski. He needed a water taxi to swing in low and pick him up. He needed help.

His gaze turned east, toward the buildings. Head there, he decided. Knock on doors, turn himself in, explain everything. Maybe they would radio the *USPP* to come back.

He ran down the arrival promenade. Surely a park policeman would challenge him. But no uniform appeared. A sign on the promenade read:

THE NATIONAL PARK SERVICE
WELCOMES YOU TO
STATUE OF LIBERTY
NATIONAL MONUMENT

Welcome was good. But what he needed was deliverance.

He followed the arrows, hurrying to the main door of the visitors' center, knocking loudly. No one answered. He pounded with both fists. He tried the handles. Locked. If the island was closed to visitors, why would the visitors' center be open? Beneath a driving rain, he hastened to the dining concession area, where he found the entrance secured with a chain and padlock. He peered through the darkened panes, hoping for a surprise. He found none. Chairs were turned upside down on tables. Serving windows were boarded. It had the winter look of the Dairy Queen down the highway from his father's station.

He recrossed the promenade, detouring north to inspect a gated area with tractors and grass-cutting equipment. Under an adjacent roof he spied the same wooden crates, wire spools, and metal drums that had concealed him on the *USPP*. "Hello!" he yelled into the rain. No answer. He cut behind an open-sided shed, rain cascading off its roof, two jeeps parked there, both dry.

"Can anyone hear me?"

Daylight faded. Soon it would be dark. He needed to find someone. He needed to turn himself in, call Miss Cutter, and get to the bus station.

He entered the residential area. "Anybody here?" he called through cupped hands. An unlatched screen door swung on squeaky hinges. The seats of a swing set pendulated with invisible swingers. Every window was dark. Every door he tried was bolted. He approached a building with tall antennae on its roof. Was this the administration building? He tried the door. Locked. He pummeled the door. Nothing. He took a coin from his pocket and rapped sharply on a window. No answer. He shouted, "Please, somebody, open up!"

The rain roared. The wind shrilled in the trees. Where were the park police? Who was protecting Miss Liberty? Who was getting him home? "Please, somebody answer!"

But no one did. He was alone. Or so it seemed.

He returned to the dock. If another boat arrived, he needed to be there to catch it. The wind propelled him down the arrival promenade, his jacket a sail, his legs trying to keep up. When he reached the abutment, he abruptly halted. The face of the sea had changed. Steel waves taller than a man clawed at the dock. The abutment shuddered. And the rocks—the ones jumped an hour before—they had disappeared beneath a churning surf that reached the barrier wall, its onslaught white and thunderous. Mohammed backed off the pier. The sky and the sea had become one, no line between them. He peered through the fading daylight. Minutes ticked off his watch. He looked toward New Jersey. Nothing. The rain drilled the dock. No boat would tie up, he realized. Not in this sea.

He retreated up the promenade, muscling the wind. Broken branches littered the lawns. The cherry trees tossed their naked limbs in violent flurries. He made another round of the complex, trying doors again, calling out, and peering through windows before he circled back to the administration building. Rain pounded the roofs. The wind howled in the oaks. He pulled his Yankees cap tighter on his head and stared into the gathering dusk. No boat. No police. No one had found him. Was it possible he was alone? There was one place he hadn't checked.

He headed for the monument.

Her figure rose like a colossal specter in the darkening sky, a shadow cast by something larger. She looked borrowed from a dream.

He followed the promenade east to the flagpole circle, where the boundary hedges waved madly from side to side. He saw trees upended, shrubbery flattened, and signs knocked over. The roar of the surf was close. The wind tore at his jacket and cap. The rain beat down his gaze.

On the central mall the water reached his knees. *This had to be the sea.* He approached the fort entrance conspicuously, wanting to be seen. He pulled his hands from his pockets. Didn't the police always want to see your hands? Surely the guard had a gun.

Yards from the stairway, he stopped and cupped his hands. "Hello!" No one stepped out to challenge him. He inched closer. The fort wall blunted the wind. Above him the pedestal eclipsed the sky like a giant umbrella deflecting the rain. "Can somebody help me?"

He ascended the west steps and paused on the landing. "Hello!" A illuminated alcove opened into the rusticated stone wall of the fort. At the rear of the recess stood a pair of large double doors—the centennial doors—the main entrance. He called out again. "Is anyone here?"

The alcove was empty, the doors unguarded. *Surely there are cameras,* he thought. *Surely this is the one door on the island I can't touch without triggering an alarm.*

He entered the recess and stepped to the centennial doors, where he pushed purposefully on the decorative bronze panels. He pulled the handles. Nothing happened. The recess was well lit, but he saw no cameras. He observed a keypad with a LCD screen mounted on the wall. He pummeled the doors hard with both hands and then yanked the handles again.

He waited, imagining an alarm brought to life in a command post somewhere. The storm raged beyond the walls. Five minutes passed. Ten. He listened for the wail of sirens, but he heard only the rain. He stepped to the edge of the landing to survey the central mall and beyond. No flashing lights. No vehicles. Just rain and wind. A flood.

Something was dreadfully wrong. For the last hour he had trespassed on the grounds of a national monument closed to the public, a monument two miles from the tip of Manhattan. He had pounded doors. He had screamed like a maniac. Now he was standing at her unguarded entrance. It was beyond weird. It was creepy. No, it was scary. Scary not because he was alone. Scary because Miss Liberty was alone. He had a national treasure to himself. He could climb her. He could desecrate and vandalize. Or worse. He could plant a bomb, blow her to pieces, topple her into the harbor—the wind his only witness.

It appeared for the moment that she was in *his* custody.

When the statue's flood lamps lit, drenching the entrance with brightness, Mohammed took it for rescue. He rushed to the landing to make himself seen. Moments passed before he realized the illumination came from ground lighting on a timer. The central mall remained deserted, its flooded paving stones tinged green with statue-reflected luminosity beaten by the silver rain.

He checked his watch. Five after seven. The club was back at the hotel. By now Miss Cutter had interrogated Edgar. Next she would get the phone number of the Islamic Cultural Center of Manhattan. She would call. If not satisfied, she would hop the subway one stop to check, confirming that he wasn't there and hadn't been there. How long would she wait before she called the police?

Not good.

His clothes were soaked and dripping. His wet tracks followed him through the alcove. He removed the camera from his pocket, wondering if the film was ruined. Had his picture taking been for nothing? He fished out his Koran, cringing as he opened its cover. Soaked, too. He thumbed to al-Fatiha. He *tried* to thumb to al-Fatiha. The thin pages were stuck together, his Koran a sodden brick of paper. He remembered Yaseen Haneez's injunction from Saturday classes. *Never get it wet.* Another mark against him.

He removed the wet papers from his shirt pocket—a breakfast receipt from Howard Johnson's, the club itinerary, the paper with Miss Cutter's cell number—now washed out. He unfolded the note from Priscilla, smudged but legible: "DO IT."

Well, he had done it. Mission accomplished and more. He wondered how long Priscilla would hold out before telling Miss Cutter about the plan. "I won't tell anyone," she had promised, when she believed a kiss could bring him luck.

Soon Miss Cutter would know. Which meant the police would know. Which meant they would check the Whitehall and St. George terminals. But Miss Cutter would never guess he had actually made it to Liberty Island. Everyone in the club knew he was crazy about wanting to see the Statue of Liberty, but none would imagine just how *close* craziness had gotten him.

How could they? He could hardly believe it himself. The whole thing seemed like a dream.

Outside, the storm raged. Rain ran sideways. Treetops bent. Broken tree branches raced by like skeletal birds. Mohammed wondered if it was storming in Ohio.

On rainy days his mother cooked broths with chunks of meat and potatoes. Sometimes she made *ful nabed*—a thick bean and vegetable chowder.

His stomach growled. He realized *iftar* had passed. He could break his fast. He could eat! If he had something to eat.

He gazed at a concrete trash receptacle near the doors. The receptacle had a new plastic bag. No visitors, but a fresh trash bag? A sign above it read: "No Food or Beverages Beyond This Point." It was a long shot, but anything was possible. He approached and peered into the receptacle. Empty.

His father had once likened the fasting of Ramadan to jogging. "Each day it will get a little easier," he had said. Tonight the jog was for real. He had no food to eat, though there was plenty of water to drink—enough to drown in.

He remembered breakfast that morning. Corn Pops. Toast. Jam. Scrambled eggs. He recalled the menu board at Bernstein's Deli. That three-foot plastic pickle. It seemed like a year since he had eaten. He wondered what his family was dining on. Lentils again? Or rice and beans for the third time this week? Tonight he would have devoured three bowls without complaint. Maybe his mother had cooked lamb for dinner. Pot roast. Fried fish. Flan for dessert. Maybe the family had broken fast with the usual Ramadan multidish feast because his father was selling gas again—cars lined up at the pumps and cars parked inside the garage for repair. Maybe Delmar was back, the plywood in the station window replaced by glass, and the Ahmed Automotive sign repainted and occupying a small piece of the Ohio sky.

No. They had eaten beans again tonight.

He checked the time: eight ten. Had Miss Cutter called them? Had she let them know their only son was missing in New York? Or had she held off, hoping to find him?

He stopped listening to his stomach and decided to pray.

It would be *Isha*, a night connection, and a long one, too—to atone for missed *Fajr* in the morning, for *Zuhr* and *Asr* that afternoon, and now for *Maghrib*. He owed big-time.

He washed his hands—every other inch of him had performed *wudu* in the rain—then he removed his sneakers and cap, kneeling inside the alcove with his wet jacket as a prayer mat, aligning himself with Mecca. He didn't need the qibla compass to find it. He knew how Miss Liberty stood. She faced Mecca, too.

As he gazed at the centennial doors, he wondered if any Muslim had done this before—perform salat under the Statue of Liberty. Closing his eyes, he raised his hands to his ears and began with all his voice. *"Allahu Akbar."* No need for whispers here.

The rhythm found him quickly, his prayer flowing without interruption. Everything fell away—thoughts, sounds, the feel of wet clothes. It was the way prayer was supposed to be, though Mohammed had never experienced it so pure and unhurried. He went down for his prostration, and then up again. Outside, the roar of the sea was close. The wind raged. The rain pounded. But his connection remained strong. He prayed to the greatness of God, and he prayed to be led on a straight path. For the first time he sensed that his words were not sucked into silence. Rather, they were going *somewhere*. It was an unusual sensation, strangely comforting. He was sure Allah heard him.

When he finished, he sat motionless, reconnecting with his own presence and the noise of the storm. As he sat, he became aware of other sounds, new sounds—these not from the storm.

He listened, holding his breath. One was low-pitched, almost a groan. The other was louder, harsher. It sounded like the creak of rusted hinges on a swinging door—a very big swinging door.

He got to his feet. There was only one place such sounds could come from. How many times had he heard them in his dream? *So it was true.*

Like a giant shifting its weight from one foot to the other, Miss Liberty had begun to sway in the wind. The low-pitched groan was the sound of Eiffel's iron trestle flexing, its harmonics magnified by the cold cavern of hollowness inside the statue. The armature of ribs were astir. The screech was the sound of her thin copper skin bending, stretching, creaking. She was alive, or so it seemed, her metallic voice reverberating magically in the chilled void of wet air.

Instead of being afraid, Mohammed was thrilled. He pressed his ear to the bronze paneled doors to hear better, amazed by his timing. If he hadn't come to the island—if the storm hadn't brought him to the entrance—if there hadn't been a storm— he would never have known with certainty that Miss Liberty could sing.

His clothes went from dripping to damp. His watch said eight forty-five. He stepped to the edge of the entrance and surveyed the central mall. No vehicles approached. No flashlights probed the darkness. Had those who were here to protect her trusted their duty to the storm? Had they bet on bad weather to keep serious mischief-makers away?

He stared into the slanted rain. Would *he* be suspected of serious mischief-making?

He saw himself sitting before grim-faced detectives in some interrogation room explaining what he had been up to on Liberty Island. He heard himself talking very fast, using his hands—like his mother did. His father's frown became his frown every time his interrogators shook their heads in disbelief at some part of his story—the part about getting stuck on a crew boat, the part about getting off to take pictures, the part about the boat leaving without him. What would the detectives say when he told them he had wandered the island for hours, calling for help, finding no one?

Delmar would have called it a stretcher.

Outside, the storm battered the night without lull. The roar of the sea was close. Rain pounded the fort. The island seemed under attack. With each frenzied gust of wind, the statue's iron trestle groaned. Miss Liberty's hollow, roughly conical center had become a giant megaphone amplifying the low-pitched sound downward. Mohammed imagined the triangulated legs of the main pylon straining on their anchorage bolts, the heavy crossbeams flexing at the base of the statue. He imagined the flowing folds of her tunic buffeted by the wind, their thin metal warping then reshaping until Miss Liberty's copper clothing was suddenly transformed into fluttering robes.

Stomach growls broke his reverie. He licked his lips. Hunger was feeding his imagination.

He felt a sudden urge to hug himself. The night was cold. So were his damp clothes. He began to rub his hands together then stopped. His palms looked as if he had done push-ups on broken glass. What would he tell Miss Cutter? That he fell? Fell on his hands?

Another stretcher.

He retreated into the alcove. He was tired. His leg ached. When he lifted his pant cuff to examine his shin, the blood had washed away, but the gash still grinned. Miss Cutter was sure to see his torn pants.

He stifled a yawn. It had been a long day: wake-up call at four thirty, breakfast at six, nothing since. As Delmar liked to say, he was "running on fumes."

Mohammed recalled the gaunt and grizzled face he had seen through the Greyhound glass. Was Delmar hungry like this? Hungry all the time? He remembered his old friend's parting words at the bus station: "Give Lady Liberty a kiss for me."

Not yet. But he had kissed Priscilla Smith.

He sat on the floor in a corner of the alcove. His soggy sneakers seemed made of lead. The rest of him felt heavy, too. Except his head. It felt light. Was it hunger? Exhaustion? He yawned again, rubbing his eyes.

What is the club doing now? he wondered.

Were Teddy and company parked on the lobby sofas trying to look concerned but unanimously relieved *they* weren't the ones in trouble? Or had Miss Cutter marshaled them to alert postures of watchful waiting while she tried to track him down. And what of Priscilla? Was she worried and hating herself for letting him go? Had she secretly cried for him in the restroom?

He closed his eyes, remembering the kiss. Then his stomach grumbled, and he sat up and yawned. The lights in the recess were bright. Above him, Liberty's bending and stretching had grown rhythmic. *Creak…creak…creak.* She sounded like an old rocking chair rocked by someone too heavy for it. Mohammed listened to the roar of the sea and the serpentine hiss of its retreat. It sounded close.

Did the surf breach the barrier wall? he wondered. *Is it hitting the fort?*

He pictured the tall waves with their curling white heads reaching for the granite parapets then crashing into the facade. He could easily picture it, having seen it in his dream.

❖   ❖   ❖

Sometime later, headlamps from a jeep and the bright beam of a roaming spotlight advanced up the central mall. The jeep lights were dimmed by the rain, but the spotlight cut through the storm-driven night, sweeping toward the monument. When it acquired the fort wall, the spotlight locked on the entrance. Two million lumens of candlepower inched up the west stairway, glistening off the hand railings. The beam moved across the landing—the shadows of balusters dancing devilishly inside the illuminated recess—before it tracked the fort's stonework up to the promenade facing, then higher toward the pedestal, where quartz and mica flecks glinted in the wet granite rock. The beam dropped to the entrance again, sweeping the stairways and the landing, its light reflecting off the top panels of the centennial doors. Then it went dark. The jeep's headlamps turned west. The wind carried off the sound of the motor. The pounding rain drowned the splash of tires. Within the alcove, curled on the floor, Mohammed saw no moving lights. He heard no motor or tires. He was asleep, deep in a dream, the song of the statue filling his head.

He awoke with a start—somnolence and the chill of damp clothes gone in an instant. Something very loud had sounded. The song in his head had changed.

Quickly he was on his feet. The sea boomed. The wind shrieked. Rain blew into the alcove, puddling on the floor. Mohammed felt the room tremble, the stone bricks seeming to rise then fall as if lifted by a wave. The florescent lighting flickered. The centennial doors shook. Something was wrong.

He turned to the entrance. Beyond the balustrade, the silver lines of rain had tightened their slanted threads into a ghostly weave. The night looked strangely white and unworldly, a dreamscape. From above him came a strident metal screech that pierced the stone alcove with the sharpness of a steel spike.

Mohammed wanted to scream back. Then he only wanted to grab his ears and hide his head. Had something broken loose from the statue? Was the sea upon them?

The alcove trembled again, another groundswell under his feet. The centennial doors rattled. He half expected them to fly open and reveal something alive behind them. From the pedestal's compacted earth and concrete rose an awful sound, deeper than any groan. It was the sound of a monstrous stirring, of something awakened.

He retrieved his Koran and camera from the floor, then rushed onto the landing. Something big was happening—below or above he couldn't say—but it seemed the world might collapse at any moment.

Outside, the white night embraced him. The wind—solid now, a racing wall—swept him across the landing. He grabbed the balustrade to stay on his feet. In an instant, he was soaked. The shrill metal screech pierced his ears, but its sound was quickly eclipsed by the shock of what met his eyes. The central mall was gone—overrun by the sea!

Already the flood had reached the stairways, churning white above the first steps. Ground lighting had disappeared on the lawns. Shrubbery was submerged. When he looked beyond the bastion, he discerned the steel grin of waves lifted above the fort wall, crashing on the stonework. Was this what had moved the floor and rattled the doors?

He stood transfixed, strangely mesmerized in spite of his terror. The wind tore at his clothes. The sea's roar filled his head. The night was white. The world had tilted on its side. He had been here before.

He retreated into the alcove and waited, listening to the thunderous surf. His thoughts raced. What if the waves collapsed the wall? What if the flood rose? What if he was trapped inside? The floor of the alcove shook. The centennial doors shuddered. It was time to leave the monument.

The stairway was half submerged when he returned to the landing. Holding to the balustrade, he inched down the steps, the wind at his back. Above him, the metallic screech pierced the storm. It sounded close. Was the iron trestle buckling? Were the dunnage beams lifting from their anchors? Was that awful screech the sound of copper coming loose?

He hesitated. What if Miss Liberty fell? What if she fell on *him*? What if he was buried beneath a collapse of twisted metal? It wasn't supposed to be like this. He was supposed to be asleep on a bus to Ohio, lost in his dreams. This was a nightmare. He released his grip and let the wind pitch him down the stairway into the flood. The cold sea made him gasp. Salt water stung his eyes. He frantically reached for the steps, for anything solid. Then his knees hit the paving stones. He stood and shook himself. He grabbed his jacket pockets. The camera and his Koran were still there.

Overhead, the sky went to pieces. An enormous locomotive fell from the night, braking on steel tracks. He had to get out of the way.

He waded into the mall, shouldering the wind, the water quickly rising to his chest, its cold current pushing him toward the boundary hedges. He held himself against it, sensing trouble. Beyond the hedges the mall dropped sharply to the pedestal lawns. The water would be over his head. Branches tangled with debris raced by him, tempting him to take hold, but he resisted. Would they ferry him to higher ground? Or into the harbor? He steadied himself against the flood, fighting panic. He felt lighter, more buoyant. His legs seemed to dissolve in the frigid water. His teeth chattered. His hands were white.

The current pressed him with compelling authority. Should he retreat? The mall's flooded expanse stretched into darkness. What if the whole island lay underwater? What if she was the only high ground? He had not looked back, not daring, afraid of what he might see—afraid the horror might be real.

An earsplitting screech sliced the wail of the wind, its sound ripped from a metallic sky torn in half. Mohammed froze and dropped his head. *"Allahu Akbar,"* he whispered, holding against the current, knowing what he had heard was not the world coming to an end but the fall of a statue.

The taut metal twang of failing trestlework came next—a sound of girders wrenching, of an iron armature compressing under too much weight. Then the water darkened. Mohammed held his breath, unsure what he was seeing. The blackness widened in a pool around him. Seconds later it took shape. It was a shadow on the water, her shadow cast in the white darkness. As the strident chords of fatigued metal played in his head, he turned to look—expectant, breathless, terrified.

She hung—she loomed—frighteningly off-center, her arm outstretched, her crown lighted. She seemed to be coming around, pivoting to her right, as if intent on pointing her torch toward Manhattan. Her shadow had found him first.

Mohammed stood looking up into the rain. Her figure appeared perfectly clear in the white darkness, almost too clear. He saw her drapery move—the bunched folds of her tunic sliding from her shoulder—but he knew copper robes didn't do that.

She continued to pivot in a slow, slanted pirouette, the weight of her torch driving her spiral motion, bringing her around. Beneath her robes, some part of her held fast to the pedestal, preventing a sudden topple—prolonging her screwlike descent.

Her buckling trusswork cried out. Her torch led an imaginary charge into the storm. The rays of her crown rotated like some fantastic windmill. Mohammed made out the lighted observation windows. He could almost see her face. He didn't move.

She tilted toward him, bearing down on her shadow. He stood looking up, his panic gone, his terror fled. Something fixed him to the flooded mall. *Something he had to do.* All those dreams, all the trouble since the eleventh, his father's trouble, his own trouble, everything fell away—the storm, the cold, the numbness in his legs, the clamor of contorting metal, any thoughts of self-preservation—everything but her. He was connected—as if in prayer. She was close. He was hers. They were one, and not even the white night could wedge itself between them. A breakthrough realization came to him. Suddenly he knew why he was there.

With a horrific shriek that made the black water ripple, her pylon broke loose from the pedestal and she began to topple. As if from the clouds she descended without haste, defying gravity somehow, the wheeling momentum of her torch arm rolling her face into view. She dropped straight to the spot where he stood—a statue yet. As her shadow darkened around him, he ran—but not to get way, not to save himself. He ran to *catch* her. Deaf to the metallic cry, he raised his hands as he ran, preparing to receive her, unflinching beneath the cascading torrents of water and the rush of driven air. Unlike in prayer, he did not close his eyes to see. He felt ready, at his center, strangely empowered.

The soggy landfill of Liberty Island shook with the cataclysmic shudder of a tall building driving itself into the ground. Mohammed didn't feel it. He leaped from the water to catch her, arcing above the flood with uplifted arms, a boy stretched beyond his dreams. And when he came down, he held her in both hands, and she weighed nothing. Nothing.

She had stopped short of coming full circle—back to the skeletal predecessor of herself—to copper sheets and iron beams strewn on the ground. Her tablet and torch fell from her grasp. The clasp of her cloak slid off her shoulder. Slowly, her drapery settled into the flood.

He held her face above the water with extended arms. He felt her breath—warm and smelling of the sea. He heard her sigh. From beneath the water her torch cast a dim, yellowish glow into the night. Her crown held fast to her head, the nimbus rays intact, their tips grazing the wet expanse. As Mohammed stared into her eyes, the rain coursing down her copper cheeks fell on him like tears.

The sea lapped at his chin, the taste of it on his lips. Standing on his tiptoes, he knew what came next. Catching her had been only the start. There was no letting go now. Without fear or hesitation, he pushed himself off the submerged paving stones, holding her above him, kicking wet sneakers mightily. He swam, his arms holding her above the flood, their faces close. Suddenly, a voice sprang from his throat, exhilarating and triumphant, a voice unlike his own, challenging disbelief. *"Allahu Akbar!"* it cried into the storm.

It was all he needed—all she needed—a voice crying faith, hands to hold her high, and the strength of one tempest-tossed son.

She stirred. Held aloft by small hands, she rolled right, freeing one arm, then the other. Mohammed clung to her soft metal even as she started to rise, allowing himself to be lifted wide-armed like a child grasping his mother. When he could hold her no longer, his lips touched her cheek before he dropped back to the flood.

Then she was on one knee, reaching for her torch, its light bright out of the water, too bright to look at. She retrieved her tablet, unbroken from beyond the hedge tops, its shadow passing across him as she clasped it to her bosom. The folds of her tunics clung to her figure, unruffled by the wind.

Mohammed gazed through the rain, staring at her face. She did not smile. Her eyes did not meet his. The tears streaming down her cheeks looked lifelike. In a single motion she stepped onto her pedestal, the folds of her garments settling into place. Her torch rose to the end of her outstretched arm, and she turned to face the harbor, her back to him once more.

It was over. Her beacon glowed. She was okay.

He shook himself and rubbed his eyes. The storm raged. Through the driving rain, he gazed aloft at the statue. No twisted iron beams protruded from the pedestal. No jagged edges of copper gaped at the base. She was perfectly in place.

Had it been a dream? A miracle?

His heart pounded. His arms felt heavy. He was out of breath. There was a taste on his lips, but it wasn't the sea. The flavor was faintly metallic. He surveyed the dark water, remembering the last hour. He had slept in the alcove near the doors. He had awakened to the sound of something loud. He had walked to the landing, slid down the stairway, waded into the mall, fighting the current. Then her shadow, black as ink, had fallen over him.

Something wet in his chest triggered a cough. How long had he been standing here? He reached to press the light on his watch but found nothing to press. He felt his wrist. The watch was gone. Immediately he touched his jacket pockets, feeling for the bulges, finding one—the Koran. His camera was gone, too. Mrs. Heath's gift. His photos. Lost.

He coughed again, then shivered. His feet felt numb. His hands were white. An overwhelming lethargy invited him to recline on the water and float back to Ohio. The dark current seemed to beckon. He hugged himself, trying to make warmth. Languor was trouble. So was the lead in his legs.

His gaze returned to Miss Liberty, to the night no longer white. It was time to move—to find shelter, to survive, to return to Ohio, to his family, to school, to life with its troubles—troubles that suddenly didn't seem that large. Real or imagined, Miss Liberty had been in bigger trouble.

Maybe he would never really know how much.

He was headed to the building with the antennae—determined to break in—when the sweeping lamp of the Park Service police officer found him on the promenade path.

"Freeze!" shouted the rough voice behind the blinding light. Another voice, the one in his head, said, "Run!" So he ran. He would never be able to explain why. Was it the rough voice behind the light? Was he spooked by detection or befuddled by events? He had searched so long for help, it would have made sense to embrace rescue, not run from it. But nothing had gone the way it should have—including rescues.

The chase followed. Then came the dock and the raging sea, a turn onto the perimeter path, gunshots splitting the storm, and a gigantic wave suddenly rising before him, the faces of his father and mother and Nura Maryam—everyone he loved—rising with it, turning him around, sending him straight to the park officer to be saved.

The rest was the pursuit of truth. And truth was mostly found.

OHIO

Only Priscilla was awake when the FBI car delivered them to the Days Inn at five that morning. The boys drowsed on the lobby sofas.

"Now there's a worried crew," observed Miss Cutter as she entered.

Priscilla rushed from the front desk to meet them. For a moment Mohammed thought she might hug him. But no. He was dreaming.

"Hamed, where have you been?" she asked, the familiar vehemence back in her voice.

He waited for their eyes to meet. In a single, meaningful look, he would telegraph triumph. The plan—*their* plan—had worked. He had done it. She would be blown away.

Priscilla put her hands on her hips. Her face said she wasn't ready to be blown away. She wasn't even ready to listen. "We're not going to be back in time," she protested irritably. "It's Sunday. I'm going to miss my fellowship meeting."

"Meeting?" echoed Mohammed. And the meeting of their eyes—what of that?

"The Anointed Youth Christian Fellowship. I'll be marked absent."

Something chillier than harbor water drenched him. "Sorry. I didn't know," he offered.

Priscilla shook her head. "I'm tired of being in charge. Edgar went out after I told him not to. Teddy and Bernie did nothing but play on the elevators. No one listened to me. Why did you take so long?"

Was she pretending for Miss Cutter? Had a missed meeting really ruined her day? Her question grounded him. Why had he taken so long?

"I got lost," he replied simply.

So much for welcoming hugs. So much for tears secretly shed in the restroom. Not all dreams came true. At least he had that kiss. (And what luck it had brought him!) Could he really blame her for not holding on to it as he had?

"Lost? What do you mean lost? You couldn't get lost." Priscilla sniffed, wrinkling her nose. "Hamed, you smell like the sea."

"That's enough," interrupted Miss Cutter. "Please wake up the others." She beckoned him to the front desk. "This young man needs to change," she told the clerk.

Inside the room with the computer desk, he shed stiff clothes, changed out of damp socks, then wet his face and hair in the bathroom. When he finished, he rolled his sea-scented clothes and cap inside the prayer mat. What would his mother say when she smelled them?

Back in the lobby the boys were up. "Hamed, dude!" shouted Teddy.

In moments the YEPS had gathered in an inquisitorial circle, sleep chased from their faces. "Man, you scared the bejesus out of me," Edgar declared.

They knew he had taken the ferry. Nothing more.

"You should have seen Cutter. She was hyper."

"So what happened? Did the ferry sink?"

When he explained about getting lost, the word echoed loudly in the lobby.

"*Lost?*"

Speculation ran in circles, saving Mohammed from elaboration. Everyone talked at once.

"Lost where?"

"Did he say lost?"

"In the rain, stupid."

"I know that! But on Staten Island?"

"Where else? How can you get lost on a ferry?"

"You could."

"Shut up, dink."

"What happened to your pants, Hamed?"

"Luggage, people," announced Miss Cutter from the front desk. "We have a bus to catch."

On the subway ride to the bus terminal, a man sitting across from him was reading *USA Today*. Mohammed scanned the front page but saw nothing about an incident on Liberty Island. Had it happened too late to make the papers?

Then Teddy leaned over and spoke in a conspiratorial whisper. "I don't buy that lost thing, dude. I *know* where you went."

Mohammed looked at Teddy. "You do?"

"You can't fool me," he said, his voice low. "You caught the queen, didn't you?"

"The queen?" He kept his gaze on Teddy. His face gave away nothing.

"Don't play dumb, Hamed. I'm talking about Jenna Jameson, the spiderweb lady!" Teddy winked. "Man, I wish I looked legal. The places I would go..."

Mohammed said, "I don't know what you're talking about, Teddy."

"Come on, fess up. I know you saw her. I won't tell anyone."

He knew Teddy wouldn't shut up until he heard what he wanted to hear. "Okay. I went. But not to see her."

"Not Jenna?"

"I saw another lady. Nicer."

"You dude, you. I knew it." Teddy grinned. "So how was she?"

"Beautiful," answered Mohammed.

Teddy shot a glance at Miss Cutter, then drew the curves of a female figure with his hands. "Bigger than Jenna?"

Mohammed nodded. "Much bigger. Bigger than you can imagine. She was the most beautiful woman I've ever laid my eyes on."

Teddy White licked his lips. "Hamed, you dude, you."

In the Port Authority Bus Terminal, he eyed the Sunday papers at a newsstand. Not one mentioned a terrorist scare at the Statue of Liberty. He picked up the *New York Times* and skimmed the headlines. "WTC Fund Dispenses $24.4 Million More to Families"; "Bin Laden's Whereabouts Unknown, Taliban Envoy Says." Same news, different day.

After the club bought their tickets, Miss Cutter announced there was time for a breakfast snack. "Due to our delay, I'm sure Mohammed will understand if any of you wish to buy something to eat on the bus."

Mohammed understood. If the club had been in Ohio this morning, their fasting would have been over.

"That's my ship," said Edgar.

"Yeah, bus food," agreed Bernie.

Boys moved off to refreshment cubicles and vending machines. Priscilla declared that she *absolutely* had to have some yogurt. Miss Cutter turned to Mohammed. "You, young man, had better eat something before it gets light."

His stomach growled as he stared at plastic-wrapped deli sandwiches inside a refrigerated case. Removing a damp ten-dollar bill from his pocket, he did the math for an egg salad sandwich and two cartons of milk. Then he remembered he had bought no souvenirs to take to Ohio.

He returned to the newsstand, where he found a New York City pen for his father, a postcard for Nura Maryam, and key rings for Delmar and Mrs. Heath. From a carousel display of refrigerator magnets, he looked for one his mother would like. When he asked the lady at the cash register for a magnet with the Statue of Liberty, she said they were sold out.

"Fact is, I heard they caught some terrorist trying to blow her up last night," she added conversationally.

Mohammed froze at the magnet display. *How did she know?*

"It was on the news," the lady said, as if he had asked the question aloud. "But that's not why the magnets are sold out."

A small television behind her was tuned to a news program. The lady followed his eyes, misreading the alarm on his face. "Don't worry," she reassured him. "The guy didn't do diddly-squat."

"Good," he croaked, glancing behind him to make sure no one from the club was listening.

The newsstand lady rotated the display, doubt on her face. "There might be one of just her head," she said, inspecting magnets. "Since nine eleven we've had a real run on Liberty stuff."

Mohammed feigned the voice of adolescent insouciance. "Did they say who it was?" he asked.

Magnets spun on their carousel, the lady still searching. "Who?"

"The man they caught."

"Oh. He was one of those terrorists, like the hijackers. They didn't give his name. Wouldn't have been able to pronounce it if they had. Those Arab names all sound alike."

He nodded. "And he tried to blow her up, you said?"

The lady interrupted her search. "Well, they didn't say that exactly. But what else could he have been up to? Do you think he was out there trying to keep her warm?"

Her frank look of incredulity forced Mohammed's gaze back to the magnets.

"Wouldn't surprise me if we never find out what he was up to," she said. "You know how hush-hush the government is about everything."

He nodded again, remembering Chief Perez's injunction of an hour before when he asked Miss Cutter not to share the events of that evening. *We don't want to give our enemies new ideas.* Now Mohammed understood what Chief Perez had really meant about giving the incident a low profile. He didn't want news of a *kid* getting to the Statue of Liberty to become a big story. The newsstand lady was right. It was hush-hush.

"Of course they've got their reasons for telling us what's convenient," she said. "It's how they catch 'em—the terrorists— by being secret, you know."

As his gaze returned to the TV, the truth finally dawned on him. His name wasn't going to come out in news reports. Not today. Not tomorrow. It couldn't. A sketchy incident would remain just that—sketchy, unconfirmed, under investigation. America was being protected.

"They've probably sent the joker off to Camp X-Ray already," added the newsstand lady.

"Camp X-Ray?"

"Where they send the Taliban—bin Laden's buddies— the ones captured in Afghanistan. Camp X-Ray, they call it. Someplace in Cuba, I think."

Mohammed turned to the display.

"If you ask me, the government ought to drown them," the newsstand lady opined.

He fingered the magnets, settling on one without buildings. It read: "I  NY."

"Can't go wrong with that," said the lady. "Everybody loves New York."

Mohammed paid with the damp ten-dollar bill. *So much for predawn egg salad and two cartons of milk*, he told himself. Wasn't Ramadan about sacrifice?

❖   ❖   ❖

It was Fuzzy Thornton who told him about Miss Cutter and Priscilla crying at Ground Zero. The Fuzz sat next to him (Edgar had found a seat to himself) as their Greyhound motored out of the city. "She tried to hide it behind her shades, but you could tell," he said. "Her nose was red, and she was sniffing. The Pris started to bawl, too. It was awful."

Awful Ground Zero or awful the sight of Miss Cutter crying? wondered Mohammed.

"When we got there, the line was really long, but you could already smell something funny, like the ground was cooking. Everyone was real quiet, whispering. Even Teddy shut up. When we got closer, on a ramp, there was this wall with flowers and the pictures of the people who died. There were messages written on shirts and posters. 'God Bless America,' stuff like that. One said, 'Daddy, please come home.'"

Mohammed listened, saying nothing.

"Then after like three hours it was our turn to look, and let me tell you, I thought it was going to be cool, but it wasn't. It was real. Remember when we saw it in Mac's class—when they fell?"

He nodded. The images from the television were seared into his memory.

"Well, it looks like it just happened. And there was this smell, like I said. It reminded me of when my dad throws water on the grill after he has barbecued. That smell."

Beneath them, the Greyhound tires whined.

"Anyway, we stood there staring at the ruins and the excavators and the cranes. There were firefighters with rakes and shovels standing by as the cranes pulled out a steel beam or a hunk of concrete. Then, while we were watching, one of the machines stopped, and the firefighters crowded over something in the pile. Teddy wanted me to ask Cutter for her binoculars so he could see if it was a body, but we didn't need them. The firefighters *had* found someone—or a piece of someone—because we saw them bring over a stretcher and huddle over it. Then a flag appeared and it was put over the stretcher, and when it was carried out, all the firefighters took off their helmets and stood at attention. Everyone on the platform got real quiet. That's when we heard Cutter cry. None of us dared to look at her. I mean, Miss Cutter crying? I just couldn't."

The Fuzz paused to spit his gum into a wrapper. "Man, you were lucky you didn't have to see it. It was awful."

Mohammed moved his head, but not because he agreed. He finally understood what Fuzzy Thornton had meant by "awful."

"So when we left, we saw this bike on the sidewalk surrounded by flowers. People were stopping to stare at it. When we read the sign, we found out why. The bike had been left by this guy, a messenger, who went into the towers just before the attacks and never came out. And the amazing thing is nothing happened to his bike. Tons of building fell around it, but not a single piece hit it. I mean, it's ready to ride—except for some dust—and it's like the bike is waiting for the guy to come back, still locked to its rack just the way he left it."

The Fuzz turned his gaze toward the gray daybreak over Newark. "I can still see it. It wasn't even a new bike. It was a worn-out bike with one of those little 'ding, ding' bells on the handlebars. Teddy called it a miracle bike—for not getting hit—and that was true, but I couldn't stop thinking about the guy. Even after we got back to the hotel and I heard you were lost, and Cutter was running around, I still kept thinking about this messenger not coming back, about the bike waiting for him." He shook his head, turning to look at Mohammed. "I mean, the guy rode it to the World Trade Center, Hamed. Do you see it? A *bicycle* to the *World Trade Center*. And then the World Trade Center fell on him—but not his bike. I still can't figure it out. But you know how sometimes—not very often, in fact, almost never—you see something, and as soon as you see it, you know it's never gonna leave you, that you'll see it over and over again, even in your dreams? Have you ever had that happen?

Mohammed nodded.

"Yeah. Well, that's what it did to me. I know it's weird, but I can't let it go. Like three thousand people died there—one of them this guy—and all I can think about is *him*. I mean, I don't even know his name. And now he's following me around with his bicycle. Crazy, isn't it?"

This time Mohammed didn't even answer with his head. He couldn't. The Fuzz had taken him beyond answers, back to a sunny Tuesday morning in early September when the leaves on their oak tree were still green, when he had eaten waffles for breakfast and joked with Norman on the bus. Middle school corridors had been filled with the sweet morning smell of freshly packed lunches while somewhere on the streets of New York an anonymous messenger had pedaled his way under severe blue skies to a world about to change. Crazy? No. On the other side of crazy? Maybe, if there was such a place—one where lives cut short became the makers of other men's dreams.

The Fuzz said, "I understand now why you didn't want to go. You didn't want to bring back anything like that, right?"

"Right," Mohammed mouthed. Gerald Fuzzy Thornton, the one member of the YEPS least inclined to deep thinking—the Fuzz—had somehow touched the raw substance of unalterable events.

"So how was it?" he asked. "The ferry, I mean. Was it cool?"

Finally all of Mohammed could agree. "The coolest, Fuzz. You wouldn't believe it."

"Yeah, well, don't tell anyone what I told you, okay? About the bike. The guys might laugh. And if my mom heard, she'd want me to get therapy or something. So it's just between us. Deal?"

"Deal," he agreed.

They rode through flatland New Jersey, Mohammed gazing out the window. The hum of bus tires and the cradle rock of the interstate eventually overcame him. Somewhere east of Allentown he slept without remembrance, drained of dreams. When he awoke, late afternoon was in a sky he recognized. Beyond the bus windows stretched the familiar Ohio landscape. A voice nearby was talking about turkey—turkey gravy and turkey stuffing—Edgar anticipating Thanksgiving. Then he heard Miss Cutter's voice. "We all have much to be thankful for."

He sat up in his seat, remembering he hadn't prayed. His last salat had been *Isha* on the island, in the middle of the storm, under the statue. He was remiss again. By the time he got home, the sun would be down, the hour too late for the afternoon prayer. Would his father hold off *iftar* until he arrived, waiting for them to pray together?

Mohammed braced himself for parental hugs and inquiries. When they asked about his hands, he would say he fell running in the rain. His torn pants? The same. His watch? Lost in the storm. The camera? Lost, too. The truth. If they asked about what had been on the news, the incident on Liberty Island, he would answer that he didn't know what had happened. The truth. Dream? Miracle? Did it matter which? Weren't some mysteries better left to the power of wonder?

Outside, familiar landmarks sped by the bus window—farms, bridges, and highway signs. They were close now. He watched kids in sweatshirts and dungarees playing American football on the brown-stubble grass of front yards. He caught the scent of burning leaves. He saw a man in a red hunting jacket stacking firewood. Everything seemed normal.

When the bus passed his father's station, Teddy yelled, "Hey, Hamed, your old man's sign is gone."

Everyone faced the windows. The bus slowed, even the driver glancing. Mohammed looked, too, surveying the deserted gas pumps, the office with its plywood window.

"Jeez, what happened?" asked Edgar, gazing at the naked sign poles.

Mohammed said nothing. The Fuzz offered an explanation. "It was the storm, man. Didn't you hear that wind last night? We must have got it, too. It could have knocked over anything."

Heads nodded, gazes abandoned the windows. The bus motored on.

"Bad luck, Hamed," said someone.

"Yeah, sorry about that, Hamed."

He listened for Priscilla to add her voice, but no. Silence until Miss Cutter spoke. "Let us hope it will soon be fixed," she said, loud enough for everyone to hear.

EPILOGUE

Officers Slocomb, Glovsky, and the three National Park Service policemen from an earlier shift were placed on unpaid administrative leave pending an investigation into the incident on Liberty Island. A month later an internal review board would determine that the five men had failed to follow standard NPS procedures for securing the monument on the afternoon and evening of November 17 and on the morning of November 18. Each officer would be docked two weeks' salary and put on six months' probation. Bob Slocomb's wife—the only person other than the participants who knew the true facts of the case—never breathed a word of what her husband had related at their breakfast table that morning. Her man was in enough trouble already.

The "wiring" of Liberty Island by the security contractors would be completed in the last days of December. It would become fully operational at the end of March 2002.

The day after the storm, National Park Service maintenance mechanic Leo D'Angelo was on the statue washing the crown's observation windows from the outside. A small, wiry man with a sure grip and a soft touch, D'Angelo had washed Liberty's windows and cleaned her spikes for thirty years.

He had repaired leaks, rescued injured seagulls (when they crashed into the Lady), thrown snowballs from her diadem, and on September 11 he had been at work in the crown when the second hijacked plane flew low and fast over the statue. As the only Park Service employee allowed in the torch, he had the exclusive job of cleaning Liberty's flame and changing her lights—all eight hundred of them.

From news reports he had heard about the incident of the day before. First he had heard *terrorist*. Then *trespasser*. This morning he had heard nothing, not even a name. Around the coffeepot at the building-and-grounds headquarters, some of the guys said the incident hadn't happened at all. They said the whole thing had been staged by NPS brass to build a fire under the security contractors so they'd hurry up and finish wiring the island. Funny how stories changed.

The observation windows were scummed with sea salt from the storm. Leo D'Angelo finished the west windows and was about to drop to the statue's shoulder to switch his belay, when he noticed something on Liberty's face, just below the lips—two small marks in her patina. They looked like handprints. He descended for a closer look.

Bracing himself between the shoulder folds of Liberty's stola and the right side of her chin, he leaned out to study the marks, struck by the oddity of their location. Their resemblance to handprints was queer, but upon closer examination he decided the digit shapes only looked like fingers. He saw now they were just smudges, probably left from airborne debris. Or a bird strike. Three hundred feet of statue picked up a lot of low-flying objects in a gale.

Overhead, a pair of National Guard fighters swept low across the harbor, banking toward Manhattan. D'Angelo looked up. The blue sky was cloudless, the sun shining. It was a stunning November morning—except for the mess. The island looked like a freight train had run over it. A dozen freight trains. There were uprooted trees, knocked-down signs, flattened hedges. But the Old Girl had come through just fine.

He had always considered it a privilege to be assigned to the statue, but of late he had come to think of it as an honor. America was at war. Liberty was being defended. And his nineteen-year-old son had just left for Afghanistan to fight the Taliban and hunt down bin Laden and his Muslim pack of al-Qaeda murderers. Payback time was at hand.

As he gazed at Liberty's stern profile, he said a silent prayer for the safe return of his son. He prayed for America, too—his habit since the eleventh when he found himself alone with Miss Liberty. He was not a religious man, but he feared God, and saying his prayers before the Statue of Liberty somehow made him feel they were being heard.

America needed prayers. It needed brave sons.

GLOSSARY

ISLAMIC AND ARABIC TERMS

Al-Fatiha: the first chapter of the Koran.

Asr: the late afternoon prayer.

As-salamu alaykum: "Peace be upon you." The Muslim greeting of peace.

Alhamdulillah: Arabic for "All praise is due to Allah." In everyday speech it means "Thank God."

Allah: the one and only God in Islam

Allahu Akbar: God is greater.

Dhikr: The Muslim version of the rosary: remembering God by repeating religious phrases.

Du'a: supplication; a personal request of God.

Fajr: the morning prayer made before sunrise.

Five Pillars: the five duties incumbent on every Muslim: (1) declaring allegiance to God; (2) daily prayer; 3) charity to the poor; (4) fasting during Ramadan; (5) the pilgrimage to Mecca.

Ful nabed: Egyptian bean-and-vegetable chowder.

Hajj: a pilgrimage to Mecca that every able-bodied Muslim is obliged to make at least once in his or her lifetime; one of the Five Pillars.

Halal: lawful—allowed to eat or engage in according to Islamic law.

Haram: unlawful—forbidden to eat or engage in according to Islamic law.

Hijab: a head scarf placed over the hair and traditionally worn by Muslim women.

Iftar: the meal Muslims eat at sunset to break their fast during Ramadan.

Imam: spiritual leader of a masjid and a Muslim community who leads prayer during Islamic gatherings.

Isha: the night prayer.

Jinni: hidden ones; a class of invisible spirits mentioned often in the Koran; they inhabit another dimension and can communicate with humans through their minds; they can be both good and evil.

Juz-Amma: the thirtieth part of the Koran.

Khamsin: the hot southwesterly wind in Egypt blowing from the Sahara.

Maghrib: the prayer made just after sunset.

Masjid: the place of worship for followers of Islam.

Mecca: a city in Saudi Arabia and birthplace of the Prophet Muhammad; it is the holiest meeting site of the Islamic religion.

Mihrab: a niche in the wall of a masjid that indicates the direction of the Kaaba in Mecca and hence the direction that Muslims should face when praying.

Muhammad: founder of Islam and regarded by Muslims as a messenger and prophet of God.

Mushbooh: suspicious—an object or activity whose halal or haram status is unknown, and hence is suspect or doubtful to eat or engage in.

Niqab: a veil which covers the face; worn by Muslim women.

Qibla compass: a modified compass designed to indicate the direction of prayer.

Koran: Muslim holy book.

Rak'at (also spelled *rak'ah*): one unit of Islamic prayer including prescribed movements and words.

Ramadan: ninth month of the Islamic calendar; a month of fasting in which Muslims refrain from eating, drinking, and indulging in anything that is in excess or ill-natured, from dawn until sunset.

Ramadan Mubarak: A greeting spoken during Ramadan, which means, "Have a blessed Ramadan."

Salat: the ritualistic prayers of Islam performed five times daily; one of the Five Pillars.

Salat al-Jumu'ah: "gathering" prayer; a congregational prayer held every Friday.

Sunni: the largest sect of Islam that claims to follow the words and actions of the Prophet Muhammad.

Tajwid: proper pronunciation during recitation; a set of rules that govern how the Koran should be read.

Tarawih: extra prayers offered during the month of Ramadan.

Wudu: the ritualistic washing of hands, face, and feet before Muslim prayer.

Zakat: alms giving, usually the annual mandatory charity from Muslim adults; one of the Five Pillars.

Zuhr: the noontime prayer.

M. S. HOLM lives in Mexico.